"Tabbie's original and unusual pl(really intriguing read."
Dave Andrews, Presenter, *BBC Radio Leicester*

"The master of supernatural suspense."
Peter J Bennett, *Author*

"The books are catching, they keep you thinking, and make you 'look outside the box'. I enjoy reading Tabbie's books in my limited down time."
Anne Royle and Spook (my four legged glasses).
Founder *Pathfinder Guide Dog Programme*

*For Carolyn
Best Wishes
Tabbie*

A Bit
Of
Spare

Other Books by this Author

White Noise is Heavenly Blue (Book One of The Jenny Trilogy)
The Spiral (Book Two of The Jenny Trilogy)
Choler (Book Three of The Jenny Trilogy)
A Fair Collection
The Unforgiveable Error
No-Don't!
Above The Call
A Bit Of Fresh

Visit the author's website at:
www.tabbiebrowneauthor.com

A Bit Of Spare

Tabbie Browne

Copyright © 2016 Tabbie Browne

All rights reserved, including the right to reproduce this book, or portions thereof in any form. No part of this text may be reproduced, transmitted, downloaded, decompiled, reverse engineered, or stored, in any form or introduced into any information storage and retrieval system, in any form or by any means, whether electronic or mechanical without the express written permission of the author.

This is a work of fiction. Names and characters are the product of the author's imagination and any resemblance to actual persons, living or dead, is entirely coincidental.

The views expressed in this work are solely those of the author and do not necessarily reflect the views of the publisher, and the publisher hereby disclaims any responsibility for them.

ISBN: 978-1-326-83866-9

PublishNation
www.publishnation.co.uk

THIS BOOK IS DEDICATED TO

KATH BROWN

1939—2016

My friend for over 48 years

My adoptive sister

The first proof reader and the other half of my brain

The night before she went into hospital, she insisted we finished the third proofing, keeping me up until 11pm! She will always be so much part of this book

Before she died, she said that as readers had asked me to write one about cats, she would come and help with it.

I said "Are you going to write the books now?"

Humour was always part of everything

A MESSAGE FROM THE AUTHOR

This story is for those who like a challenge.
Although it may appear a little complicated at first,
all will be revealed,
but can you sort out the evil from the good?
Beware of false leads, and stay focused.
Hope I see you at the end, or do I?

Chapter 1

"Well, I don't know what came over me!"

The sexual innuendo was blatantly obvious but completely ignored. There was a significant pause as the group surrounding the wayward spirit, let the air settle before continuing.

"You have not been recalled to pursue your physical needs, you are here to be knocked into shape before you are allowed to take further charge of your body."

Julius, the chief guardian spirit was in no mood for flippancy. He had taken the unusual step of removing Kam from his physical with the view to cleansing him from his obsession and then, when it was deemed fit, return him to finish his earth life. This procedure was only used after much deliberation and could take two forms. Either the subject would be placed in a coma for many years, and then appear to wake as they re-entered their body, or they would be removed for a longer term. To put it bluntly they died. But that meant they were either reborn and had to start from scratch, or they may appear at another location and live their next phase, continuing from the age they were when they were taken. This involved taking over another identity from a soul whose life had been unexpectedly cut short, and the procedure had to be very carefully planned and not undertaken unless absolutely necessary.

Kam fell into the latter and would be returned to complete his current allotted time span. He had been born into a well to do family, never felt he needed to work and filled his life bedding as many females as possible. But when boredom set in, he was always looking for that bit of extra excitement.

Simple sex held no thrill, so his whole attention was geared to finding something to give him a 'jolt' as he put it.

But, while the devil may find work for idle hands, it also finds entertainment for idle dicks and here was a prime candidate.

"Oh aren't I a naughty boy. Do I get my wrists slapped again?"

"This is not a game." The reply was harsh. "As has been explained, you are only here to cleanse your mind and spirit and then, and only then you will be returned to live the rest of your earth time in a productive manner."

"But I am productive. You ask any of the bearers of my offspring." Kam followed this with a laugh but it soon faded.

"You will be in the hands of these two guardians from now on and I would advise you to obey them."

Julius gave a silent message to each and was gone.

"Ooh, thinks he's God doesn't he? Is he always like that?" Kam was still not taking his situation seriously.

"Would you have felt differently if he had been female?" Vard was weighing this new arrival from every angle.

Kam was trying to keep his attention on this spirit which seemed to be all round him and constantly moving.

"Keep still, where are you?" then almost in despair replied "What difference would it have made? He's bossy, or if she had been bossy, oh I don't know."

The second guard seemed to have moved directly into his line of vision.

"You like a bit of bossy don't you?" The voice was almost seductive and swept over him in a very soothing way.

"Who are you?" Then after a moment "You're a woman, now that's more like it." Kam brightened at the thought. Perhaps things weren't going to be so bad after all. He never had a problem with the ladies and if he got this one on his side it could be a very enjoyable interlude.

"What's your name love?" he ventured.

"What name would you like?" There was humour in the reply.

Vard was suddenly in front of him now. "Enough. You're not here to play, you have to learn to work."

"Woah, I don't work. Don't forget big man, I'm dead." The reply was spat out with vengeance.

"And it's very different being 'dead' as you put it. Here we are all workers in some way or another."

"Not this boy." Kam turn his attention to the other guard. "You still haven't told me your name."

Vard answered instead. "Powl. The name is Powl."

There was a moment's pause while Kam took this in, then he asked "Did you say Pole?"

"The name is unimportant, we only have them for you to understand, we don't need them."

"But Pole, the only pole I know is one you ladies dance with." He replied turning his attention back to the female.

It was at this point he realised that, although he had been conversing with the two spirits that were with him, he hadn't actually seen an image of either of them. For the first time since arriving, he was beginning to feel alone. There was nobody he knew and everything in this existence was so different to what he had always imagined. As if reading his thoughts they flanked him and moved him to another area which seemed to be filled with other newly passed souls, some with one guardian but some with several.

"Where is this?" He tried to take stock of his whereabouts but everything seemed to be floating and he was becoming disorientated.

"You'll be fine," Powl whispered "just takes a bit of adjustment."

She seemed nice and understanding, but he wasn't too sure about Vard. He seemed like one that would become another Julius one day, so every success would give him another boost up the ladder.

"Do you mean we have to work every day?"

She laughed. "There's no day or night here. We work most of the time. Every so often we take a break to cleanse ourselves but if there's a major problem we see it through to the end."

"What? And I'm expected to go along with that. Well, forget it, I do not work."

What surprised Kam was the fact that although he was now totally in spirit, he was still getting the sexual urges that had become the main part of his earthly life. At this moment he was feeling the desperate need to relieve himself and could even sense the stiffness in the usual place. But how could that be? This was confusing. To his amazement he was now being taken to another area which bore the resemblance of individual rooms and he was thrust inside one of them.

"You will remain here for a while to gather your thoughts, and realise this is not a holiday. Your cleansing period starts now." Vard snapped out the words giving a command rather than information.

All was dark and very still. If Kam attempted to shout, swear or even move, everything seemed to echo in a sphere and any movement seemed to reverberate from all sides. He felt he was going mad, his mind churning, until suddenly everything went very still and he was conscious of someone behind him. He tried to turn round but it was as if he was no longer in control of himself and he had no physical body to obey him. Slowly he felt as if two arms were enclosing him and the feeling was creeping back all over him so that he was aware of every inch of his mortal shape, especially the sensitive areas. It was as though he was materialising, but as it was still dark he couldn't see what was going on.

"Who's there?" he thought.

"Be still. I am here to help." The words came on a gentle breeze which was now caressing his entire form.

"I need to see you." He was getting a little agitated. What if there wasn't only one spirit present, and how did he know he could trust whoever or whatever this was.

"Oh I get it. You're all playing with my mind." He tried to laugh but nothing happened. So what was going on? Something very nice and feminine was arousing a body he hadn't got, whispering without words and he couldn't respond.

How long it continued he had no idea, but he was sure his companion was Powl as there was something vaguely familiar about her. The darkness seemed to be lifting slightly and he could just make out the most beautiful naked lady standing in front of him her arms outstretched beckoning him to her. He didn't stop to ask any questions, this was too good to ignore and he floated over to join her. As he moved he felt the weight of his familiar body returning and as they met everything sprang into action.

He was now lying on a bed with her taking charge, working on every part of him that would react sexually, and before he knew it he had delivered more than a sperm whale in one shoot, or at least it felt like it.

Many men would have accepted the delights without even asking why, but Kam was not in a normal situation.

"I don't understand." He was musing. "The god man said I was here to work, but then, well, this. I mean if this is work, bring it on."

He had no sooner uttered the words than he was aware of two new arrivals taking over from the first.

"Where's Powl?" he asked.

"Who?" they chorused.

"My guardian. She was here just now."

"No, you're mistaken, just another therapist."

"Therapist!" he shouted. "What is this?"

"Oh just one of the pre cleansing programmes."

They were starting to work on him simultaneously but he hadn't recovered from the last session to respond.

Trying to push them away he yelled "What is this? I don't get it."

"Oh you will sonny, don't you worry about that." The laughter was snide and quite sinister.

He was panicking now. How could this be happening? If he was dead, he was dead and that was the end of it. He must be ill. That was it. He was in hospital somewhere, unconscious and he was probably attached to tubes and equipment. Of course, he was hallucinating, so it wasn't real, it was all a horrible dream and that's why he couldn't feel his body all the time. But he could feel it now, only too well as the females were trying to strain every drop of love juice from him. In normal circumstances he wouldn't have complained but this was anything but pleasant.

"I'm not a lab rat, you can't just keep milking me off, I can't do it. You're hurting me now."

Silence. Darkness. He was alone, very alone.

Julius, and the other two guardians had been observing everything with mixed feelings.

"Don't think he'll stand much of this phase." Vard said. "They don't mind dishing it out down there, but overkill it and they soon squeal for mercy."

"I wouldn't be too sure." Julius was musing. "Don't forget the sex wasn't just ruling his body, it was an absolute obsession that was poisoning his mind and even his soul."

Powl agreed. "Remember, he's still adjusting. He wants to play by his rules and he is rebelling because he isn't in charge. If you gave him time to recover then lined up an array of beauties, he'd go for it."

"I still think he's a wimp." Vard wasn't convinced.

"Oh, I can tell you really like him." Powl sneered.

"Can't stand the little prick." Was the reply.

Julius cut in. "All right. Let's put him straight onto a course of actual work, but I assure you it won't last. He will have to get his end away, spiritual or not, and you know where that kind of frustration leads."

Vard couldn't resist a dig at Powl. "We all know you'd have kept him on the 'too much of a good thing' regime."

"We'll see." Was all she would offer.

The news of the lazy playboy's sudden departure was gradually creeping around the area surrounding his parents' estate, starting with the villages and it had reached the nearest small town by the time the media had got hold of it. Although the family had tried to keep it as quiet as possible and asked for privacy, the general reports didn't paint Kameron, to give him his birth name, in a very good light. In fact he was described as a no good parasite, a lecher, and they were the mild descriptions.

His parents had despaired of him years ago, but whatever they tried, it fell on deaf ears and he continued to lead his life of pleasure at whatever cost. When he collapsed suddenly, thankfully not on the job at the time, a heart attack taking a young man in his thirties, came as a complete shock. The scandal mongers wasted no time in saying they weren't surprised and you couldn't go burning the candle at both ends without the wick giving out. Most of the young women he had poked were in agreement, that he had merely satisfied his own needs without a thought of love or commitment, and when he had drunk his fill with each one, he merely moved on and opened another bottle, so to speak. There were even unkind remarks that it was a good thing and may he rot in hell.

The only young lady who took it to heart more than the others was a local girl who was employed on the estate as a domestic. Amy had spent more time than she should working in his bedroom, caressing his belongings in his absence, and caressing him when he was there. She was under the delusion that when he had finished his philandering, he would realise that she was the one for him and settle down with her. The fact she would then be part of the family and no longer be a servant would have been uppermost in the minds of the fortune seekers, but to her, he was the prize and she would have him all to herself.

She was now in turmoil. Although she was glad to be able to remain working at his home, there was another problem. His room had been closed off with instructions it remained locked and nobody was to enter. It was as though a knife had been plunged into her stomach, for she was seeking comfort in being close to his belongings, to be able to hold his clothes close to her, to smell his aftershave and melt into his memory. Her sexual urges were almost as strong as his, but whereas he was always looking for his bit of spare, she only wanted him and nobody else would do and although it may all have seemed innocent, and in a way pathetic, there was a much more sinister side to this obsession than anyone realised. But she must remain on the property, so for now she must stay in the background and go about her work almost unnoticed.

Due to her job requirements there was no need for her to live in, and she cycled to work every morning from Narrow Brook, the nearest village where she shared her late parents' small house with her unmarried brother Bryn. He'd been named Brian, but could never say it so Bryn had stuck. He was a farmhand and always up early to go off to work and although they didn't see a lot of each other due to their employment, they had always got on very well. Amy always hoped he'd end up with a nice local girl, but none of them seemed to fancy him, so he plodded along, not bothering anyone, did his job properly and seemed to be respected by the farmer.

"Sees ya later kiddo." He called as he left. "Don't ya go worryin' now mind."

He'd noticed how much the death had affected her, but didn't know quite what to say.

"I'll be fine Bryn, just gets on wi' me work. They'll all be busy arranging the funeral."

With a little smile and a nod he was gone.

Obviously he had been questioned by other men at work regarding the incident, but he always shrugged it off and said he knew 'nowt'. He'd never been happy that his sister had become one of the chap's playthings, as he called them, and he hoped that now she would settle a bit and maybe find a decent fellow who would really love her.

She arrived for work as usual and immediately noticed a difference in the atmosphere. The tension was everywhere. The head domestic almost hustled her downstairs giving instructions over her shoulder as they went.

"Get your coat hung up and your apron on, quick as you can now."

"What's going on Maud?" Amy quickly donned her uniform.

"Just mind your 'p's and 'q's today, that's all." Then with an afterthought "And do exactly as I tell you. Alright?"

"Yes, of course, but…"

"You ready? Let me look at you." Maud checked the way the apron was tied and patted the little cap. "Right, come along."

They both hurried up the stairs, past the ground floor and up to the first. Amy's heart was racing. This was where his bedroom was and they seemed to be heading straight for it. As they approached the door, Maud stopped and whispered.

"The master wants Mr Kameron's best suit and favourite tie to be put on the bed along with a white shirt, oh and a pair of black socks and his best shoes. Thomas will polish them if you take them down to him."

Amy was feeling faint. Much as she wanted to be among his belongings, the thought of selecting the clothes in front of someone made her feel sick.

"Couldn't Thomas put them out?"

Maud looked shocked. "It's our job, and the only reason I'm telling you to do it is that…well…" she coughed uncomfortably "to put it bluntly, I imagine you would know exactly which to choose. Oh and don't forget a set of underwear as well."

Amy was visibly trembling. "I…I…"

"I'll be back shortly, and keep the door closed. We don't want everyone to see what you're doing. The undertakers will be here at ten. Put everything neatly on the bed and I will pack it into a small case. The suit can go in a hanging bag."

"Where is the master?"

"The family are out at present. So look sharp, and don't forget to take the shoes down."

The door was closed behind her leaving Amy still wondering why she was being put through this ordeal. Maud had always frowned upon the relationship and it would have made sense to do this job herself, thus keeping the girl out of the arrangements. But maybe this was the bitch's way of getting her revenge for she knew just how much distress it would cause and at the same time rub in the fact that Kameron was dead. No more frolicking.

The tears began to flow as Amy sorted out the most suitable pair of shoes, covered them with a towel and hurried with them down to the basement where Thomas was waiting. As he took them, he gave her a gentle pat on the shoulder and told her to keep her chin up.

When she returned to the bedroom she went to the underwear drawer to choose a pair of boxers, no need to look for a vest as he never wore one. The memories were flooding back as she went through the pants but settled on a sensible pair that wouldn't raise any eyebrows with the undertakers. She paused, then went to the door and listened. All was quiet. This may be the only chance she would ever have to take a keepsake. She selected a thong on which she had played many a tune, and was about to stuff it into her pocket when she stopped.

"Better hide it where nobody will see it." she thought, and went into the en suite where she popped it into her own pants, making sure there was no obvious bulge.

She had only just got the other items together when Maud came bustling in.

"Right, Hang the shirt with the suit and put it into the suit bag." She ordered. "We won't need a case so the rest can go in an overnight bag." She looked around. "Shoes, where are the shoes?"

"I'll go and fetch them." Amy disappeared and soon came back with a gleaming pair.

Maud wrapped them and put them in the bag then took plastic bags and wrapped the other things separately before laying them on top. Zipping it up as if she was glad the job was over, she said "They will be left here for the funeral directors. You can go about your normal duties and remember, this is private. Don't gossip."

Amy left with mixed emotions. She would willingly have stayed in that room forever on her own, but she couldn't get out quick enough when anyone else was around. Had she had more time, and had been able to look in other drawers, she may have felt very different.

Although Kam had enjoyed many women such as Amy, they were simply a way of releasing the tension and draining his tanks. There was no love or attachment on his part and he expected no ties in return, so had he not died, the situation could have become rather difficult, for Amy wasn't about to let go.

But there was another side to his sexual requirements of which she was completely unaware. In a locked chest in his room lay a number of items used with those who were willing participants. When a simple sex act had become boring he had gradually sunk to depths of depravity which many would have found shocking. He owned quite an array of strange pieces of equipment and would sometimes use a combination of them if the need arose. These were yet to be discovered, as the key was also hidden in a place known only to him, but he was dead.

"Time for work." Vard was one side and Powl the other as Kam was moved at speed away from his holding zone.

"Where are we going?"

"Work. You were told." Vard was in no mood for any resistance.

"No, I told you, I don't work. I thought I made that clear."

They halted abruptly and Kam felt Vard in front of him.

"Now, get this straight you long streak of useless piss. You do not make the rules. You do not order us. You work."

As quickly as they had stopped they were on the move again. Kam tried another approach.

"Well, call yourselves guards. Hasn't it occurred to you that your work, as you call it, well, I wouldn't have a clue as to how to even start, not that I have any intention of trying."

Powl seemed to be leaning on him almost as if she was taking his arm.

"There are people in distress." The words came as a whisper.

"Not my problem."

"They need help passing over." She went on.

"Oh, well ha ha, I pity them, if they are going to get the same treatment I got. Can I tell them to stay where they are? Ha ha what a bloody joke."

Vard stopped again.

"You had better alter your attitude or you will be here for a very long time."

"Oh, you mean my sex life will be on hold. Haven't you forgotten? I'm going back when I've met your standards and then I will carry on where I left off."

The tone was sinister now as Vard answered "We will see. You haven't got the balls for what we have to deal with. You are nothing."

"Well right on one count old man, I think I did leave my balls behind now you mention it. Hang on though. No, I can definitely feel the plums dangling."

Vard had had enough and they were again travelling at speed. Although he and Powl could have transported instantly in thought, this student needed taking by the cumbersome route. They were now over an earthquake zone and many helpers were already taking souls into their care whilst others were comforting those trapped but still in body.

"What the hell are you doing to me? I don't need this!" Kam was horrified.

"But they do." Powl indicated to a group just below them. "Come, we must work."

Although the guardian angels were in presence, there was always a call for souls to be helped through trauma such as this and many spirits devoted there entire existence to the job, while others would come for a while then move to other tasks.

Vard and Powl grabbed Kam and pulled him down to the earth and began teaching him how to react and help those crying, not understanding what was happening to them and not wanting to be parted from their loved ones.

He could never have said how long it lasted, but if it had been an exam, he would have failed miserably on all counts. There was no compassion, no pity for others only himself and the effect it was having on him. Eventually when the guardians returned him to base he was in a very belligerent mood. He was left alone in a holding place to ponder his reactions but the hate was foremost for being subjected to this when he could have been left on earth to live his life as he wanted. He was like a junkie with no drugs. He needed sex, lots of it, but back where he was in charge, not with the weird lot up here, if indeed this was up. Perhaps he was in hell, it felt like it.

So he now made up his mind what he would do and they could get stuffed, to put it politely. He felt his power rising. Up to now he was in a strange place and had just gone along with whatever shit they threw at him, but they didn't know what they were up against.

"Look out." he thought. "Get ready. I'm coming back."

As his determination rose, so did his unstoppable urges and even though he had no physical body, his mind was still trying to satisfy his sexual needs to such an extent that it became an urgent problem that had to be relieved. His subconscious was desperately trying to figure out how, in his current state he was going to deal with it. Up to now he had only fed his desires on an earthly basis, but hadn't realised just how sick his mind had become and there seemed to be no answers in this existence. That left only one choice. Somehow he had to visit the physical world again to feed his habit but he had no idea how to attempt it plus the fact those blasted guards must be watching and they would thwart any plan he would try to put into place. His ego said that he could outwit them but he must be on the alert at all times and even fool them into trusting him.

That was fine in general but he must get some relief now, so sinking into his own self he went through all the mental stages of climaxing to the highest level almost shouting his pleasure with such gusto that anyone in the vicinity would have no doubt as to his antics.

Little did he know that help was on the way from an unexpected source.

Chapter 2

Kameron's parents had requested a small family funeral with as little fuss as possible and although a small buffet had been arranged for the few mourners, most of the staff had been instructed to keep their distance. The atmosphere around the whole place was heavy and almost like the lull before a storm.

"It's as if something's going to blow up any minute. You mark my words." Maud was sounding off to Thomas in the kitchen.

"Perhaps it's just the shock." He replied not wanting to get drawn into one of her lengthy surmises.

"Oh there's more to it than that I can tell you. What do you think Cook?" she turned to face the matronly figure who was intent on making pastry.

"What I think is that anyone who's not got any business in here should get about their duties and keep their noses out of what don't concern them. That's what I think."

"Oo, don't tell me you aren't curious." Maud snapped back as she gathered up her things, and muttered under her breath as she left "don't expect any snippets from me lady."

She hated not knowing everything that was going on in the house and was annoyed if she wasn't the first to find out the latest gossip. Her reason for getting Amy to sort Kameron's clothes had been to get first hand information about their relationship, but that hadn't proved very profitable. Well, there was plenty of time, she would find out in due course. She had her ways, devious they might be but they were usually fruitful and she had a strange feeling that this girl would open the doors to many a tasty bit of knowledge.

A few days had passed and all the staff expected there to be some movement regarding the young master's bedroom but the door had been locked with instructions that no one was to enter. Maud had be told to return the key they had been using which she did very reluctantly as she felt that if she could get Amy to work in there, the girl would pour out her feelings whilst surrounded by Kameron's personal items. This now meant she would have to resort to other methods.

It was dinner time and some of the staff were having lunch in a small room leading off the kitchen.

"You're looking a bit peeky Amy." Maud said casually. "Don't you think so Thomas?"

The man carried on eating and grunted while giving a little wave indicating he didn't want to give an opinion.

Cook was used to Maud's probing ways and didn't trust the woman's supposedly casual remarks.

"You're starting to show your age lately I've noticed." She said without looking up.

"What?" Maud wasn't only annoyed at the remark but the attention had cleverly been drawn away from Amy.

"You 'eard." Came out like a bolt from a gun.

Not to be outdone Maud went back to her original statement. "I was only saying, to Amy," she emphasised "that I thought she was a bit pale which is understandable in the circumstances."

"I'm alright, honestly, please don't make a fuss." Amy looked on the point of tears.

"You see," Maud jumped in, "I told you. She's not well. Probably a chill dear."

"Will you leave the lass alone woman." This was an order and Cook brought her fist down on the table as she spoke.

Amy was far from pale now, her cheeks were flushed and her pulse was racing. Something seemed to be enveloping her from all sides and at first she thought it was just the pressure that Maud was piling on but it wasn't like that. This was different and it reminded her of someone. With a quick 'excuse me please' she got up and hurried from the table to the little area the staff used as a cloakroom, made her way to the toilet, went in and locked the door. She could feel her heart beating as though trying to escape but what was this? There were hands up her skirt, but there was nobody there.

Then the very familiar smell she knew only too well filled the tiny room. It was that certain aftershave which was at present sitting in his bathroom upstairs. Now the hand with the distinctive ring caressed her lady garden until it was replaced by the familiar warm sausage that could only belong to Kameron. Suddenly she was swung round until she was bending over the toilet her hands on the rim for support while he inserted his length in and out until she felt the final push and imagined she heard the cry 'Jeronimo' as he delivered his load.

As she regained her normal feelings she wondered if her grief had taken over and she was hallucinating. There was no semen so nothing had actually happened, yet it had all been so real.

"Are you alright? Are you going to be much longer?" Maud's voice brought her back to earth.

"No, just coming now." She called.

"The hell you did." Kam thought as he returned to base then smugly added, "Well I fooled them, didn't think it would be so easy."

"You didn't think what would be easy?" The question made him jump.

"Oh nothing, just thinking." He realised Powl was with him but couldn't quite make out where. He wished these spirits would stay in one place especially when they were communicating with you.

"You think you've been somewhere?" she almost purred.

He still thought he had got one over on her. "No, just letting my imagination run riot."

"Don't take us for fools Kam." Vard had joined them and was only too keen to put this 'prick' in his place.

"Oh I might have known you'd be around." Kam didn't hide his disappointment.

Vard paused for a moment then said very deliberately. "Perhaps you would like to tell us exactly what you have been doing."

"None of your frigging business. I fooled you. Call yourselves guardians. Ha. Leaving people alone. What do you expect?" The phrases came out in short bursts like arrows hitting a target.

"You shagged your woman in a toilet." Vard shot back at him.

For a moment Kam was stunned but regained his composure. "Well, if you know, why did you ask?"

"Did you enjoy it?"

"You tell me you voyeur. Did you sell tickets?" He then turned to where he thought Powl was. "And were you there as well?"

"Of course."

"Oh I see. You all followed along for the entertainment." Kam was getting fed up with this.

Powl was at his side now. "We didn't follow." She said quietly.

Kam was getting angry and the sarcasm was taking over. "Oh I see, you have spiritual cameras all over the place, or have you got very high powered binoculars?"

"It isn't like that." She purred.

Vard cut in. "You didn't escape. Get it into your mind. You do not make the rules, you go where we say, under our control. Now do you get it?"

"You mean, you were there all the time?"

Vard gave the impression of a sigh and directed his remark to Powl. "Not very quick on the uptake is he?" Then to Kam he said "We let you take the lead and we followed, and when you had satisfied yourself we brought you back. But get this straight, if we had decided you weren't going, you wouldn't. You had no say in any of it."

"Alright." Kam was calm now. "Tell me, where were you exactly I mean, while I was doing the act?"

"It's not important." Vard dismissed it.

"Oh but it is. Come on. Where were you both?"

Powl and Vard exchanged a silent message but did not reply to him.

Kam was getting a picture in his head that was not pleasant so he decided to go for the kill.

"Would you like me to tell you what I think?" Without waiting for a reply he continued. "You are supposed to be cleansing me? Well I don't need treatment from two perverts. Come on now, which one was using me and which one of you took over the girl?"

The whole atmosphere went deathly still.

"You will be given time to contemplate your actions and your remarks. When we consider you are ready, your next process will be put into operation." Vard's words were like ice as the two guardians left Kam alone.

This was a strange experience for a young man who lived one day to the next, enjoying all the physical pleasures with little thought for anyone but himself, and the idea that he was now a puppet performing for the enjoyment of others, rankled him. He always made the rules. Women danced to his tune, and when they had served their purpose, he ditched them. He revelled in those who were keen to experiment with something new and the likes of Amy were just treated as fill ins, or his bit of spare as he called them.

Everything was churning over in his mind and he couldn't understand what the purpose was to move him around from different situations without seeming to finish one thing before starting another. And what was the latest test supposed to prove? The idea came back that these so call guardians were not all they seemed and somehow he had got into the wrong hands. Well, there was only one thing for it. He must find some way of getting out of this place, whatever, or wherever it was, and so he began to formulate a new plan of attack.

"Well, what did you make of that?" Julius was quizzing the pair.

"He's a complete waste of space." Vard felt he had better subjects to help.

"We know how you feel about him," Powl answered, "but you don't give up straight away. What's so different about this one?" She knew her partner wasn't coming clean.

"He's a prick."

Julius cut in. "Yes, you've made that clear but I think we would both like you to be more explicit." His tone implied no nonsense and he waited for a reply.

"He doesn't want to be helped."

There was silence for a moment then Julius said very slowly "You speak with experience."

Vard knew he wouldn't get away with his delaying tactics and admitted reluctantly "Because I've had him before."

Powl exclaimed "Is that all? I thought you had some dark secret you were trying to hide."

Julius gave her a moment then replied "I don't think you quite get the meaning."

She turned from one to the other then stopped. "Not in body? You had him while you were on earth?"

It wasn't like any of them to be easily shocked but this certainly put a new aspect on things. As Vard seemed unwilling to elaborate further Julius took over.

"He was a female in that life but Kam was a similar male to what he is now, that is using women for his own ends. It was many years ago and things were different then."

"Go on." Powl wanted to know everything.

Julius faced Vard who indicated for him to continue.

"It started with simple sex but when he couldn't get enough from decent ladies he turned to prostitutes who satisfied his need for a time, but then even that wasn't enough."

"Can I ask which you were?" Powl almost whispered.

There was a pause before Vard answered. "The latter."

Julius gave this a moment to sink in then said "He got violent, it gave him that extra thrill, and I don't just mean masochism, it went further than that. When he was in full swing," he stopped before explaining "it wasn't enough to cause pain, he killed them."

There was a long pause before anyone communicated. Then Powl realised the truth.

"He was the 'Midlands Murderer' as he became known. He was hanged wasn't he?"

"Not by the law." Vard spoke now. "They got to him first."

"They?" She wanted confirmation.

"Friends, families, who knows? But when he was found, he could hardly be identified."

After a time Powl said "You can't wipe the memories can you? That's why all this is painful."

He agreed. "I had to see for myself that this was the same person, and now I'm sure. Having witnessed his session with Amy there is no doubt in my mind. It's him."

Julius asked if he wanted to remain on the case as he could be replaced, but Vard replied that if something wasn't done to his spirit now, it may be too late as the creature was gaining strength all the time.

"He's played a very clever game hiding his identity in his various lives," Julius pointed out, "but now we have him we can't let him give us the slip."

Powl wondered "Does he really know who he is, only he doesn't seem to be reacting the way I would have expected, knowing what I do now?"

Vard answered her. "He can cloak his own soul so that for a time he will really imagine he is the hard-done-to victim that can't understand why we are being so unkind to him."

"We had to get him out of his current life for the reason of a sex clean up anyway, regardless of his true self, but in a way we still have to go through that process initially before we can even try to cure his soul for good. And it may not happen." Julius delivered the final blow slowly to make sure they knew just what may lie ahead.

There was a very different atmosphere when Julius had left, but the two guardians knew they had to clear their minds so that Kam couldn't pick up any thoughts they may transmit, and for now he hadn't recognised Vard, so it was essential to keep up the mental barrier at all times.

When Amy went home after her spiritual intercourse session, she was floating on air. He hadn't left her and hopefully would keep coming back for more. In her mind she belonged to him now and he could have her whenever and as often as he liked. Bryn was already at home and was pottering in the garden.

"I've done the spuds," He called as she passed "and Mrs 'wallflowers' has given me some home made sausages."

He never called people by their names but always tagged them with something he remembered them by. It could be quite amusing but he could have his own little conversation with his sister without people knowing who they were talking about. The lady in question had always been a friend of their parents and liked to send little gifts of home made produce because the siblings had always helped her in many ways.

"Lovely," she called as she went into the house, her mind still on her pleasurable moment. Instinctively she went straight to the bathroom and washed herself as if it had only just happened then went into her room to play with his thong for a moment, imagining he was still in it. She had made up her mind that she must acquire as many of his belongings as possible but that was proving difficult at the moment. However she would bide her time and keep her eyes open for any opportunity, after all who would miss anything, and most of them wouldn't even know what he had, especially his underwear.

Bryn was a quiet plodder but didn't miss as much as most people thought. The spring in Amy's step hadn't gone unnoticed but he had mixed feelings. He would be more than pleased if she had met some nice hard working man but hoped it wasn't someone like the young master. Although he had never been told, he had worked out what was going on there and was relieved the waster was out of the picture, not that he wanted him dead or anything, just nice to have him out of her life. Little did he know what was imminent and how it would affect his quiet existence.

They had just finished their meal, and as Amy was clearing the table Bryn asked casually "Things settling down at the house now?"

"What? Oh yes. The family are going away for a few days. Want to get away from it all I expect."

He looked at her closely as he handed her his plate.

"And how are the staff coping?"

She stopped, surprised at the questions as he never seemed to take too much interest in the place and hardly said anything about his own work.

"Alright really." Then as if to put him off added "It was very sad of course but we have to move on don't we. Can't do any good moping."

He gave her a quizzical look and just uttered a short "Hmm" in reply.

When somebody has something to hide they tend to get a little suspicious if they feel they are being giving a third degree, however mild, and Amy felt rather uncomfortable at this sudden interest by her brother. She made up her mind that from then on she must not give away any sign that there was any connection between her and Kameron, after all nobody could prove anything physically.

Kam wasn't convinced that what he was being told by his captors, as he now called them, was the truth. He had found his own way of contacting Amy and he didn't believe for one minute that they had manipulated him into it. This gave him a boost as he felt he had got one over on them. But the fact remained that he still was under their control or he wouldn't have been returned to his 'cell' to meditate. Also he wanted to know what the next thing would be on their agenda. They seemed to be testing him with all sorts of situations to see how he reacted, not as a punishment, but more as a case study.

"Well, you've picked on the wrong one," he thought but then his mind took a different route.

"Ok, bring it on. You want to play your little games. Well, we'll just see who is the cleverest."

As the thoughts left his mind he felt his strength rising and he was ready for battle. His moments with his bit of spare would satisfy his needs for now but it would only be temporary. He knew he had a direct route to the woman, he'd just proved it, but the 'wham bam thank you ma'am' didn't hold much of a thrill in the long run. He must look much further afield where the catch would be plentiful.

It had occurred to him that these guards were no better than he was, and were simply using him for their own gratification and the remarks that he had thrown at them were actually his true feelings instead of just idle retorts. Everything was now taking on a new look and he could turn it to his advantage, for if he groomed it properly and found this world provided deeper satisfaction, who could force him to return to the basic earthly existence? He was like a phoenix rising from the ashes, his new pleasures started from here.

Powl had been watching Kam closely and knew there was a change in him which needed to be carefully monitored. She had taken quite a liking to this spirit which was not the accepted thing so she had to keep her feelings hidden. When the truth came out about his past it had hit her quite hard and she was trying to see him how he really was and accept the job she had been given. It was obvious that Vard wanted to procure the maximum punishment and wouldn't give up until it had been achieved, then he would feel that justice had been done.

She placed herself behind Kam to see how soon he reacted.

Immediately he turned and said "What have you got up your dirty little sleeves this time?"

"What makes you think that?" she purred.

"Look, I don't know who you are or what your game is and I don't really care, so you can clear off and leave me on my own."

She felt the strength coming out of his spirit in waves and she was being pushed away. This wasn't right. Her message went out and Vard was at her side instantly.

"Now what are you playing at?" he snapped at Kam.

"Oh, sending for the big guns are we?" Can't you manage me on your own?" he directed at Powl, but turned on Vard "Well you are nothing more than a water pistol, so don't come the heavy with me."

It was as though a light had been turned on and Kam realised he was surrounded by spirits in all directions and they were closing in on him almost crushing him.

"Hey, what the……?" he tried to cry out but there were too many and he couldn't fight this force.

Somewhere above him a voice seemed to penetrate through every spirit

"You have many lessons to learn. Until you have, you will be confined."

The spirits slowly melted into the air yet the force was still there, unseen but holding him in one position. He was aware of a voice, whispering at first then speaking in soft tones to calm him trying to get him to understand he did not make the rules. Using all his force he emitted such a wave of energy that he felt space around him again and the bellow that came from him echoed out from the area and vibrated throughout the surrounding atmosphere.

"You cannot stop me. I know what I am. You will never beat me."

With a tremendous surge he rose upwards scattering every entity in his path leaving his holding cell completely void except for the vilest smell imaginable. No fart emitted could have come close to his parting shot and it would take a long time before that area could be used again.

Vard was furious at losing his charge and was determined to track the creature down but was warned against it by Julius who insisted this could not be a personal vendetta and would have to be dealt with by much higher and more powerful levels. Kam had taken many forms in the past and was always driven by extreme sexual requirements and although nothing had changed, his increasing demands would crush anything in his path. They had hoped this time he could be detoxed but as his true self rose to the surface there was no stopping him. The job now was to track him down by powers highly skilled at such work or the outcome would be unthinkable.

Julius was interacting with the level above and although it may have seemed that a weak group had been sent to cleanse a much more powerful entity, all the events had been closely monitored. Kam was not an easy subject to deal with and would always be hunted by some force or other. He had left a trail covering many centuries but when he reappeared under a new identity, the good forces had to be sure they had the right spirit and not some amateur emulating him. He had acquired many followers in his time and used these as a smoke screen when it suited. But he seemed to have been taken in by his recent captors, regarding them as ham fisted half wits without actually looking deeper than the surface.

When Julius returned he had a surprise for both of the guardians.

"Your work is done on this one Powl, you may return to your chosen image now."

She brightened, watching Vard as she transformed into a very handsome young man and after waiting for the shock to sink in asked "Well, what's your opinion of me now?"

"So what was that supposed to achieve?" his reply was cold.

Julius looked from one to the other with amusement then said "We needed a female to keep Kam's attention and Powl volunteered."

"Well he wouldn't have fancied me if I'd looked like this, would he?" The retort was smug as Powl was now looking at him with desire.

Vard looked shocked at the question. "Christ Almighty. Haven't we got enough suitable females?" Then realised what he had said.

Julius laughed for in spirit they were sexless and just took on whatever form they wished, or knew earth relatives would recognise them by.

"Isn't it time you came clean?" he asked Vard who looked rather uncomfortable under Powl's admiring glances.

"Why not, I can't stand his lecherous leering any longer." Vard hadn't liked him as a woman and this was worse so he placed himself in front of the junior and transformed his image into that of a woman, not particularly beautiful but one that sent out the message that she would stand no nonsense.

"Now fancy me if you dare." He spat at Powl who's reaction was priceless.

Turning to Julius he stated "Don't ever put me with this creep again."

It was time for Powl to be sent to another assignment and as he left he blew a kiss to Vard who completely ignored him.

Left alone Julius confirmed that Vard, who had now reverted to his former male image, was the best one to positively identify Kam and requested he stay on the case but cloaking his previous identity to which he agreed.

"I want to be in at the kill." He answered "He's spread too much evil around the earth, it's time he got his just rewards."

"Won't be easy." Julius was deep in thought. "The powers 'upstairs' have him monitored so he hasn't escaped completely, but we are letting him think he is safe, then he'll make his mistakes. But he has become much wiser through the years."

"And more evil." Vard added.

As they left the area, Julius couldn't hide his amusement.

"That was a rotten trick you pulled on Powl."

"Stopped him though." Vard was satisfied.

"You've confused many with your sex swaps and there will be plenty more times when it will be necessary."

Vard was aware of what his job entailed but muttered "I'll hang on to this one for now if that's Ok with you."

The years had taken its toll on many of the larger houses in the area, and the staff at Kameron's home had been reduced to the very minimum. Apart from Amy, Maud, Cook and Thomas the only other regular member was Mr Dawkins who was over the staff and acted as private secretary. There were no maids as such and all the jobs had to be covered by the remaining few. Nobody complained as they didn't want to look for work elsewhere, and always wondered who might be next for the chop. Several rooms had been closed out of necessity and the only entertaining was for family or close friends, but they seemed to be dwindling off as can happen when people consider you have slipped down the social scale. A local man was used to keep the gardens and grounds in a reasonable state but they had lost their glory over the years.

Amy was quite content with the situation knowing that when the time came to sort through the young master's things, she would be involved. Her hopes had been dashed of marrying him and becoming lady of the manor which would never have happened considering the current state of the place, and Kameron wouldn't have been able to make it a profitable venture even if he had been willing. But since her encounter in the toilet, she knew that she had a hold on this place and nothing would tear her from it. She even felt it gave her the edge over the rest of the staff, and she made up her mind that things would be a little different from now on, and she should be treated with respect. In fact, in many ways she and Kameron made a good pair. Both were deceived with delusions of grandeur.

Maud had sensed a difference in her manner and didn't like it.

"Getting a bit up herself if you ask me." She confided to Cook.

"Well as long as everyone gets on with their work and doesn't hang around here messing up the place while I'm trying to bake."

There was finality in the retort that Maud didn't appreciate. Didn't anyone know anything anymore? At one time the place was full of snippets of information but now you couldn't find out anything. She was about to leave when Thomas came in.

"See how that goes," he handed Cook a saucepan, "handle should hold now."

"Very good of you Thomas." She smiled "Could you just hang it on the hook for me? I've got my hands in this sausage meat."

Maud left thinking "A few manners wouldn't have gone amiss."

She made her way to the sitting room where Amy was dusting.

"Do you think Cook is alright?" She opened the conversation.

Amy carried on without turning "I expect so. Why do you ask?"

"Oh nothing, didn't seem herself." She sidled up to Amy. "I think it's all getting a bit too much for her don't you?"

"Seems Ok to me. Why? You after her job now?" She had turned to face Maud and stared her in the eye.

"I said no such thing! And you had better watch yourself lady, or you'll be the next out."

Amy stopped dusting and gave a very sarcastic smile. "Oh I don't think so Maud, and I'd be very careful what you go spreading around if I was you."

This wasn't what the older woman was expecting. "And just what do you mean by that miss?"

Amy just smiled and carried on with her work but Maud wasn't leaving it there.

"I asked you a question."

"Well, let me see." Amy was playing for effect. "Seems there was a lot going on in this place long before I came, amongst the staff if you know what I mean. So before anyone starts pointing any fingers anywhere, they'd best clean up their own back yard. If you get my meaning."

Maud was taken aback but not going to be outdone.

"Oh you mean similar to what was going on when the young master, God rest his soul, was alive. Ah I see what you are driving at." She gave a false laugh as if to lighten the atmosphere and left the room with a "very interesting" whispered just loud enough to hear.

Amy stopped dusting. What was this woman playing at? Until she found out, it may be best to get along with her for now as she could spell trouble.

Chapter 3

Kam was in high spirits. He had learned a lot during his period of captivity and studied the way the good spirits operated. It had taken a while to shake off his recent earthly image because when he took on a new form he threw himself into it completely which was what made it so hard for him to be detected. There were few that could be so much in control of their thoughts and actions and he always needed a short cooling off period to regain his normal self.

His 'race' although in spirit, had to return regularly to earth to satisfy their sexual needs as though it was the food to keep them alive and he was furious that the good powers had intervened and brought this last episode to an abrupt halt. But the annoyance turned to concern, because up to now he had been in total control of his movements and the fact that the other lot had crept in and taken over even for a short time, was a serious matter. It also became obvious that they had been studying him.

"Well, I gave you the slip." He thought smugly but turned his attention to the next step. "As you have cut my pleasure short, I will have to seek it elsewhere. Or will I?"

He wondered just how astute they had become but guessed the patrols were already alerted to track him down. The answer was worth a try, and the game had only just begun, then they would see who was the master of deception and king of all things sexual.

Powl had been seconded to a group of experienced spirits who used their time protecting rather than consoling. Wherever there was a predator threatening an area, they were in force to try to prevent any further casualties. It could be abuse, both mental and physical, stalkers and sexual attackers. Even before a report hit the news they patrolled the area and the earthlings never realised just how many people had been spared. The unfortunate ones who had come into the firing line never knew how much of a battle between the good and evil forces had taken place around them and sadly sometimes the evil had won on that occasion. This was why it was an ongoing essential job for this kind of group.

"You won't be on your own at first," Natt the senior spirit told Powl, "and always take the advice you are given."

"Must think I'm inexperienced." He thought but knew he had to bow to his superiors.

"Of course." He answered and was immediately transported to an area where some vicious attacks were taking place. "Can I ask what's been happening?"

"By all means. We aren't sure if there is only one, or a group but there have been a number of serious assaults on the edge of this town. The women have been robbed and sexually assaulted."

"What age?" Powl asked.

"Any, apart from elderly as they aren't usually out alone at night." Natt said.

Powl thought for a moment then asked "Why aren't you sure how many there are?"

"I see your thinking. Yes the MO is the same but there are slight differences. A bit confusing, but, well you will see."

They were in an alley between some shops when a middle aged woman hurried towards them.

"Keep your senses on high." Natt imparted.

Sure enough, within seconds the figure of a man appeared hurrying after her. She quickened her pace but he was gaining on her.

"Now!" The command came from the leader of the group. Immediately Natt pulled Powl to help make a barrier between the woman and her would be attacker, while the rest formed a power wall to stop him. The man was spiritually strong and fought against them with such a force they had to keep the barrier on high power until the others had moved the woman to safety. As they returned to the alley Powl was staggered at what he saw. The spirit group had almost pulled the man's soul from his body and were giving it a cleansing process.

"He's not the one, or part of any previous attacks." Natt explained.

"New one on the block?" Powl asked.

"That's what they're finding out."

When the group reformed, the leader stated quickly that it wasn't a local man and maybe a copycat prowler, but he had been up to no good and was armed with a knife, although not the same as the ones used recently. Something was niggling at Natt.

"I'm sure I've come across him before."

They all agreed there was something familiar about him but his spirit hadn't been identified as one they knew. This always gave cause for caution as some of these evil beings could shift shape, not just their bodily image, but their very soul. In view of his recent experience, Powl began to wonder just who this could have been. Surely Kam hadn't stooped to these levels just to get his relief, but he pushed the thought away as he figured that Kam was only after sex and didn't go in for vicious attacks like the one who was now being transported out of the area. He made up his mind not to let his imagination run away with him and just look at the facts that were presented.

Reading his thought patterns, the leader of the group knew that this young spirit, willing as he was, had an awful lot to learn, but it would have to come from experience.

Bryn was always hoping that one day the right girl would come along for him, but that gave him cause to worry. While engrossed in his work on the farm, his mind was mulling everything over.

"If I gets a nice lass, what about Amy? Suppose we could all live in the house at a push, but don't reckon she'd take kindly to it."

Then his mind turned to his suspicions about her and the young master.

"Nah, he'd never have married her, I know his kind. Love 'em and leave 'em."

But something was stirring in Bryn's lower regions and recently he had given in to pleasuring himself in bed or in the bathroom if Amy was still at work. But it seemed to be getting more demanding, and sometimes he had to find a place out of view to perform an extra toss. A feeling of guilt always followed as he had been brought up to consider anything in that area was very private, not to be spoken of and certainly not to be fiddled with. Their father had given him a very strict talking to and warned that the devil would punish him if he used it for anything other than its proper purpose. If it hadn't been for the lads talking among themselves, he could have grown up thinking it was only to pee from or stir his tea. But he knew better and didn't respect his father for his attitudes.

"Surprised we were even born." He often thought to himself and wondered if Amy had received the same treatment from their mother which could account for her finding so much out for herself.

Although Amy was in her early thirties, Bryn was in his mid forties and time was passing him by. As the village was very small, there weren't many of his age to choose from, and he'd never appealed to the local girls who found their husbands by going to nearby towns to check out the talent. Even socialising with the local lads didn't work as they tended to go a bit loopy when they'd had a few drinks and the last stag night had put him off as he felt they went too far by leaving the groom tied up in the middle of the brook. They began to feel as though he was a drag on their amusement and after a while they stopped asking him to go.

Little did he realise that he had now been targeted by unseen forces who specialised in breaking in virgins, and his life was about to change drastically.

Julius was aware of the fact that Kam was capable of not only laying a false trail to confuse his trackers, but could continue to keep it alive even though he was far from the scene. At the moment the higher powers were letting it be known that they had two leads but weren't sure which was the true one. It was intended that the information would soon filter back to Kam, for although he worked alone, he continuously picked up all the spiritual gossip going. Danny and Abe from the upper levels had an interest in this as their paths had crossed with Kam on more than one occasion, and although they had been instrumental in bringing about his downfall at the time, they knew he would inevitably always pop up again somewhere.

It was their practice to always have scouts who not only helped to spread false titbits, but who could pick up on the slightest clue as to Kam's identity. These were masters in their own right and worked undercover but in plain sight so that no passing spirit gave them a second glance. Several had been in position since Kam had been born into his current life and little had escaped their notice.

When Abe had stage managed Kam's so called cleansing recall, there was more to it than either Vard or Powl could have imagined but it was important that they were only fed the essential details until the subject had regained his true self, by which time it was too late for him to return to his current body. Although in such cases the person would be repositioned at a later date, Abe had no intention of this happening to Kam. He was a bad enough entity to cope with in the spiritual area without letting him loose on the earthlings.

"Better bring Julius up to speed." Abe was in conference with Danny, who was also still using a body to keep in physical touch with earthly happenings, but spent most of his time 'upstairs' as he called it.

"Didn't think you were going to just yet."

"I think we may need to be on extra alert and not much escapes his notice."

Danny almost guessed what was coming next so asked. "And you'd like me to do it?"

"Well, as you've offered…."

There was no need to finish the sentence and Abe explained that he had a few leads he wanted to follow up so Danny left to put Julius in the picture. There would be no need to include Vard at this point for good as he was, he hadn't reached the level that would convince Kam in extreme circumstances.

The staff had been gathered in the servant's room adjoining the kitchen and there was a certain amount of muttering as they awaited Mr Dawkins.

"Well I saw it coming. It was only a matter of time." Maud was in full swing.

"What was?" Amy asked.

"It's obvious of course. Another one will be going, you mark my words." Maud gave a sniff and her usual shrug and looked round the small group.

"Probably me." Thomas looked sad. He'd worked as general handyman for the parents of the current employers and knew his number must be up.

"Nonsense Thomas, who would do your work, and on your wages?" Maud was adamant. "No I think we all know who is most likely." Her mouth formed into a pursed self satisfied shape.

"We'll see what we shall see," Cook muttered then added quite forcibly "when we are told, that is."

Amy had sat quietly through all this finding it very amusing. If someone was for the chop it certainly wouldn't be her, not with what she knew. It wouldn't be good for the family name if she was to start blabbing to the newspapers. Young master Kameron would be painted in a very poor light along with others who would most certainly be named. She'd see to that. You couldn't beat a bit of smut to bring the pounds in and she wasn't likely to get much from these employers.

Dawkins appeared and motioned everyone to remain seated while he stood at the end of the table.

"I don't have to dwell upon the sad passing which has had a devastating effect upon this family, our employers." He began.

"Oh get on with it," Maud thought but kept her mouth shut.

After a nervous cough Dawkins continued,

"It appears that necessary changes will have to be made."

He opened a file and held it high enough that only he could see the contents, hence the reason for him remaining standing.

"It has been decided, after much deliberation that the house will be sold."

There was a hush and he waited for the blow to sink in before continuing.

"In the meantime you will all remain in your current employment but I have to make one thing clear. With the exception of Cook, the rest of you will be obliged to undertake anything you are requested to do without question."

There was a confused muttering but he ignored it and continued.

"It has been decided," he looked at Cook "that you remain in the kitchen but your hours may be slightly reduced when the family are away."

"Oh." She looked staggered. "What does that mean? May I ask?"

Dawkins looked uneasy and coughed.

"Well, as I say, when the family are away, um, you will be required to prepare one meal for the staff at lunchtime."

There was silence all round.

"What are you saying?" Maud cut in guessing what was coming next.

Dawkins coughed again. "When the family are in residence, everything will carry on as normal, but when they are away, Cook is only required to cook you a dinner but then it will be up to you."

"You mean they will be let loose on my kitchen?" Cook was horrified.

"And we have to fend for ourselves?" Maud was aghast.

Wishing to take the emphasis off this bombshell Dawkins carried on "The rest of you will be given specific tasks on a daily basis and I repeat you will do them without question."

He closed the file and said "For now, go about your normal duties. Thank you."

He left as though he couldn't get out quick enough. There might only be four of them but they made a formidable bunch and he knew the air would be electric in his absence.

The truth of the matter was that, not only was the house becoming too expensive to keep, but Kameron's parents wanted to leave the area for good. They had another home in Corfu that they kept for holidays and were seriously considering moving there permanently. But they knew they had to let the grief period pass before making too many drastic decisions hence the current rules for the staff. Cook and

Dawkins were the only ones who had rooms in the servant's quarters, while Maud and Thomas, like Amy lived nearby but a change loomed for all of them and there was a general feeling of uncertainty throughout the house.

As Amy went about her duties she felt a strange feeling creeping over her. At first she thought Kameron was visiting her again and made sure she was in a room where she could be private while he did his deed. Checking that Maud was well out of the way she started to lift her dress in readiness for the familiar feel of his equipment. In a second she felt herself thrown on her back to the floor, hot breath almost scorching her neck and something had almost ripped her clothes away and was now right inside her pumping away as if it was blowing up a dinghy. She beat her fists on its back, but there was nothing solid there and yet she could feel the ramrod almost ripping her membranes.

She daren't cry out for help and just when she was at her wits end as to what to do, it shot out with such a sucking noise, one could have imagined a horse pulling its hoof out of mud. Schlurp. Gently her hand felt round her groin to see if there was any physical evidence of the being's ejaculation, but there was none. It took her a minute to pull herself together and as her mouth was so dry she decided to go and get a drink of water. Trying not to disturb Cook she slid over to the sink, grabbed a glass from the drainer and filled it from the tap.

"I hope you're going to wash that." Cook said without looking up.

"Of course."

Amy gulped as she swilled it under the tap but as she went to leave the room Cook added "I didn't mean the glass."

Not stopping to ask what the woman meant, Amy instinctively checked her clothing and everything seemed to be alright but she couldn't see the back of her dress where there were some very distinctive white marks.

Kam was annoyed. He knew he had to slide under the radar of the good forces, especially their beady eyed scouts, but while he had always been his own master, and in control of his movements on the earthly place, something now seemed to be manipulating him.

Some wayward spirits, as they gain power during their existence, don't realise that they send out a beacon to much more sadistic and manipulative entities who delight in adding them to their chattels, and in time are totally pulling the strings. The frustrating part is that the likes of Kam are perfectly aware of all that is going on but have no way of escaping the clutches and have been known to end up trapped for eternity.

As soon as Kam had left Julius and co, he had been stalked for a short while until the evil pounced on him, hiding him from being traced. At first he thought they were doing him a favour, but he soon learned that he was now a plaything in their special sect and he had no control over anything, even his will power.

For as many good forces that abide in the various levels of existence, there are equal numbers of bad ones always trying to take over and rule, which means the good have to be on constant watch in their fight for supremacy. Although they require no names in their world but are recognised by memory and thought communication, for the purpose of identification, the group now holding Kam will be referred to as Dark Demons, a name often used by those in body who have been on the receiving end of their attacks.

This group had manipulated Kam to have sex with Amy along with another of their sect, which hid his identity from any scouts who may be watching, but bewildered Amy for she had picked up Kam's nearness. While it was used as an initiation test for the spirit, it had not only confused Amy but frightened her more than she realised. But they didn't bargain on the fact that she wasn't about to let her young prize go that easily. She had been reading about contacting the departed and was keen to try out some of the information on her own. Sadly, as she didn't confide in anyone, there was nobody to warn her of the dangers of meddling in what she didn't understand but she had heard many tales of fakes that took your money but didn't really tell you anything, so what was the harm?

On returning to base, Kam made up his mind he had to escape from these predators, for that's what they were. They lined up their targets then went in for the kill.

"So," one of the Demons was prodding at Kam's mind "you didn't appear to enjoy that."

"I don't like company." He almost spat back. "And I have my own ways of doing things."

There was a ripple of amusement in the group.

"You don't have any ways, unless we approve." The tone was menacing.

"Oh you're going to tell me how to screw a bird after all my experience?"

There was a pause and he began to feel very uncomfortable. This wasn't just about having sex for his enjoyment, it was deeper and more sinister than that.

A figure emerged that seemed to be much larger than the others but all he could make out was that it was just a very dark shape with no limbs or features.

"Who the hell are you?" he yelled but no sooner had the thought had left him than he felt a resounding force knock him sideways, stand him back in the upright position then spin him until he didn't know which way he was.

"You will learn not to disrespect your elders." The voice seemed to boom from all sides.

He was terrified but had to answer. "Look, I don't know who you lot are but I seem to have been brought here by mistake. Now if you'd just like to…….."

The sentence was cut short as he was now surrounded by many demons as though he was in the middle of a ball.

"You complain. You lived for sex, now you have it for ever, in whichever position, place, or person we choose."

"But I –I."

"Oh take the simpering fool away." The command indicated no argument and Kam was immediately transported back to the earth to perform again, this time with a prostitute for the sadistic pleasure of his captors.

Bryn's mind seemed to be intent on discovering the joys of sex but as he was having his wash after leaving work he knew he had a problem. It would be obvious to any woman that he was a novice and they would laugh at him. Even the thought of a stranger holding his tackle was a bit daunting. He undid his trousers, slipped his pants down and looked at what he had. Was it a normal size? Would someone think it was too small? Couldn't be too big could it? As he stood there with it in his hand it started to stand up and he went over the questions again and did they judge it on when it was up or down? Ah, the lads always bragged about when it was hard so that was it. He looked again. His must surely be a good size, but you couldn't go round asking folks what they thought of your willy.

"Well only one way to find out." he decided. He'd just got to take the plunge and find someone to go out with but then another problem arose. When did you do it? It seemed to be the thing to do it on the first date nowadays, but he didn't fancy that.

"Probably shit myself in fright." He thought.

The sound of the front door opening made him jump.

"Oh Christ, it's Amy." He'd completely forgotten the time.

"I'm home Bryn." She called up the stairs before making her way to the kitchen hoping he wouldn't be too long in the bathroom as she felt the need for a good wash. He appeared within a couple of minutes and if she hadn't been so wrapped up in her own thoughts, she would have noticed the slight flush on his face.

He was glad to have a moment to compose himself and set about doing the potatoes for dinner trying to keep his mind on what he was doing and not on the limp sausage which was safely tucked out of sight.

Danny was eager to converse with Abe for he had received word that Kam, although supposedly hidden by his guard had enjoyed another poke at Amy already.

"Don't think she minded." Abe seemed to be already aware of what had gone on.

"Might have known you'd be one step ahead." Danny shouldn't have been surprised but was eager to compare notes. "There's a source keeping careful watch close by isn't there?"

Abe agreed "If only he knew just how near. But apart from that, the passing sentinels picked up the vibes, only momentarily but they were there."

"Wonder why he is still stalking her when he could have his pick of anyone." Danny wondered, "After all she wasn't his first choice, we know that for a fact."

"Oh, the bit of spare comes in useful to keep your hand in," Abe was aware of the innuendo so before Danny could add anything he said "but that's merely an audition with the group that I believe have snatched him, and if he doesn't perform to their standards, he will be out."

Danny was aware that sects such as the Dark Demons didn't just tell you that you had hadn't made the grade. So that any inside knowledge could never be divulged, the way they permanently disposed of the failures was beyond description, suffice to say it was like being confined to eternal torture. Even if Kam had never led a good earth life, murdered and raped women, the high powers would still not have wished for him to meet such an end which meant that his soul would never be at rest.

"One thing is paramount," Abe was very serious, "it is essential that the close watchers remain in place."
"Already on to it, although the current situation isn't looking favourable, but we will stick with it."
They parted in an instant knowing the battle had only just begun.

Kam could never make out what form his captors took as they seemed to he changing constantly and often only appeared in a cloud. He felt he was never alone and the feeling of being watched was beginning to annoy him. He turned on the one nearest to him.
"You get a kick out of watching don't you, and you let me do the work while you come along for the ride, I've already told you I prefer my privacy so you can all sod off."
"And you have been told that you do as we command. You have no will power so the sooner you learn it the better."
The voice came from all around him and he was being spun in all directions similar to the capsule an astronaut trains in. If he had been in body, to say that he vomited in all directions would have been an understatement, for although he was in spirit he felt extremely ill. Such was the mind control these demons possessed for they could provoke all emotions and feelings until the spirit mind was completely unstable. Although Kam had been aware that such groups existed he had never been in contact with one especially at such close range.

But he had been a prime target and although the good forces had done their utmost to prevent it, he had still been taken. Whether he would ever return to normal was unlikely.

With all the teachings and warnings of the good powers, some souls always think they know best, but many wish they could go back and warn others in similar circumstances that if they didn't listen, they were on their way to an existence worse than any hell they had ever imagined. And it was a one way ticket.

"We've got a job for you, breaking in a virgin." The voice was giving a command.

Kam was about to object but was still feeling the effects of the last turmoil so thought that although this wasn't his first choice he'd better go along with it.

"Don't suppose I'll be on my own with the poor creature?" he thought.

The fact that there was no answer just confirmed his suspicions.

"Oh well, let's get on with it."

He was transported to his old home which confused him because Amy certainly wasn't untouched by any means but then a horrible thought came to him.

"Oh no not Maud." But he had some recollection of something going on years ago concerning her so he dismissed the thought but the next one hit him even harder.

"Not Cook. Please tell me it's not her."

So intent was he upon the remaining women servants that he didn't realise the demons had changed his appearance and he was now a woman himself.

"What the f…" he started to exclaim but also realised he was no longer in the big house but in a small one nearby and he was in the bedroom of a man.

"Oh, No, sorry not this." He was back peddling.

"Get to it."

He was thrust forward until he was almost on top of Bryn who was busy massaging his 'pitchfork' and only too ready to be given a bit of assistance as his hand was getting tired.

"No!"

But as Bryn felt the gentle touch of a woman's body on top of him, he was too far gone to ask any questions and Kam had been positioned to give him the works. It didn't take long and immediately he struggled to detach himself before the man realised he had been broken in by a spirit. Again, Kam felt nauseated but there was no relief in that existence and it was a very sorry looking specimen that was returned to base.

Amy had been lying in bed going over and over in her mind what had happened at the house. She still felt as though Kameron was there but it was so different and she thought it was time for her to take charge. Suddenly she heard a noise coming from her brother's room and if she didn't know better would swear he had a woman in there. But she smiled at the thought.

"He should be so lucky."

She lay there wondering if he was having a little private moment, then his door was opened quietly and he went to the bathroom. Somehow, although she knew it was possible she couldn't think of her brother actually having a jerky as she called it, so she pushed the thought away and snuggled down planning her next move. If spirits could make contact with her, then why shouldn't she be able to return the favour?

The main house had settled down for the night. The master and mistress were at home at the moment although nobody knew for how long this time. The servants quarters were at the top of the house and as Dawkins and Cook were the only residents, they had turned one of the little bedrooms into a place where they could sit and have a drink before retiring themselves.

"How long do you think we've got?" she asked, sipping her cocoa.

"Who can say?"

"These stairs are getting a bit much for me now."

He smiled "A bit too late to ask for a stair lift."

She sat musing. "The memories we've had in this place. Some good." She didn't finish but he knew what she meant.

"Ah," he sighed "who'd have thought it?"

They both sat for a while with their own thoughts of how history seemed to repeat itself, but with time, the change in attitudes made some things almost acceptable now but which had brought about staff losing their jobs in the past, that is the ones who were caught. There were some things they could remember only too well, but neither chose to gossip and there were things that were best left and not discussed by idle tongues, even if there were daily reminders right under their noses.

As Vard had shown a lot of promise, Abe and Danny had decided to let Julius groom him in some of the more in depth skills. Obviously it would take time to master some things which were only achieved as a spirit rose to higher levels, but prospective candidates were selected for special tuition, although they would only succeed if it was proved they had the ability to acquire the delicate and often dangerous skills they were required to perfect. Kam hadn't been far off the mark when he thought that Vard would be another Julius one day.

Both Vard and Powl could shape shift at will but that was soon learned by most younger spirits, the secret was to remain undetected for long periods. When Powl had appeared as a female, he hadn't fooled anyone by his own talent but had remained covert by the intervention of Danny for the purposes of guarding Kam which was why Vard had felt cheated when this underling reverted to his chosen image.

But Julius had one main forte that Abe and Danny had used him for many times and one which they now wanted Vard to accomplish if possible. Julius was referred to as the Ace Decoy for if there was a larger plan in operation he could draw the enemy's fire to another area while the big guns carried out their investigations for attacks elsewhere. Of course he didn't use a particular image more than once so he was never suspected until it was too late, and sometimes not even then. It was therefore his job to hone Vard into such an operator by teaching him tricks that were certainly not by the book, but that was essential. It would take time, but no skill is taught or learned in five minutes, either on earth or in spirit.

The two had transported to an area away from the earth known only to the chosen ones where this kind of training took place, and Vard began to learn the first steps in his new realm of deception. One of his first lessons was that he was never to try any of the tactics alone and every move had to be under close scrutiny for that was the only way he would learn the easy traps that would expose him and ruin any operation.

Maud was getting very irritated. She still wanted to find out what had gone on between Amy and young master Kameron but the silly girl was like a clam, giving away nothing. Having just arrived for work she was talking to Thomas as she took off her coat.

"I know there's more to it. I can feel it in my water." She stated firmly. "You mark my words, there's going to be things come out that will surprise you."

He picked up his tool bag and said quietly "But what does it matter now? The young man has gone. Won't make no difference if you ask me. Best let it rest."

"Well, I'm telling you she knows something."

Thomas tried to leave but she blocked his way.

"She's been giving me some very funny looks," Maud was giving him a knowing nod as she spoke, "don't tell me you haven't noticed."

"I likes to get about my business." He almost had to push her aside to get out of the room but as he left he said "What's other folk's business is just that. That's how I like it."

"Well!" Maud was furious. "What a useless individual." She knew she had hit a brick wall with him and Cook was as bad,

"Good morning Maud." The voice made her jump.

She spun round. "Oh Mr Dawkins. Good morning."

"Amy arrived yet?" He looked round the room.

"No, I haven't seen her. I expect she's late. Again." She emphasised the last word.

"Oh, I wasn't aware that she was normally late." His tone was cutting.

"Well, you know the younger generation. Punctuality means little to them."

She tried to laugh off the remark but Dawkins held her gaze for a moment then looking at his watch he said "Well she still has ten minutes so when you are both ready meet me in the sitting room." Giving her a searching look he left, but she knew that nothing escaped him so she had better keep her wits about her.

Unfortunately Amy was currently under the impression that she had special gifts which were bringing Kameron through to her, not realising it was all coming from the other side and she was just a receptacle. But this new experience was exciting and she wasn't about to let it slip from her, whatever it took.

She was in fine spirits as she had found out that there was an elderly lady in the next village who was known as a bit of a psychic so if she could look her up, it would be a good chance to find out more about contacting the departed. Nobody knew much about her but some of the older folk remembered her telling fortunes at a local fete and everything had come true so others went to see her privately in the hopes of getting messages from loved ones. There had been many complaints about her methods as she seemed to be drawing vulnerable people into a following so she had been told in no uncertain terms to cease any practices.

From information Amy had gathered she discovered that her name was Juliette Demonet and had been given a rough idea of where she lived. Although Amy had tried to find a phone number there didn't appear to be one listed, so she made up her mind to cycle over there that evening after dinner and see if she could trace her.

As she bounced into work, Maud's expression told her it wasn't going to be an easy day.

"I thought you were going to be late." was the greeting.

Amy took off her coat, looked at her watch and said "Well you were wrong on that one." She smiled sweetly and put on her uniform.

"Don't mess about we have to meet Mr Dawkins in the sitting room."

"Ready when you are." Amy held out her arm indicating for the older woman to lead the way.

They both walked in silence, wondering what task lay ahead of them today.

"Right ladies, now pay attention. There is a lot to go over and I expect you to remember what I have said."

He stood erect, a file of notes in his hand and eyed both females closely.

"Of course Mr Dawkins." Maud's tone was precise but suggested that she would be the only one paying attention.

"Creep." Thought Amy but her expression gave nothing away.

"Ahem." He looked from one to the other. "What I have to say is not pleasant but it has to be done."

There was a moment's awkward silence before he continued.

"All the furniture has to be covered in order to protect it until such time as….well, until it is sold."

Again a pause.

"Thomas will bring the sheets up for you and put them in the appropriate rooms."

"He will be allowed in the rooms?" Maud sounded horrified.

"Unless you wish to carry them. They are very heavy." Dawkins tone was curt.

"Well, I suppose so." She muttered

He drew a long breath.

"Now we come to the more delicate matters."

"Here we go." Amy could hardly hide the smile for she guessed what was coming.

Dawkins kept his head down as he appeared to be reading the notes exactly.

"As the master and mistress will be leaving here soon, we will obviously leave their rooms for now but……we have to clear the young master's belongings and have them packed ready for transport."

"They're keeping them all?" Maud was amazed. She imagined that his clothes at least would be sent to charity.

"It is not for us to question any decision made by our employers." Dawkins answered without looking up. "I think it appropriate that you go through his things together, but anything that you find that, shall we say, you are not sure about, you call me immediately. Is that clear?"

They both nodded and almost whispered "Yes Mr Dawkins" but both had totally different feelings about doing this.

You could feel Maud's smugness in the fact that Amy wouldn't be doing the job alone, for she knew that was what the girl was hoping for, and it could be very rewarding watching as various items were handled before being packed.

Although trying to keep her face expressionless, Amy was shocked that she would have this woman constantly breathing down her neck and she was glad she had taken the thong while she had the chance. However other opportunities may arise, and if they did, she would grab them.

Dawkins left to give Cook and Thomas their latest instructions. He found all this upsetting but the years had taught him to hide his emotions and he would carry on in his usual efficient manner to the bitter end.

Chapter 4

Kam had been studying some of the ways of the Dark Demons but not always certain as to whether they were feeding him certain knowledge, and giving him enough rope before hauling him back in. It was a bit like a fish that kept getting away but was always caught again. But he was still very adept at the skills he had built up over the centuries and liked to put on a façade of being a lot simpler than he really was. The Demons weren't fooled so the game continued to see who could outwit whom.

But he had now decided to play in plain sight, and if one or more of the other side wanted to tag along, he could have as much fun running rings around them as trying to elude them. Recently he had kept an eye on his old home and wanted to be there when his belongings were rifled. He was musing about the locked chest and was deciding whether or not to direct one of the earthlings to the key's hiding place, because they would never find it without some guidance.

As he hovered over the building he was aware of quite a spiritual crowd in presence but there was something different. He focused his attention on those nearest to him and recognised three of his regular stalkers, but the others were strangers.

"Brought some trainees in?" He threw the question out.

Immediately there was consternation all around him. It seemed that the newcomers were not Dark Demon operatives and were infiltrating the entire area. They were coming from all sides and were just as powerful and before long took over and ejected them. Kam was still reeling from the onslaught, but what came next was even more staggering. They seemed to be merging so that there was half the number, then half again and so on until he was faced with one solitary force.

"Do I know you?" Kam asked, for there was something very familiar about the surrounding air and he knew he had been in this presence recently.

"No need." Was the returning thought as the entity left, leaving Kam alone.

Danny was waiting for Julius to return but was aware of the outcome of the venture.

"Not lost your touch." He greeted him.

"I keep it honed for any occasion." was the short reply.

"Well it proved you could get in easily," Danny said "they never knew what hit them. Didn't think they'd drop their guard so quickly."

"I wondered that." Julius was pondering "I expected a trap but I think the pure volume was the answer."

"But they won't fall for it again." Danny started to say but then thought "unless they are losing interest in him."

There was a moment while they tried to piece together all aspects.

"I know he has been the worst of his kind, but do you think the novelty has worn off." Danny mused.

"From the Demons?" Julius didn't agree.

"Hmm. Maybe he hasn't been quite what they expected. Yes, he was belligerent at first and now he is playing a careful little game making him seem like a useless streak of piss while they could be better employed elsewhere. But we can't underestimate either them or him. Both are masters in their own field."

"So? Watch and wait?" Julius shrugged.

"For now, but I think you could don another outfit while he's hovering around his house. He won't expect you there."

"Want me to take Vard?"

"Not that close to home. Train him elsewhere first."

"Hoped you say that."

With a brief farewell they had gone.

Bryn was getting very frustrated as his bodily needs were becoming uppermost in his mind. Previously he had concentrated on finding a nice lady but since his spiritual experience he realised that even if he did, she would have to be pretty special to come up to that standard. Now he was wondering if and when it would happen again. He was alone in the barn and paused for a second to take stock of the entire moment. He had been playing with himself when, ah was that it? Was the spirit attracted by his desperate needs and had homed in to finish the job for him? If so, she or another one might do the same again.

Even the thought of it got him aroused, and taking a quick peek out of the door to make sure nobody was around he whipped his old man out and started to give it the works. Suddenly he was on his back in the straw and he was being well and truly serviced until he could hold it back no longer and climaxed trying not to shout or gasp. This was even better than before because he was aware of not only one but more presences doing the deed until his mind was floating away.

He came to, panicked, and tried to clean himself with a rather dirty handkerchief but found it difficult trying to return his equipment to its resting place as the damn thing refused to go down. How long it took he never knew but one thing was certain, he wouldn't be searching for any physical companion in this world. He had found paradise and that's where he would be from now until the day he died.

Kam wasn't one to be beaten for long and he seemed to be gathering strength from every recent encounter. He still couldn't work out who was good or who was on his side but it didn't really matter as he preferred to work alone and as long as he could throw off the opposition he would remain intent on acting in his own way.

However, the intervention of what must have been an ally, did cause him some concern. If someone was tagging him, he wanted to know why. He didn't need their help and certainly hadn't called out for assistance. Now it was time to return to his initial project, his physical belongings.

"Look at the vultures." He sneered as he watched the women sorting his clothes and toiletries. "Could have a bit of fun here."

Although Maud seemed oblivious to any spiritual presence, Amy was certainly in tune and moved across the room to the bed.

"What are you doing?" Maud snapped without turning.

"I feel a little strange." The reply came out in a whisper.

Catching sight of her junior in the mirror, Maud swung round her face bright red.

"Have you no respect for the master, get off that bed at once, do you hear me?"

She was now face to face with Amy who merely smiled sweetly back at her.

"You have no idea, have you?" she purred.

Maud looked as though she was going to explode. "How dare you?"

"Oh, I dare. You going to watch then? Always thought you were a bit of an onlooker."

"I'm going to fetch Mr Dawkins, then we'll see who's smirking."

Before she could turn, Amy served her ace. "Oh, you're all as bad as one another then. All want to watch do you? Well, let's make it a party!"

Her voice was getting so loud that Maud was afraid it would travel through the house so she brought her nose within inches of the other woman's face.

"Do not play your disgusting little games with me miss or you will be out on your ear."

Kam was watching this with great amusement and decided it was time to really stir things up. With a gentle shove he pushed Maud until she fell face down at the side of Amy.

"Oh, decided to join in have you?"

As she struggled to get up Maud hissed "I slipped you little fool so don't go making something out of nothing again."

"In which case," Amy grinned, "why aren't you getting up?"

"Isn't it obvious? I can't. My back must have locked."

This was what Amy had been waiting for.

"And not for the first time, from what I've been told."

"Keep you mouth shut and don't speak about what you don't know." The voice was muffled due to Maud still lying face down.

"Well…..maybe I should fetch Mr Dawkins." The emphasis on the 'I' was poignant. "After all you were going, but now I could do it for you." The air reeked with sarcasm.

"Get me up. Get me up."

Kam was still holding her in position but then turned his attention to Amy.

"Shame to waste an opportunity when the bit of spare is so willing." He mused.

Not only was she willing, she was gasping for him and even her senior lying on the bed wasn't going to stand in the way of a moment's erotic pleasure.

It was a pity there was no one there to film the next scene as it would have been a scorcher. As Amy made herself available to her lover, Maud being inches away was bounced up and down on the bed with every thrust, and with each gasp and moan echoing in her ears until she was nearly at screaming point.

When Kam decided it was time for the ultimate moment, he made sure Amy was as voluble as possible, describing every single moment in lurid detail until Maud forced her head up and yelled.

"Stop it, stop it do you hear?"

This made the copulating pair carry on even beyond the delivery.

Suddenly Maud felt herself released from the invisible bonds that held her.

"Don't you understand?" she jumped away from the bed. "That's how you were conceived in the first place."

All went very quiet. Amy sat up feeling quite dizzy.

"What you rambling on about? I was born from a spirit? Don't talk bollocks."

"I will ignore that remark as it is what I would expect from your kind."

If Maud was expecting it to be left there, she should have known better.

"No. Come on. You can't say that and not explain to me what you're getting at."

Maud was regretting the outburst and certainly had no intention of explaining herself.

"Forget it. I was merely using you as an example."

But Amy was having none of it.

"Oh No! You said that for a reason. And I wants to know what that is."

Knowing she had to give some sort of excuse Maud sighed then said quietly "There are many things that go on in a house such as this, but it is up to reliable and loyal servants to keep them private."

Amy was looking at her as though she wasn't impressed and expected more.

"Well we had better be getting on, now tidy yourself and let's be about our business and we'll say no more about it."

She pulled open a drawer and started to remove the contents. Amy was about to argue but before she had chance, Maud spotted something unusual in the corner.

"I wonder what this could be." She almost whispered.

Jumping off the bed now and pulling her clothes straight, Amy joined her and peered at the small object.

"That's strange."

Maud carefully lifted it out and held it up for them both to see.

"Looks like a container of some sort."

Even turning it on all sides didn't show any kind of opening.

"I bet it's one of those foreign things." Amy suggested. "You know, when the Captain was abroad he used to bring stuff back."

"Hm, it's possible."

Maud was giving it a gentle shake now.

"It doesn't rattle, so it must be empty."

"What shall we do with it?" Amy was peering closely at it.

"Well, put it with the young master's belongings of course. What a stupid question."

As it was put on the top of the dressing table, it moved slightly. Both women jumped. Then as they watched, it moved sideways only an inch or so, but it moved on its own.

"I'm not sure I like this." Maud was going a bit pale.

Amy had suspicions that Kameron was behind this and couldn't resist a bit of fun.

"Try talking to it." she whispered.

"What? Don't be so silly." Maud was getting back on form.

Knowing she had the upper hand, and praying that Kameron would co-operate Amy leaned forward and whispered "Is there anybody there?"

"Oh now you're turning this into a farce. This isn't a séance for goodness sake."

Maud reached out to snatch the thing but just as her hand reached it, it slid across the surface and stopped just short of the edge.

Amy continued "Are you a musical box?" trying to hide her giggles and remain sombre.

The box started to spin where it stood and a faint sound seemed to be coming from it.

"It's humming." Amy stood with her hands out in front of her as if she was in touch with whatever it was, knowing this would really get Maud's back up.

"That's enough. It's a trick. The young master was full of those antics. Now stop it or I will throw it in the bin."

It worked but Amy wasn't going to just let this moment go as she knew how she could get to this woman from now on.

"Do you have a message for anyone here?" she chanted

Immediately the box rose and moved over to within inches of Maud's face. That did it. She turned and ran out of the room, slamming the door behind her.

Amy grabbed the box and fell onto the bed laughing to herself. But the mood soon changed as a strong thought was placed in her mind.

"Now you have the power, use it."

She sat bolt upright.

"You aren't Kameron. Who are you?"

"Your guide. Now you have been awakened as to your powers, you can have anything you want. You are in control, but you must learn to use it properly."

After the message, she knew that whoever it was had left. There was an eerie stillness in the room and the little box was sitting motionless on the dressing table.

How many ignorant souls are led into this trap? After Kam had satisfied his pleasures he had departed only to be replaced by a very malevolent spirit just waiting to pounce on the innocent. The thought had been carefully placed in Amy's mind that she had power but must learn how to use it and she was now even more determined to seek out the medium in the next village who was the obvious person to train her. Although the good forces would try to protect her, when a soul has their mind set on a challenge, they often are oblivious to good advice and only realise the error of their ways when it is too late.

Abe and Danny were catching up on some serious happenings around the country and then had a few moments to look at some of the less urgent problems. From experience they knew they must not overlook even the smallest occurrence because it could hide a danger that could be lurking.

"We've got one attached to Bryn." Danny stated. "Do we let it run its course or oust it before the poor lad gets hurt?"

"Do we know it?" Abe wasn't too concerned.

"Not yet. But strange it should appear just as Kam is servicing Amy."

"He was doing that a long time before he came over," Abe said "but don't forget he's not that bothered about her. Just a stop gap."

Danny mused for a moment. "All the same, I'd like to put a tail on it."

"How about that young spirit in training?" Abe laughed.

"Not Powl?" Danny exploded. "You don't mean send him out alone."

"Be a good test."

"And what form do you suggest?"

Abe smirked. "How about his favourite? Another female might flush the other one out. I don't think it's that high up from what you've said. He could handle it."

"Needs monitoring."

"Julius will do that." Abe seemed to be finding it quite a joke but Danny knew better. Nothing would get past his friend and if something sinister was afoot, they would be the ones to deal with it. After all they could play the innocent as well as any other entity.

"Right. We'll send 'her' in then."

If Danny was honest he was rather looking forward to this little charade.

Kam was beginning to think he had escaped the clutches of the Dark Demons by his own talents as there seemed to be nobody following him or interfering with his movements. He still wondered who had rescued him but as there seemed to be no way he could find out, he decided to carry on to try and find as much enjoyment as he could in this new existence. He would keep his attention on the house expecting to have fun when he directed the earthlings to his private chest but that needn't be rushed although there was the time problem if all his belongings had to be packed or thrown out.

The remaining staff never knew whether their employers, Captain and Mrs Shaw were going to be in residence or not as they seemed to be there one minute and gone the next. Dawkins had given strict instructions they were not to be approached unless requested and everyone was to go about their business in the usual professional manner, not letting any of the standards slip.

He had noticed a very strained atmosphere when they were there, with hardly a word exchanged. He guessed he knew the reason but it was wrong to speculate and it would not be discussed with anyone, even cook as she would have her views and not be afraid to voice them.

Most of the clearing out and packing was being done in their absence, so it was essential that as much as possible was achieved in the time permitted. Dawkins had been aware of Maud's exit from the young master's bedroom and had questioned her as to what had been going on.

This was a golden opportunity for her to stick the knife in for Amy and prove that the sooner she went the better.

"It's that hussy." He had stopped her half way down the stairs. "Decency forbids me to described what went on in the young master's room, but I'm not used to that kind of behaviour. She is nothing more than a trollop."

"Come into my office." He directed her down the stairs.

Once inside he beckoned her to sit at the desk while he took his position opposite.

"Now, I understand you have strong feelings about this young woman, but at the moment I have only heard your side."

"But I...." she protested.

His hand went up indicating her to be quiet.

"I must hear what she has to say before I can decide what action to take."

Again she tried to speak but he would have none of it.

"I want you to go to the servant's room and wait there until I call you."

With a snort she got up, threw him a filthy look and left.

After a moment Dawkins made his way to the bedroom and stood with the door open as he addressed Amy.

"Now Amy, I am going to speak to you alone to hear what you have to say and then we are going downstairs to discuss the matter with Maud."

"Now what's she been saying? That woman doesn't like me. She wants me out you know, and she's doing all in her power to make it happen."

"Sit."

She looked bewildered.

"Sit on that chair." Dawkins indicated the chair at the far side of the bed, while he remained almost in the doorway his hand on the knob.

"Are you going to tell……" she started but he interrupted.

"Maud has indicated that something unsavoury went on in this room. Now, as there were only the two of you here, I am very curious to know what she is suggesting. Perhaps you would enlighten me."

Amy sat back in the chair.

"Oh come on Mr Dawkins. What kind of 'unsavoury' thing?"

"That's what I'm hoping you will tell me."

"Well I haven't the foggiest." Amy crossed her arms. "You do know she's losing it don't you."

"Excuse me?" He wasn't giving her any fuel to use.

"She's gone peculiar she has. Surely you must have noticed. Forgets things. Gets all up tight all the time. Makes things up."

Dawkins took a deep breath.

"We have all been affected by the recent sad occurrence." Then looking straight at her said "Some more than others. And we deal with it in different ways. Our own ways."

"Is that it then?" Amy went to get up.

"Certainly not. Sit down. You still haven't explained why Maud should have been so distressed at your apparent vulgar behaviour."

"I'm telling you, I have no idea what the old mare….. um what she's rattling on about."

"Right." He beckoned her to the door. "We will go and find out. Come."

She scurried behind him as they went down to the servant's room. Amy wasn't bothered. She knew she could talk her way out of anything and if necessary Maud would be made to look a liar. After all, what proof had she got? Come to think of it, she was lying there watching it all. Now that wouldn't sound very good would it?

As Maud waited for the pair to appear, she was going over everything in her mind. The box apparently moving on its own had freaked her out, but if she explained it as it happened, she would sound crazy and so she had blurted out that Amy had done something rude but now as she contemplated it, how was that going to sound? If she said she had been held on the bed by an unseen force, nobody in their right mind would go along with it. Well, she had better think of something quickly before Dawkins came back with the creature in tow.

The playful spirit that had been amusing herself with Amy had left to annoy someone else but intended to return to the house as this was just too easy. Some subjects took a bit more work but this woman was leaving herself wide open to any passing spirit that would use her as a puppet. The resident guardian had done its best to interfere and had ordered her never to return but she fobbed that off.

Although not particularly high in spiritual levels, these mischievous entities often stirred up trouble for their own amusement then left, rather than be ousted by higher powers. This one knew that she could play around for a while but the guardian would recognise the familiar presence and could lay a trap. But whether she came back or not, the seed had been planted and Amy now assured that she possessed the power would follow it up herself, especially as she had already decided to visit the medium.

Maud stood as Dawkins entered. He crossed the room and closed the door leading to the kitchen where cook was busy preparing vegetables.

"Please sit." He motioned to Maud. "And you." He pointed to the seat opposite her for Amy to use while he took the chair at the head of the table.

"Now, let us try and resolve this matter as soon as possible. We have a tremendous amount of work to do here and everybody is needed." He looked from one to the other to let the comment sink in.

Maud shuffled uneasily which didn't go unnoticed by either of the others.

"I am going to hear what you both have to say," Dawkins said very precisely, "and I would ask that you both conduct yourselves in a ladylike manner. Please do not speak while the other is talking."

He paused and looked at them both again.

"Now Maud, you raised the complaint, please explain your reasons."

"Well," she looked at Amy who stared back defiantly almost daring her to give a graphic account. Any previous thoughts of how she would handle this vanished as her anger rose, fuelled by the snide looks goading her on. The touch paper had been lit.

She jumped to her feet, leaning over towards Amy staring her straight in the eyes.

"I don't know what she has told you Mr Dawkins but this little liar knows full well what happened."

He was on his feet immediately.

"Maud please sit down."

He hadn't missed Amy's gloating look of satisfaction and knew there had to be more to this and he was intent on getting the truth. He waited for the elder woman to return to her seat then addressed Amy.

"I will give you the opportunity to explain, or I will ask Maud to tell me exactly what happened, for something certainly did. Now, do I get the truth?"

Amy was a bit taken aback by the outburst but was still having none of it.

"I've said my piece." She stared into the air with a faraway expression,

"You see, she can't look us in the eye." Maud was quick to notice.

Dawkins held up his hand to calm her then turned to face Amy.

"Look at me."

She turned her head slightly but looked as though, as far as she was concerned the subject was closed.

Having reached the end of his tether Dawkins raised his voice.

"Very well Maud, I think to settle this you had better explain what went on in the room and please get to the point as quickly as possible."

She stood so that she was now above Amy who was the only one still seated.

"There was something in the room, a presence and it was evil."

"What?" Dawkins wasn't expecting this.

"It's true what I'm saying. Now do you want me to elaborate?" she waited for his permission to continue.

"I think you had better."

The look on his face was of disbelief but he knew that if she didn't explain now, there may be no chance later. It was most probably imagination but strange things had happened in the past and if something had been stirred up by the recent bereavement, he had better know about it, although he prayed it wasn't so.

Amy's expression had also changed. Surely this woman wouldn't go into details. She had better think quickly and come up with an explanation. Ah! She could say she had passed out and only came round when Maud was leaving. Better hear how she related it first. This could be amusing.

Maud coughed and turned to face Dawkins.

"There was a spirit in the room and it had relations with her." She emphasised the 'her'. "It was disgusting, she was enjoying every minute of it."

"Tell me, where were you while this…um … exchange took place." Dawkins looked a bit uncomfortable.

"Oh she was on the bed as well. Didn't try and get up if I remember right." Amy couldn't resist this retort even if it did throw her original excuse out of the window.

"Quiet." Dawkins snapped. This wasn't what he expected.

"Maud?" he faced her. "Is this true?"

"I was paralysed, I was stuck there forced to watch." She appeared to be almost in tears now, her lip trembling and Dawkins told her to sit down.

There was silence for a moment, then with the two women staring at each other he said quietly "I want to put this behind us."

They shot round to his direction, each one amazed but not understanding what was going on.

"I'm sorry you had to experience this ladies, but can I just say it isn't the first time."

"But it hasn't happened before." Maud started to speak then clapped her hand over her mouth. "Oh my God, it did didn't it, only it was a long time ago."

"Before our time." Dawkins explained. "It seemed to be quite a regular occurrence for a while then it seemed to go away and nobody spoke of it.

"Is this house an attraction for that kind of thing then?" Maud asked. "Has something stirred it up?" She cast a look at Amy as she spoke but the reaction she got was not what she expected.

"You never know do you Maud? They says there's some folk who can control these things, so best not upset them I say." Amy looked self-satisfied.

Afraid this was going to turn into a slanging match, Dawkins stood up and said to both of them "As I say, I think we had better put this unfortunate incident behind us and get on with what we have to do here. Hopefully it was just isolated. Probably stirred things up with the recent sadness."

He dismissed them both with a reminder to get on amicably and not refer to it. After all none of them knew just how long their jobs would be safe.

Cook had started her pastry making and had missed nothing of what had been said in the next room.

"So, he's back. I wondered how long it'd be. Not that this was the first time by any means. Won't hang around here for long, nothing to keep his interest."

There was one question on Amy's mind and she was determined to get the answer. They had just got back to the bedroom to carry on with the sorting.

"What did you mean?"

"About what?" Maud wasn't in the mood for discussions.

"You shouted out that that's how you were conceived. Who did you mean by 'you'."

"Don't ask questions – you may not like the answer."

Amy opened her mouth to speak but Maud was ahead of her.

"And that is an end to it."

Chapter 5

Bryn had finished work and was heading home but his mind was still on the surprise visitor that had left him feeling better than he could remember. He turned his bicycle into the garden of their house, peddled up the path and went to park it against the house as usual. As he lifted his leg over the saddle he felt a warm feeling brushing against his groin. It was so pleasant and unexpected he nearly fell off his bike, but regained his balance and after putting it in its usual spot he made his way into the house. He noticed with some relief that Amy's bike wasn't there so he would be on his own and he was in urgent need of some attention to his private areas.

Powl was very taken with this rugged man and was more than pleased at being given this assignment.

"Let anyone try anything with me here." He thought and took possession immediately. The regular guardian tried to intervene saying that he had been sent to protect his charge against unwanted attention from undesirable sources.

"I can assure you that I am from a very desirable source." Powl repeated the words to make his position clear.

The guard tried to argue and say that he was most unsuitable but Powl retorted that he was ideal for the purpose, after all he had a female outlook but the strength of a man.

"I will tolerate you for as long as is absolutely necessary." Was the reply "But I would request you conduct yourself in a proper protective manner."

"You have my complete assurance, I will be more than protective." Powl turned his attention to Bryn.

"My word looks like you could do with some help."

Without warning he had transformed into the loveliest woman any man could have wanted and transmitted the image into Bryn's inner soul. The guard was taken completely by surprise but hovered as near as he could.

Julius was observing from a safe distance knowing this was going to be a disaster from start to finish. This trainee should never be let out alone. There was much better work for him where he could be under proper supervision instead of having to be spied on. It was as though he was treating this as a vacation and was going to fill every minute.

The temptation to either intervene or report back to Danny as soon as possible seemed to be the only solution. The idea was to keep other sexy spirits away, not go in and do the job for them. He thought he would watch for a while but other duties were requiring his presence so he had to make the decision to go and hoped nothing irreparable would happen until his return.

Bryn had dashed up to the bathroom, dropped his trousers and stood gasping as the image of this gorgeous creature took over his mind. Suddenly she was on the floor and he threw himself on top of her giving her his all and it was obvious this wasn't the same one that had drained him in the barn. But he wasn't questioning anything. The urge was so great that in no time he had gushed all over the mat and imagined he was still on top of her, but of course he was physically alone.

He had only just regained his breath when he heard the familiar sound of the front door opening.

"Amy!" he gasped as he struggled to get to his feet.

"I'm home." She called up the stairs.

He opened the door a fraction and called down "In the bathroom. Won't be long."

"Alright. I'll get the dinner on."

"Whew," he sighed, "good job she didn't catch us at it."

He was addressing Powl as though he could see him but if he could have witnessed Powl and the guardian having the biggest argument, he would have seen the latter threatening to request he be removed.

"Get with it, this is the real world, albeit the spiritual one." The guard snapped. "Don't tell me you haven't succumbed before now."

Powl paused then said "No, I guess you haven't. Well, they will keep me for this kind of job. Need to be versatile you see."

"The sooner you go the better. This is a decent upstanding man, and he doesn't need the likes of you tormenting him."

"So you will let any passing sex bandit come and take him, but I mustn't protect him in my way. Is that what you're saying?"

"It isn't the way we do things. We protect our charges, not corrupt them."

Powl gave a moment for effect then said "Which century do you come from mate?"

"I am not your 'mate' and time has nothing to do with it as you very well know."

"Seems you are stuck with me for now, so move over and let the big boys onto the job."

The guardian knew that this creature would have an argument for anything so decided to end the confrontation but be extra vigilant.

Bryn went downstairs and as usual asked his sister how her day had gone.

"Oh nothing out of the usual really. Still packing stuff. How about you?"

He thought before answering. "Not a bad day at all, not bad."

Was it her imagination or did she pick up a happy tone in his voice?

"What you been up to then?"

Some would have teased by saying a lovely lady had come by and he had made love to her in the barn, not expecting it to be believed but Bryn didn't think that way and just knew he had to keep his pleasure a secret from everyone.

"Oh, nothing much, just been a nice day."

She thought his cheeks looked a little redder than normal but didn't say anything.

Cook was feeling exceptionally tired, in fact she was always pretty weary these days. She was more aware than anyone that when the time came she wouldn't look for employment anywhere else. She had been in service since leaving school, starting at the bottom and working her way up to her present position.

It was time to close the kitchen for the day and head up to her room. The stairs seemed longer this evening and her steps got slower the higher she went. Just as she reached the landing she heard Dawkins coming up behind her.

"Going to sit for a while Cook?" He noticed how laboured each step had been.

"Do you know, I think that would be very nice Mr Dawkins, better than being on my own. I feel like a bit of sensible company."

"Let me." He reached past and opened the door to their little sitting room watching her closely. "Now why don't you let me do what I do best and pour you a glass of sherry?"

"Oh, well, that would go down well. Not that I would normally you understand." She sat in the chair she always used.

"Be right back."

Left alone she mused "Bit different to the old days, that would have been unheard of. Butler, as he was, waiting on me?" she gave a little laugh.

"Here we are. You enjoy that." He was still observing her, sensing she wasn't too well but knew she would never admit it.

"That's very kind of you Mr Dawkins."

They sat quietly for a moment then he said "You and I have seen and heard a lot, not only while we've been here but before, if you know what I mean."

"Now you know me Mr Dawkins, I notice things but I'm no gossip. No one could ever accuse me of being that."

"Absolutely not. That's what I've always admired about you." He was adamant but it was edging the conversation in a certain direction. She always knew when something more was afoot.

"That's why I'm speaking to you alone Cook. Wouldn't want the staff to start getting any more wound up than they already are would we?"

He gave her a moment knowing she wouldn't contribute much then continued "I expect you heard the confrontation in the kitchen earlier, even though I closed the door."

She took another sip of her sherry and looked him straight in the eye knowing what was coming.

"Go on. I know you're thinking it's started again." Her reply was little more than a whisper.

"We know it is. But the problem is what attracted it?"

She huffed. "Him of course, who else?"

"You can't be sure of that. It could easily be a new spirit that's hooked onto this being a fairly old building and residing for a while."

"Tse." She had her own way of tutting. "You know as well and I do, that everything that's ever gone on in this place has always been caused by the same person. It's got his trademark all over it!"

"But all that business before he was even born." Dawkins was insistent.

"He's like the undead. That's what he is. It doesn't matter if he's living or dead, he still creates unrest, and if it's not here it's going on somewhere else, you mark my words."

"Right." Dawkins slapped his knee. "Tell me then. When the young master was alive and living here, we didn't notice any happenings did we? How do you explain that?"

He thought he had won the argument but Cook wasn't having any of it.

"Not in this house. He wouldn't need to would he? But we don't know what dirty little deeds he was doing somewhere else, when he was asleep. And...." she continued before Dawkins had a chance to speak "......now he's gone, he's back here and having his way with, well shall I say enjoying himself with a certain person."

"I don't think you should take it that far Cook." He was indignant now.

"I know what I know and what I see." She gave a nod of satisfaction as if she had won the round.

"Yes, well, some people have a vivid imagination."

He looked away and drank his sherry. When he turned back he had the shock of his life for her head was back and there was a faraway look in her eyes and for a moment he thought she had died. Then he noticed she was breathing and her arm was rising slowly.

"What is it?" The words stuck in his mouth and his head followed her gaze. Although he could see nothing he knew there was a presence in the room and it didn't feel good. His mind shot back to Maud's experience and wondered if it could be the same force.

"Don't touch it Cook." He wanted to shout but no words were audible.

The room was icy cold now and he felt the goose pimples rising. Whatever it was seemed to be expanding until it filled the room and he was being choked as if the air was being sucked out. He couldn't see Cook now for there was a grey haze everywhere and even if he wanted to move, he wouldn't have dared. There were long fingers round his neck and as they moved over his body he felt naked, but these weren't friendly, and he realised now they were trying to kill him. How long he was held in that state he couldn't have said but gently the temperature started to rise and he was manoeuvred back to his chair.

Was it his imagination or was there a much younger female helping him and dispersing whatever had been possessing the place, but all he could make out now was Cook returning to her chair. No, that wasn't correct. The young female was sliding back into Cook's limp body which was where it had always been. He shook his head and rubbed his eyes as she opened hers.

"Oh dear, I must have nodded off, I do apologise." She gave a little yawn.

He sat with his mouth open, not knowing what to say.

"Oh," she gave a little laugh "looks like you did too," but added "wouldn't you say?"

For some reason her look told him not to ask any questions and he knew that whatever he said would be brushed aside. But what had happened made him look at her in a totally different light. Her body may be old and worn out, but her spirit was very much on the ball and pretty powerful.

In fact Cook's current life span would last until the house was sold. Physically she lived the life of the image she had been allotted and whilst awake let her brain deal with everything as she would in that situation. But when the need arose she transformed into her true self and carried out her work admirably, before returning to her job, hidden in plain sight.

Kam was taking a moment to reflect on all that had happened since being snatched from his last earth life. His arrogance let him believe he had been in control the whole time and had merely been playing with those who tried to take over. It had been very quiet of late and he smugly surmised they had got tired of not being able to have their way and the novelty had worn off. With his experience he should have realised that he wasn't only being observed by those he could easily recognise, but those who moved unseen, unheard and without leaving a wake in their trail.

He still wanted to witness the shock waves when his earthly play equipment was discovered, but in other ways his interest in the place was waning fast, and if something more interesting came up elsewhere he would abandon the place. Amy's feelings for him were unimportant and he had grown weary of her already. She'd served her purpose but there were much more satisfying 'clients' to find.

Danny had been watching him and was relaying his thought patterns to Abe who warned him not to be fooled by this obvious quest for enjoyment. The past history had proved that this was often a cover for his sadistic and murderous antics and he should still be closely monitored. He was most likely building up for something bigger this time, and it was his feeling that the Dark Demons were still lurking in the shadows ready to use him.

Bryn and Amy had finished their meal and as she cleared away the dishes she said in a quite 'matter of fact' tone "I may have a cycle over to Eastcott this evening."

"Oh, anything in particular?" He didn't look up and slowly folded the table cloth.

She called from the kitchen. "Fancied the ride. Could do with a spot of fresh air cooped up in that museum day after day."

"Oh ah."

He relished the idea of being on his own because there might be the chance that his new companion would visit him again.

Not wanting to seem too eager he called back "I has plenty of fresh air at work so I likes to relax indoors when I gets home. But you could do with a bit of colour in your face."

"That's funny," she said almost to herself "that's the second time I've been told I was pale." But here was a perfect excuse to be going off without any more explanation than she was 'going for a ride.'

Even the recent enquiries hadn't come up with much, but she did know that a woman by the fancy name of Juliette DeMonet used to do a spot of fortune telling years ago but there had been so many complaints that she had to stop. It wasn't her real name but it was a start and a couple of the older women in the village seemed to remember her but weren't sure if she still lived in Eastcott. All a bit vague but Amy wasn't put off because if she could find her, and this clairvoyant or whatever she was, did have powers she would soon spot that Amy shared her talent, for hadn't she been told so by the spirits?

The evenings were very pleasant with the warmth of late summer still evident, but the nights were drawing in slightly now so she knew she had better get going as soon as possible as it was a bit lonely on the small roads which connected the little villages, and not the best place for a woman alone in the dark.

She rode down the main road into the centre of Eastcott, stopped and looked around. There was hardly anyone about then she noticed a woman walking a dog coming towards her.

"Excuse me, would you by any chance know of an older lady that used to read fortunes?"

The dog had stopped to try and cock its leg on Amy's front wheel but the lady pulled it away and started to walk off.

"Sorry, don't know of anyone like that." She said almost without turning.

"Well that was a bit short." Amy thought, a bit surprised.

The local pub caught her eye and although she didn't want to go into the tap room as they still called it, she hoped there may be someone in the little beer garden. She leaned her bike against the wall and made her way down the side of the building. Sure enough there were a few people enjoying a drink in the fresh air. There was an elderly couple at the table nearest to her so she made her way over.

"Excuse me, would you mind if I asked you something?" she almost whispered.

They looked at each other and the man said "That depends on what you're asking."

The woman, presumably his wife cut in before Amy had chance to answer.

"You're not from here are you, but I seem to know your face."

"I'm from Narrow Brook, just along the road."

"Ah," was the reply, "it must have been your mother. You don't 'arf look like her." Turning to her husband she said "Can't you see Freda?"

"Freda? Where?"

"You know, Freda Hall." Which came out more like 'freed 'er all.'

"Oh that lass." He turned and peered at Amy who was beginning to wish she'd never spoken to them. "Not old enough."

His wife was getting agitated with him and said "Pay no heed to him. What was it you said?"

Amy sat down on the seat opposite.

"I only asked if you'd mind if I spoke to you about a lady that I was told lived here."

"Oh a lot have left you know. The village isn't what it was."

Trying not to lose the thread, Amy soldiered on.

"I've been told that an elderly lady called Juliette Demonet lived or lives here, in this village."

There was silence as they couple looked at each other, back at her then concentrated on their drinks. It was obvious they knew but didn't want to tell her anything.

She continued "Only I really need to speak to her you see. It's very important."

"Can't help." The man muttered but added "And you'd best do same if you know what's good for you."

His wife nudged him heavily then looked at Amy.

"He rambles sometimes. Don't take no notice of him."

She finished her drink and stood up saying to him "Best be going."

"Ah." He agreed, downed his last dregs and they left.

"Thank you anyway." Amy called after them but all she got was his hand raised in a wave without turning.

She looked around to see who else might help. There were a few young lads who didn't look as though they would know and she was about to leave when a two ladies came and sat at the table the couple had just left. Should she have another go? The decision was made for her.

"Can we help you?" one called softly as they sat down.

Amy lost no time in joining them.

"Yes, thank you."

One indicated for her to sit and asked "Would you like to join us in a drink?"

"Well that's very kind of you but I wasn't stopping long."

"We always have a bitter lemon, you'd have time for that wouldn't you?" As she spoke, the one doing all the talking nodded to her friend who disappeared to get the drinks.

Left alone the woman eyed Amy up and down which made her feel a little uncomfortable so she thought she had better say something, anything.

"Um, I was enquiring……"

"About Janet. Yes we heard."

Amy was confused.

"No, that isn't the one I was asking about."

The smile crept over the other woman's face.

"I think you'll find it was."

"Oh I see, that's her real name is it?"

There was a pause but the reply came as another question.

"Don't really know anything about her do you?"

"Well no, that's why, I mean that's what I'm trying to find out."

The other lady returned with the drinks and placed them on the table.

"Thank you very much." Amy said as she was handed hers.

She received a nod in acknowledgement then the first lady continued.

"I take it you are seeking her, or someone like her for some answers, or maybe help."

Amy paused with her drink in her hand.

"What makes you think that?"

Her defences were coming up. This woman seemed to have an insight into the reason for her being here, but she had told no one so how could anybody possibly know? Unless……of course, this person now addressing her must have the gift as well. Could she possibly be Juliette, or whatever the name was?

"Oh come on, you don't need to play games." The voice was very low and would not be heard by anyone especially the lads who were making their own noise.

"I'm not quite sure what you're getting at."

The two sat looking straight at Amy for a few moments and she was about to take her leave when the 'speaker' said "I think you know exactly what I mean. Now do you want help or not?"

"Well, it's quite simple, I just need to know where to find this Janet, or whatever you call her." The tone was quite curt and didn't go unnoticed.

The ladies cast a knowing look at each other. Finished their drinks and stood up.

"You won't." Was the remark as they left. "Not with your attitude."

Amy hurried to follow them.

"I'm sorry if I sounded rude. I didn't mean to be only I do need to find her. I can't tell you why."

She wasn't sure why she said that because she sensed they knew all about her.

They walked from the beer garden in silence in step as though they were one, even turning at precisely the same time.

"Must be sisters, could even be twins only not identical," thought Amy as she found herself following them at a distance. "Strange only one of them spoke, perhaps the other's dumb."

She could never have explained why she tailed them and felt they knew she was there. At first she was afraid of them turning round but then realised they wouldn't need to. They were walking on a small footpath alongside a few cottages and she expected them to turn into one of the gardens because in a couple of hundred yards they would be out of the village completely. There was no sign of a car so they had come on foot.

All this was churning through her head as she followed, then suddenly she remembered she had left her bicycle at the pub but she couldn't go back at this moment as she felt compelled to keep following as though she was being drawn along with them.

"I'll have to go back for it." she thought. "Hope it's still there."

She knew there was no gate to secure the garden area but someone could pinch it. But that didn't seem as important as possibly being led to some place for a reason.

As her mind was momentarily on the bike, her concentration lapsed for a split second and she tripped on something, only just regaining her balance or she would have ended up sprawled across the path. She self-consciously hoped nobody had seen her and as she looked ahead to the women, the road was empty. She stopped, looked all around but she was completely alone.

"They must have gone into one of the cottages."

It seemed the obvious explanation but then it made following them for no apparent reason apart from instinct, seem to be a futile action.

"I'd better go and get my bike." She decided, feeling a little sheepish at acting without thinking.

As she went to turn round she noticed she had stopped at a small alley way between two of the cottages. There was just a sandy path with grass growing naturally at each side and it was only wide enough for a car or small van.

"Perhaps it leads to a house that's set back or a footpath through to the fields."

Still concerned about her bicycle, yet very curious about this little lane, she decided to hurry back, collect her bike and ride it back here to have a closer look. In a few minute she had returned and stood in the same spot wondering if she should venture down there. Suddenly something hit her. When she had been asking around her own village, one elderly lady had said that this Juliette person lived in a house that was set back from the rest, not visible from the road, and you had to go down a little path to it.

"Now why did I forget that?" she almost scolded herself. "This has to be it."

As she waited for a moment to decide what she should say if this Juliette still lived there, another fact came into her mind. How strange that she was made to follow the two women, and then something happened so that she didn't see where they went. All of a sudden she felt uneasy as though she wasn't in control of her own actions but was being played like a puppet.

If she had only listened to the good forces who were trying to lead her away from this place and telling her to stop now and go home, she would not have to regret her own actions for the rest of her life. But the force pulling her towards the dwelling was so strong that even the wheels on the bike seemed to be rolling away and she had to hang on to stay in control of it. Her guardians may not have been able to stop her but they certainly did not leave her and called for backup to strengthen their powers, such was the evil force that now had Amy on the brink of no return.

Powl wasted no time taking Bryn into his clutches again. It was like training the uninitiated and made a pleasant change from the experienced ones he usually had. They had just started the evening session when Bryn felt his new partner being pulled off him. He reached out in despair trying to pull 'her' back onto him, for he was playing the underdog this time.

"What have you been told?" Danny and Julius were in presence and had flanked him as he was roughly removed.

"I do it my way. While I've got him, nobody but nobody can get near him." Powl was insistent.

"Carry on like this and you will be relocated." Danny was furious and the air trembled.

Sadly Bryn thought it was his doing and believed it was a new way of climaxing, poor soul.

"You're crap!" Julius added.

"And you are the expert of course." Powl was having none of this 'I'm superior' attitude. "Well you are no better than I am and I don't take orders from you."

"Enough!" Danny ordered, "You have been warned and ignored it. You are not fit to go solo yet."

"Or ever." Julius added.

Before Powl could object, Danny had departed with him in tow leaving Julius in situ temporarily until the replacement arrived.

The interchange between them when they got to their holding zone was not fit for even the most hardened souls to witness, needless to say Powl came out much the worse for wear and was sent into the charge of a very butch, no nonsense matronly type of tutor. It was something he would never forget.

Bryn wasn't sure what was happening. He knew his female had gone which surprised and disappointed him and when he reached out calling for more all he received was the equivalent of a spiritual cold flannel on his 'cucumber and tomatoes'.

Julius was aware of the willing spirits eager to partake of this opportunity but he was clever enough to outwit them all and guarded Bryn with such a powerful force that the lesser ones shrunk away instantly while the more experienced had the sense to back off while he was in charge.

Bryn may have been somewhat disappointed but at least he was in protective hands and Danny and Abe were adamant he stayed that way.

Amy came to an abrupt halt in front of a panelled gate set into a stone wall which must have been at least eight feet high meaning she had no idea what lay on the other side. She was clutching the handlebars of her bicycle as if it gave her some protection. Her instinct was telling her to turn round and never come back but her curiosity, knowing that she could be within yards of the very woman she had come to see, made her try the latch on the gate. It creaked as it opened slightly and she tried to peer through to see what it was like before opening it fully and venturing in.

What she could see came as a bit of a shock. The imposing wall gave the impression of a spooky house covered in cobwebs but in fact she was looking at a well maintained bungalow set in a very pleasant garden. This made her relax enough to rest her bike against the wall and walk along the little winding path leading to the front door. As she moved slowly along she couldn't help looking at the plants, and it soon became apparent they were all of the old fashioned varieties such as her grandmother had liked. The roses gave off the scent she hadn't smelled for years, pansies grew where they wanted and the lavender bush in one corner was loaded. And so it went on. Although not everything was in bloom she recognised the foliage of lily of the valley, hollyhocks and honesty which brought back many memories.

Suddenly she remembered why she was here and looked round to see if she was being watched as she slowly approached the door. Her hand went up a couple of times before she actually used the little brass knocker. She was just debating as to whether to knock again when she heard a key being turned in the lock. The door opened a fraction.

"Who are you?"

The voice was female and didn't sound young so it was looking hopeful.

"Um excuse me." Amy almost whispered. "I'm looking for a lady and wonder if you might be her."

"Why would you come here? I don't have visitors."

The door opened a few more inches and the top of a head appeared as far as the eyes, but the rest remained hidden.

"Someone told me you lived down a little lane and this is the only one I've seen."

Amy knew this was sounding a bit tame but she wasn't going to give up now.

"Well, I think you've come to the wrong place. Good Bye."

Amy couldn't let it end there.

"No please listen. I'm looking for a lady who called herself Juliette but her name was Janet and I really do have to see her. It's very important."

She knew she was rambling but was doing anything to stop the door being closed because she knew it would not be opened again.

"You can't believe everything that people tell you."

The door was still open so there was hope. She took the chance.

"I know you don't know me. My name is Amy. Amy Hall and I live in Narrow Brook with my brother."

There was a pause, then the door opened a bit further.

"You look familiar."

Amy gave a nervous laugh.

"Yes someone just told me I look just like my Mother, only she is in heaven now."

Again there was silence while the woman came into full view and looked her up and down. Her expression changed from suspicious to one of horror.

"I can't help you. Go away and never come here again. Do you understand? Go back to your home and forget you were ever here." With that she slammed the door shut and Amy was left standing there very bewildered. Much as she would have liked to knock again, she knew it was out of the question. There was nothing for it, she must go, just when she had got so near for she was certain this was the woman she had been seeking.

The gate loomed as she approached and she went to open it.

"I don't remember it being that stiff when I came in." she thought but realised that from the outside she was pushing it whereas now she was trying to pull it. The wall was too high to attempt to climb over so she looked round to see if by chance there was another exit from the place that led back to the road. Being aware that she could still be observed she held her head up and walked to the side of the bungalow but the wall continued as far round as she could see.

What she couldn't see was the fight going on between her guardians who were trying to procure her escape and the demons who had the gate securely closed, thus trapping her in. One guard was at her side constantly to protect her, and if she possessed the power she had been led to believe she had, she would have been aware of it. But she was a merely an innocent little puppet with unseen forces pulling her strings.

Chapter 6

Captain Shaw had sent word that they would be returning home for a short period on Friday, arriving in the evening, and apart from a light meal they didn't wish to be disturbed until the following morning when they would have a meeting with Dawkins to discuss ongoing arrangements.

"Well, that puts paid to me getting my feet up early." Cook was muttering to herself as she busied about the kitchen. She was learning that the master and his good lady were arriving and departing at any time with no particular pattern emerging so everyone had to be on their toes, just in case.

Thomas had been assigned to general cleaning especially the parts the Captain and Mrs Shaw would see. There seemed little point on wasting valuable staff time on other areas when there was all the clearing out and packing to be done.

It was Wednesday, the day after Amy had cycled to Eastcott and at the moment she hadn't arrived for work.

"Well I'm not surprised." Maud was in her usual belligerent manner. "You won't get much work out of her now."

Dawkins wanted no more hassle especially after his experience in the upstairs sitting room.

"Let's remember what was agreed Maud. Everyone has to work together and make sure they are doing their own job, and letting others take responsibility for theirs."

"Ought to have been a politician," she thought "he rambles on like one."

Giving her a severe look he continued.

"I'm separating you today. You will make sure everything is immaculate for the master and mistress in their rooms and Amy, when she arrives will continue with the clearing and packing.

"Well, if you're sure Mr Dawkins, but I would have thought……"

"As I have said quite clearly, I am allocating you the job of seeing to it that everything is satisfactory for the master. Do I make myself clear?"

Even Maud recognised the tone and answered simply "Of course."

He wasn't going to let her have the pleasure of watching for Amy to arrive and then reporting if she was late, so he packed her off upstairs well away from Kameron's room.

It was usual, especially now with everything upside down and changing by the moment, for Dawkins to allocate the daily tasks at an informal meeting in the servants room, but he was finding it was easier to inform each one on their own what he had planned for them on that particular day. He was aware of the tension going on and was doing his best to keep the waters calm until such time that they all left for the last time. He was also haunted by Cook's transformation and didn't want to be in her company in front of the others any more than was necessary. There were a lot of strange things going on and in a way he would leave the place eventually with very mixed feelings.

As he made his way across the hallway he saw Amy disappearing upstairs. It wasn't his manner to shout in the house, even if it was practically empty but he called up to her as quietly as possible.

"Amy."

She stopped without turning round. He figured that although he would normally have asked her to come back down to be briefed, it would save valuable time if she got on with her work immediately.

"I want you to carry on alone with what you have been doing. Maud is required elsewhere."

Her arm rose and she gave an acknowledgment of the hand to show she had understood, but still didn't turn. He watched her disappear onto the landing.

"She's getting very obstinate and insolent," he thought, "it's as well we are all going or she would have to be dismissed with that attitude."

His mind went back to when she first came and they had taught her how to speak and how to conduct herself. She had learned well but would never have risen to the position of being in charge of new servants. There was still a disrespectful side to her that came to the surface when she was annoyed. But he had given her more chances than some would and he always tried to be fair and not just take everything Maud said.

As he went about his business he pondered.

"Hm. Didn't even get a Good Morning Mr Dawkins." In fact, come to think of it, she hadn't spoken at all, and he hadn't seen her face. He would check as soon as he could to see if she was alright because that wasn't like her.

Unbeknown to him, Cook had monitored her from a distance the moment she appeared on the stairs, for she left no trace of entering the house. Apart from very high levels, all spirits, especially inexperienced ones cannot cover their tracks and so leave a definite wake behind them which makes them easy to trace. On examination, Amy's came from above. Something was very wrong and had to be investigated with haste, but Cook dare not expose her identity yet.

At times like these, such entities call upon decoy backup to nose about without drawing attention, and Abe, who had been monitoring this, chose the best one, Julius.

Replacement guardians were immediately despatched to protect Bryn while Danny was briefing Julius regarding the situation at the house.

"It's not coincidence is it?" he stated more than asked. "You knew all paths would lead back to Kam the minute he was brought over."

Danny wasn't very forthcoming. "It was always a possibility."

"And you had selected us knowing we would all have a role somewhere along the way."

"There's always a certain amount of planning but we have to be open to adjustment as you very well know."

Julius knew he wouldn't get a lot out of him and wondered just how much the big guns really knew. He tried another approach.

"Bit of a sly move though."

Danny wasn't easily caught out.

"Not really. You were in the neighbourhood and we thought you'd enjoy a bit of detective work."

Julius was still prodding. "Who alerted us?"

"A watcher."

"Oh, on the premises of course."

Danny was finding this amusing. ""Let me know when you've identified the intruder, oh and by the way."

"Yes?"

"You can't go in as yourself. They'd spot you straight away. We could be dealing with something a bit deeper that it appears."

Julius was smelling a rat.

"Oh No. What are you suggesting?"

Danny indicated below.

"Time to go. Assume your disguise."

As they watched, the image of a cat strolled into the kitchen from the rear garden, looked at Cook, then waited for her to open the door leading into the house.

"That's not a bodily form." Julius realised what Danny was directing him to do.

Although a master of decoy in his own right, there were times when those overseeing the whole picture would request a certain approach which they felt would be the most appropriate and produce the best results for the longest time. There was no good being recognised quickly before a spirit had chance to assess a situation especially when it wasn't certain as to the power of the intruder. This was definitely a case of softly, softly.

Cook waited for the image to be replaced by that of the one Julius had adopted, then slowly opened the door. She refrained from any other communication and kept the protection of her 'cook' image fully protected. She simply muttered something about cats and fleas and got on with her work.

Amy woke slowly. Everything looked strange, she wasn't in her own room but lying on a bed. She tried hard to remember everything and thought she must have had a dream about a house, a woman and some strong people who had dragged her away from her Mother. But how long had she been here, wherever it was? Slowly the recognition of the walled garden, the bungalow and her not being able to get out filtered back into her mind. But what had happened after that?

She was aware of many souls floating about around her, some seemed to be calming her but some were intent on trying to annoy her. Suddenly she was aware of a physical person near her.

"How are you feeling now my dear?" The voice was vaguely familiar.

Amy tried to sit up but her head was spinning.

"Be careful, you had a nasty fall."

"Where am I? Who are you?"

The woman's face was getting clearer and Amy jumped as she recognised who it was.

"You're the lady in the bungalow. You sent me away, but…."

"You tripped over in the garden. I hope you haven't hurt yourself to much. You seemed to bang your head on the wall, but there's no sign of a bruise."

Amy pulled herself up realising she was still fully clothed. She put her hand to her head and felt round.

"I haven't cut myself." Her head was spinning.

"No. Just take your time. You don't want to be riding your bicycle until you feel better. You might have an accident."

The last sentence sounded almost like a warning or a threat.

"What time is it? Only I have to be getting home."

"Have some tea." The woman handed her a beaker.

"Thank you."

After a few sips Amy started to feel a little more normal.

"I'm sorry if I have been a nuisance to you." She whispered, still feeling very uncertain as to what had actually happened.

"That is perfectly alright, my dear. Now when you feel like it we will have a little chat."

"Thank you." Amy was becoming more anxious as she still wasn't sure what time of day it was and now she wondered if Bryn was getting worried about her.

As she got off the bed, her mind started to try and piece things together. It was evening when she arrived and knew she had to get home before dark but now it appeared to be morning. Panic set in.

"I must get home, my brother will be worried."

"Of course." the woman said as she led her downstairs.

Rather than ask what time it was, Amy looked around for a clock and was horrified to see it was almost six o'clock in the morning. This didn't go unnoticed by the woman who explained that someone had phoned her home and said that she had met the lady she was looking for and had been talking longer than expected, so as it was getting very dark they had suggested she cycle home first thing in the morning.

Amy didn't feel very comfortable with this and imagined Bryn would think it strange but she was assured that when she got home he would confirm it. In normal circumstances Bryn may have queried it but he was in a new world of satisfaction which was taking over his emotions, but there was also another factor. What the woman had omitted to say was that the voice on the phone appeared to be Amy's, so he didn't question it.

As he always left early for work on the farm, she may get home just after he had gone but would see him that evening, which he accepted. Some men may not have been taken in by the ruse, but this was Bryn.

Before she left, Amy was determined to get answers to her questions. She had refused the offer of breakfast and just wanted to get away from this place.

"How did I get upstairs if I was so, um….well, knocked out?"

"Don't you remember dear? I helped you. Of course you were very stunned. I wanted to fetch the doctor but you said not to."

"I don't remember that one bit." Amy was getting annoyed. Something told her there was more going on here than this woman was admitting.

"And another thing." Amy's belligerence was working for her and very evident in her tone. "How did you see me?"

"See you? Why, from the window of course. I saw you trip."

"Well I don't remember tripping."

Before she could answer Amy followed up with her next question.

"When I asked if you were someone called Juliette, you didn't admit it and told me to go away, but that is you isn't it? You are Juliette or Janet or whatever your name is."

"Oh I've had many names in my time dear, what is a name after all?"

"I wish I'd never come, you aren't what I was expecting."

Amy made her way to the door.

"And why did you come?" the woman's tone was sharp. "I'll tell you. You came because you think you have powers and you want to know how to use them."

"Well, if you know, or think you know, there's nothing more to be said."

Amy still tried to leave but somehow the woman was at the door before her and was baring the way.

"You are an obstinate one. You have much to learn but I will tell you this. Yes, I recognised it when I first saw you and I thought you were here to flush me out."

"You knew?" Amy wasn't sure if she liked the way this was going.

"Of course. But if you want to go your own way, that's up to you. But I had better warn you. You will get into deep trouble without someone who knows about these things."

She stood back from the door indicating Amy could leave.

"Just a minute. What are you talking about.?"

The woman had her attention now.

"No, No, it's not for me to influence you."

"I've been told I have powers as it happens, and I intend to use them. For my own purpose." Amy was insistent.

"Fine! Just don't come running back here when you can't handle it."

Amy stood for a moment.

"In what way exactly?"

"If you have the power, you will know. That's all I can say on the subject."

Juliette had played on Amy's inquisitive side and knew she had her in the palm of her hand now. She could use this novice to her own ends. Unfortunately, she had no more power than Amy, but had been used by unsavoury spirits for their pleasure and entertainment for so long that she thought it was she who was calling the shots. If Amy didn't get out now, she would also be a toy, believing she was in control when in fact her eternal fate could be in the hands of beings she would never know.

"Feel free to come back whenever you want." Was the parting shot as Amy went out of the door and much to her surprise found her bike just outside. She made her way to the gate which opened straight away. Again something was niggling in her mind, but if this woman could help her get through to Kam, she may just give it one go, then she was free to leave it alone if she wanted.

The cat had been very careful not to be seen which wasn't too difficult with the few staff spread conveniently about the building. Cook had been expecting some help, but from experience had learned never to be surprised at whatever or whoever arrived. It didn't have to be an army of spirits who came blustering in, and generally was the most insignificant being who was much more experienced than the current passing trouble makers.

Julius, after getting over the initial shock, adapted very well to this role, and although knew he would have to check out the physical side, was keen to know what spiritual force was here.

The watchers had passed on the latest details about Amy, so he decided to find her image and locate its source as a priority. Keeping his true self well cloaked he picked up the disturbance of the wake that the image had left and knew a spirit had been placed.

When a good or bad force wants to suggest to a person in body that someone is there when in fact they are not, a likeness, similar to a hologram can be projected into the receiver's mind. In this case, as there is no spirit presence, no wake will have been left.

But when Abe and Danny learned that the image of Amy had left a wake, not on the ground but coming from above, they knew this was not a 'hologram' type, but a presence was there for a reason. It was urgent now that they must find out not only who, but why.

Julius was following the path left by the visitor, but veering off every so often to give the impression he wasn't tailing it. When he reached Kameron's room, the feeling was stronger and he knew the entity was inside. Gently he leaned against the door, with his body, and the door opened slowly just enough for him to get through.

From the floor level, his view was limited and he dare not expose his powers yet so he merely wandered in and jumped onto the bed, examined the piles of clothes waiting to be packed, then curled up near the pillow.

He was very conscious of three beings hovering around the locked chest, and using the common knowledge that cats can see spirits when humans can't, he looked straight at them, just waving his tail gently.

One of them alerted the others who all turned their attention to him for a moment, then decided he must live there so got on with the business in hand. None of them resembled Amy's image so that had been used purely to throw Dawkins off the scent. They were all very nondescript very hazy things but one thing soon became apparent. There was only one trail so only one spirit was present but could split to spread its power.

Julius pretended he was nodding off, but his senses were picking up everything. The thing was obviously concentrating on the chest and nothing else. It was now inside and was rummaging through the sex toys Kam had carefully locked away. Suddenly he realised there was something very familiar about this being and he immediately added protection to his image to prevent him from being recognised. For the visitor was no stranger to this room, it was Kam himself.

Under his extra protection, one question was being sent to Danny. Why would Kam display a likeness of Amy? One possible answer was that he had to come back for some reason, and realising she wasn't there, took on her form to give himself the chance to root around with nobody to disturb him.

Abe was concerned over Amy's visit to Janet, to give her true name, not only for the danger in which she was placing herself, but the evil entities in situ at the bungalow were a nasty sadistic lot and would put innocent souls through anything to provide their pleasure. In the past Janet's overworked guardians had pulled her from the clutches of one group, only for her to seek out another. There had been many happenings which resulted in her having to lie low and not practice her 'talents' on local people. The hovering spirits found her an easy tool while she was deluded enough to believe she had special powers.

Amy was now believing she could contact Kam through this source, but it meant she would be heading into disaster and extra protective guards were needed before she was beyond recall. But unfortunately she believed she would walk away whenever she chose.

"How many fall into that trap." Abe and Danny said this every time a new candidate signed their soul away without realising it, when there was still time to get out. But these two wouldn't give up on Amy and would fight to the bitter end to secure her eternal peace.

The day rolled on at the house with Dawkins checking briefly on everyone at regular intervals. Maud had made sure that Thomas had cleaned the master's private quarters, as they were called, long before she dealt with the linen and finer points.

She even tried to explain that he should now work his way down the stairs and then concentrate on the entrance hall because that was the first thing they would notice.

"I've had my orders from Mr Dawkins."

Thomas slowly picked up the vacuum and his bag of cleaning materials, looked her straight in the eye, then made his way slowly out of the room.

"Well!" Her face was a picture. "Someone else getting above themselves."

Dawkins was still a bit bewildered by Amy's apparent attitude when she had arrived, but he had been too busy to check on her much, and every time he did she was busying about either just disappearing at the end of a corridor or going down the stairs. Eventually he caught up with her in master Kameron's room.

"Ah Amy. I don't seem to have been able to converse with you today, but I see you've been busy."

Kam, in Amy's form now emulated her voice.

"Well, there is a lot to do Mr Dawkins. Especially in here." The last bit was added almost to draw his attention to it.

Julius had jumped to the floor and was out of sight on the far side of the bed but was watching Kam's spirit as it changed with his reactions. This soul was nervous which seemed a bit unusual for the pompous, self-opinionated character he had always been. So what was bothering him?

Dawkins looked around the room, but sensed that not much had been done today. His 'nose' told him that something was going on but unfortunately he hadn't got the time to spend in here while he got to the bottom of it.

"Well don't worry Amy," he looked her in the eye, "the master and mistress won't be here for long and as soon as they have departed I will have Maud or Thomas help you."

"But….."

This was the last thing Kam wanted. This may be his only chance to carry out what he needed to do, and he couldn't have the place littered up with busy bodies. He was fully aware of Amy's current situation and her temporary absence had given him a golden opportunity.

"Just do your best for now."

Dawkins tone made it clear that this wasn't open for discussion and had a gut feeling that there was something very unsavoury in this room. His attention was being drawn to the locked chest, little knowing that Julius was making him aware that this article was about to play a very significant role. His glance was not missed by Kam, who knew time was now of the essence.

Although he had sensed something evil in there, he was unable to identify it, and if it could cloak itself at such close range, it had to be pretty powerful. He was scanning through his past lives and was only too well aware of the trail of horror he had left behind him, and was always aware that, at any time, some of it would catch up with him. Was he about to meet his fate now, here in his own room?

Amy had been asleep most of the day and woke wondering what had actually happened, and what had been a dream or simply her imagination. She looked at the clock.

"Heavens above!" she squealed. "I should have been at work."

As she sat up she couldn't understand why nobody from the house had rung to ask where she was.

"What do I do?" she was even more confused. It was almost time for Bryn to come home from work. She wasn't sure what had happened that morning and why he had gone off without question. It was if something had wiped her entire knowledge and this frightened her. She got out of bed and looked at herself in the long mirror. What a mess. She was in her underwear, her hair all over the place and dark circles under both eyes. She had a vague recollection of going to Eastcott and meeting a woman, and also knew that she had to go back. But she couldn't remember coming home, going to bed, or talking to Bryn. Everything was spinning.

She went to the bathroom and had a wash, then got into a skirt and top, combed her hair and went downstairs. As she made a cup of tea and tried to sort out some vegetables for dinner, she was wondering what excuse she could make at work the next day. Of course Maud would already have put her two pennyworth in, she was sure of that.

The sound of her brother coming in made her jump. Expecting him to start by asking questions, she was amazed when he put his bag down with a simple "I'm off for a wash."

The tea was working. Slowly she was remembering bits of what happened although there were too many gaps, but she knew she had been asked back so that she could make contact with the spirit world and in particular, Kam. Sad to say, she was only recalling what the evil entities surrounding Janet's place were allowing her to remember.

The dinner was on the way by the time Bryn returned. She looked at him hoping he could throw some light on things.

"You had a good time then?" he said smiling.

"Um, what makes you say that?" She was at a loss for words.

"Well you sounded happy enough when you said you was staying over there and coming back this morning."

"I what?" Terror was filling her now. "I rang you?"

"Don't be daft girl. Course you did."

That was enough. She sat at the table her head in her hands sobbing like a child. He was at her side immediately.

"Hey what's going on? I not seen you like this."

"I think I'm losing my mind." She cried. "I can hardly remember anything Bryn, and I haven't been to work and nobody's asked where I was and I seem to have been asleep since I came home, and I can't even remember how I did that and……"

"Now, now. Just calm down a bit." His voice was soft and very soothing. "Let's take it one bit at a time."

Slowly she related meeting the people at the pub and following the two women and even finding the little lane leading to the wall. But after that, it seemed unreal. She could remember a lady called Janet who seemed to want to help her and had asked her back again.

"Help you with what?" He wasn't understanding this at all.

"Um, with something I was looking into to."

"What was that then?"

She didn't think he would understand if she told him the truth. Most men would have pointed out that she had just met a stranger and stayed the night with them which made the whole situation sound a bit fishy. With the best will in the world, Bryn hadn't even thought of that.

"About the history round here. There's a lot gone on in the past you know."

He sat for a moment then looked her in the face.

"Well, sounds like you been ill. You best see doc."

"Oh no I don't think he could help, anyway I feel better now."

"Seems funny to me."

She wiped her face and went to check the cooking. Without turning she asked "What's funny."

"Well, I may not be the rosiest apple in the barrel but you just said you can't remember much after you met this woman."

"That's right."

"But you see, you phoned me and you can't remember that."

He had a point but she had no answer so he continued as though he was sorting it all through in his mind.

"So what I wants to know is, what did she give you to drink?"

"What are you saying?"

"Ah, slipped you a mickey. But why would she want to do that? I know. She gave you something you're not used to, so" he paused as though a light had hit him "you were blind drunk, that's why you couldn't ride your bike home last night." He was triumphant.

Amy looked round now.

"And how did I sound on the phone?"

Cold water had been poured on his result.

"Ok. You sounded Ok."

She paused before delivering her punch line.

"So I didn't sound drunk then?"

His balloon had been burst.

"No, you sounded…."

"Go on. How did I sound Bryn?" she was at the table now.

"You just spoke then put the phone down."

"We didn't chat?"

"No, you just told me you weren't coming home because it was dark and I said 'Ok'. That was all."

As she looked at him, she felt he knew now that something hadn't been quite right but it hadn't occurred to him until she said.

"So, I was either plastered, or not, or….it wasn't me."

"But it was you. I heard you."

She knew it was no good going any further with this, he just wouldn't understand and if she told him what she did remember he would tell her never to go again. But she had to, this was her big chance of honing her talents so she had to risk it and go back.

Abe was getting rather concerned the way events were shaping and had called Danny for a discussion.

"The two characters in this are dancing round each other and it can only spell disaster." Abe was referring to Kam's interest in the chest and Amy's intention to communicate with him.

Danny was thoughtful.

"Can we separate them for a moment?"

"Say what you are thinking."

Danny tried to put it as simply as possible.

"Amy, believing she has powers will use the Janet woman to get through to him, but at the moment she is fairly safe. The evil calling the shots haven't got her in their clutches yet. She isn't aware just how close Kam is and if she knew he had used her image, well, that would have been a shock. Now to concentrate on him. Julius fed back some pretty interesting but scary facts."

"What was in the chest with the sex toys?" Abe was ahead of him.

"Exactly."

"And you would like to go and find out?"

Danny was a bit hesitant. "Very much so, but not knowing what could be lurking, it had better be someone high up. Don't want to send Julius, let's keep him undercover for now."

"Agree. It will have to be someone who can do an instant appraisal in less than a second."

"Shall I do it then?"

There was a pause and Danny wondered what Abe was planning.

"We'll both go. But not together."

"Explain please."

Abe drew a mental picture of the house, zoomed in to the room, then the chest then the toys.

"Right. When he was using this stuff he wasn't always alone. Sometimes females were just as much a part of his rituals, and it wasn't just in this life. There had been instances where tragedies had occurred and you can imagine the families were out for his blood."

Danny was getting the picture. "But not just in that particular earth life?"

"Exactly. Some of them have been following him through his existence which is why he always has to stay at least one step ahead."

"So there could be some from way back, when he was the Midlands Murderer." This was more than Danny had imagined.

"Very much so. Hence the moment of fear that Julius picked up."

"So am I right in thinking the sex things are the base for some of these people? They are attached to them until they attack."

Abe was silent for a while. "I'm afraid it may not be that simple."

"You mean there's more?"

"To put it bluntly, an evil magnet. The ones who centre round the stuff would be a beacon to attract more just for the hell of it, nothing personal. They wouldn't care who the target was."

Danny took up the idea. "So the ones with a grudge would wait until Kam used them for his pleasure and then…."

"Give him a taste of his own medicine."

"But there's one thing I don't understand." Danny was trying to make sense of Kam's previous actions. "Correct me if I'm wrong but wasn't he gloating about the effect it could have on those who found the chest. And wasn't he going to lead them to the key?"

"He was." Abe confirmed. "But I think at that point he wasn't aware of the interest that had been growing, and the Dark Demons for example could have found this to be a possible ready made situation."

"And when he had a quick look to check that everything was normal, so to speak and got a shock to find it wasn't."

"Even the likes of Kam recognise the enormity of what could be lying in wait."

"But surely they aren't trapped in there. If they are that powerful, they could get out whenever they choose."

Abe reminded him of one basic fact.

"But what is time? There is no rush. It will have much more effect to appear to come out of the locked chest and everyone in its path will think that evil has been released. Oh no my friend, it is merely waiting."

They were in conference for a while and the decision was made that Abe would take the first look but accompanied by two other like powers, then Danny would follow after a while also with similar back up. The idea of having more than one was to distract anything in situ to cause a little confusion so that the two main ones could observe, but the operation would be so instantaneous and hopefully catch the evil unawares. But they still didn't know just how powerful it could be so there was no room for complacency.

Amy was a bit apprehensive about reporting for work on Thursday and as she cycled up the drive she was trying to find a good excuse for her absence. She would say, quite honestly that she had slept most of the day and had woken feeling unwell but couldn't remember much of it which was about all there was. Anything she made up would sound false. She just prayed that Maud wouldn't jump on her as usual and give her a third degree.

As she went into the servant's room to hang up her coat she expected Cook to make some remark but she merely nodded in her own way and got on with what she was doing. Maud came bustling in but still said nothing about it which made Amy start to feel very uncomfortable.

Dawkins arrived and said they were to carry on as before, but as soon as Maud had finished prepared the master's rooms, she was to come and join Amy with the sorting out. He was careful not to say 'help her' as Maud would have definitely taken exception to that. He told Thomas that there were a few maintenance jobs that needed attention and would go through those with him.

Amy was completely bewildered now. Why wasn't anyone saying anything? She decided to test the waters. As she and Maud left the room, she said quietly "I feel a bit better today. Was really poorly yesterday, you know, time of the month and that."

Maud gave her a passing glance. "That would account for the fact you did very little being left on your own. Well we shall see about that when I have completed the master and mistress's rooms. That packing should have been finished long ago."

This was creepy. Hadn't anybody missed her? It was obvious they had all been stretched through the house but this was a bit weird to say the least. Well, for some reason she had got away with it so she decided not to worry too much and made her way to Kameron's room.

Chapter 7

Thomas had been with the family for more years than anyone could remember. He was glad to have secured the job for it hadn't been easy to get work. His family were from the Caribbean and attitudes were not always in his favour. It was believed that Captain Shaw's father had brought him back from one of his escapades abroad having taken a liking to the man. He had proved himself to be a hard worker, would do anything required of him but asked for no favours in return. It was understood that he would be employed at the house for as long as he could work and then adequate arrangements were to be made for him to have sufficient care for the rest of his days.

A lot of the younger staff queried why he had been taken into the employment in the first place. Nobody knew much about him, he was a loner who seemed to have no family and didn't discuss his own affairs. Every day he would leave work, and go to his lodgings near the estate, then return for work early the next day.

But if the staff through the years had known his real purpose for being there, they wouldn't have felt so easy about his presence in the house.

It had all been carefully planned, for this place held more secrets than any one generation could know. Of course there were rumours of various activities, but there was never any proof. Captain Shaw's father had been targeted, and Thomas put directly in his path so that he would be invited into the household.

It makes a big difference as to whether a spirit, be it good or evil, enters by its own means or is welcomed into a place, not necessarily a building, but any space area. When once they have received the invitation it is very difficult to remove them at a later stage. Therefore Thomas was safe and had been for all his time there.

But there was one thing that Cook had always been very wary of. To date she still wasn't sure on which side of the fence he played. Keeping her identity well under cover, she had observed him many times and knew he was there just waiting for either instructions, or the right time to fulfil his own objective. She hadn't been fooled by his outer image for one minute, but daren't probe too deeply to reveal what he was hiding, without giving herself away. The incident when Dawkins had a taste of her power didn't matter, for he wouldn't dare mention it for fear of looking silly. But she knew things were about to come to a head, then they would all see just what was living in their midst.

Thomas was walking along the corridor leading to Kameron's room and he saw Amy alone, standing by the chest. She was running her hand over the locks as though she could open them with her thoughts. As he made his way into the room he stopped suddenly.

"What's that doing there?" he jumped as he saw the cat on the bed.

"Don't know. Just wandered in I'm told. He's not hurting anything, are you puss?" She stroked Julius' head.

"It shouldn't be here." Thomas was forceful.

Amy turned to face him. "And who says so?"

"Because… they have mange and ticks and the like."

"Well, you shouldn't be in here anyway. Go away."

She stared him out but the look he was returning showed a very different side to the quiet insignificant man she had worked with all these years.

"I've been given a job." He stood his ground.

"Not in here."

He put his bag on the floor with a thud.

"When Mr Dawkins gets here, I'm to open that chest."

"But....but you don't know what's in there. It's private."

He gave a strange smile.

"Yes it was. But the owner is no longer with us is he, and Mr Dawkins wants to know what's inside."

She was fighting for time. She needed to take some of Kameron's belongings as she believed they would help her make contact with him. She had read it somewhere so it must be right. But she needed time on her own, and it was bad enough that Maud was going to be snooping around again, let alone this maintenance man.

"Mr Dawkins, Mr Dawkins," she snapped "well he isn't here yet so there's no point in you hanging around so take your tool bag and go."

Julius rose from his curled up position and made his way to the edge of the bed, then sat staring at Thomas.

"You can get rid of that thing for a start."

As he pointed to the cat it raised itself to a standing position its back arched, the ears were streamlined and the eyes were peering into the man's very soul.

"You see, he doesn't like you." Amy was pointing to Julius but yelling at Thomas.

Grabbing his bag, he muttered "It had better be gone by the time I get back." Then added very pointedly "With Mr Dawkins."

Amy sat on the bed with her arm round Julius and assured him the nasty man had gone, but after a few seconds the cat had jumped down and ran out of the door. The message had gone out and Thomas was now being observed from a much higher level.

"Didn't think we'd flush him out so soon." Danny was watching closely.

Abe mused. "He's very well cloaked and has been all this time but the cracks are showing. Keep Julius around for as long as possible but we may have to change his image."

"That was strange," Danny thought "he was really unnerved by his presence and I don't think it was just because he doesn't like cats."

"No, I think he picked something up. He'll be on his guard now."

"Ok I'll get the cat out and replace him with something completely different."

"Be careful," Abe warned. "it may not be coincidence that this is the time for the chest to be opened."

"I have just the very thing." Danny left to put the next stage into action.

Kam had retreated to consider. He had used various pieces of equipment throughout the years, including items of torture. In his life as the Midlands Murderer he was such a sadistic character that he didn't stop when he had put his victims through physical and mental horror, but carried on mutilating them when they had thankfully passed on. He even believed that he hadn't actually killed them. If you take a gun and shoot someone or take a knife and stab them, that was murder, but not when they died through various activities. That was just by accident. Also his twisted mind was under the illusion they were enjoying it and only crying out with pleasure. But that was long ago and now he found there was added satisfaction in causing pain, as long as it wasn't directed at him.

He was desperate for a full blown sexual thrill but that would have to be put on hold for the moment, for learning that his private chest was about to be forced open meant that immediate action had to be taken. It was bad enough that his sex toys would be discovered in this way without his control as to who saw them, but that wasn't the main problem. Normally he would have watched with delight at the expressions of horror as each piece was lifted out with disgust.

But there was something else in the chest, something so innocent that it had been overlooked by everyone, and it was nothing to do with the evil entities already residing in there. But Abe was about to make his first call, and it would be very obvious to him as soon as he came in contact with it.

Janet knew that Amy would come back because she had sent out signals calling her. The evil occupying her bungalow had seen to that the minute she had pushed her bicycle through the gate in the wall but this fake medium truly believed it was she who pulled the strings.

"It won't be long," she smiled "she'll be back."

There had been a few visitors over the years but she had been forced to receive them covertly so as not to draw attention. There were no group séances or anything of that nature, but she had fleeced a couple of people who had more money than sense and were desperate to contact loved ones. Others didn't come very often for one reason or another but this was a fresh new face and held promise. The evil watchers sensed Amy's eagerness to contact Kam and knew they could provide her with what she wanted with little or no effort.

Money hadn't come into it on the recent visit, but Janet knew that once she had her victim hooked it would be no problem. She'd take her for whatever she could and it would be good practice to keep her hand in.

"Hope I haven't lost my touch," she laughed. "why should I? Always been alright before."

She made her way to a small back room. It was furnished with the usual things one might expect. Small round table in the middle of the room covered with heavy cloth and even heavier curtains to keep out every speck of light. But then Janet had come up to date for some reason. Instead of a crystal ball or a candle on the table, there were numerous small colour changing lights around the outside of the room. They were on any surface available, on a bookcase, a side table, even a pile of books. When the main light was turned off, the effect was soothing at first but as the colours changed so did the shadows and when anyone was in conference it had a peculiar effect. After a while, sitters became disorientated and their attention wasn't always on Janet and some became quite dizzy. The effect wasn't caused by the lights themselves but by the attending evil which was on constant standby to pluck the innocent souls and take them under their control. This was the reason some of Janet's clients never came back.

Amy would be returning but having no idea that she was a sacrificial lamb.

Bryn spent a very uneventful day at work, his mind split. He was eager to know when his next loving session was going to be and also his gut feeling told him that something wasn't quite right with his sister. He went over and over in his mind about the phone call and her not coming home. His guardian spirit was trying to tell him to ask more questions, but he couldn't seem to sort it out. He made his way into the barn where his previous encounter had taken place. Disappointment crept over him as he felt the emptiness around him. His groin was aching for relief and he knew he had to do something about it.

As he stood there he felt a familiar hand caressing him under his clothes and he almost cried out with expectation, but as soon as he felt the warmth it was snatched away and he was left almost bursting to finish the job. Immediately a cold feeling came over him and his equipment shrank back to normal. He couldn't cope with this. What was going on? If something had intervened he wished it would keep its nose out and let his visitor get on with doing what he was desperate for.

The passing spirit had been ousted as soon as it attempted to seduce him. Powl's replacement was having none of it, and disappointing though it may be for Bryn, this is how it would be as long as this one was on duty. But, once having tasted the delights, if a person's desire is strong enough, it will go to any lengths to secure what it wants.

Dawkins, knowing the young master's history, was a bit loathe for the female staff to be in the room when the chest was opened, so he ordered Maud, who had now arrived, and Amy to wait in the next room and do some dusting or whatever would be useful.

"But why?" Amy protested. "Bet I've seen it all before, even if she hasn't." she indicated to Maud.

"It wasn't a request young lady, it was an order." Dawkins face was set.

Thomas arrived with his toolbag and looked immediately to the bed.

"Has that cat gone?"

Amy did an overacted search of the room, pulling up every cover and moving pillows.

"Yes, yes," Dawkins kept his cool, "I think we have established there is no cat here."

Amy sneered at Thomas.

"Afraid of them are you?"

Dawkins called them to order.

"We have very little time, now ladies please do as you have been told and wait until you are called."

Very reluctantly Maud left the room followed by Amy who still gave Thomas a very searching look which he ignored.

"Right Thomas, there are two locks on the lid and another one on this flap which comes down. Please be careful as we don't want any damage to the chest itself as it is very old." Dawkins wanted this done as soon as possible now.

Abe had visited already and Danny had just left but their movements were so instantaneous anything would have to have been of a much higher level to notice that they had even been in the area. The evil lurking was aware that the lid was going to be forcibly opened when the padlocks were cut and decided to lay in wait for the moment.

Thomas moved closer and put his bag on the floor. Suddenly the door to the room slammed shut. Dawkins was surprised as he was sure the women had closed it behind them. Obviously not. Thomas had shot round as if he had seen something but Dawkins urged him to get on with it. He was now getting the feeling they weren't wanted there and the sooner they got the job done and got out the better.

"Must have been the wind." He tried to make it sound casual but was getting very unsettled.

"These aren't old locks." Thomas was examining them closely. "Not the original ones, much too modern."

"Well maybe that's a blessing." Dawkins didn't mind cutting through something that could be replaced without devaluing the object.

"Pity I never learned how to pick them." Thomas tried to make light of it but he wasn't feeling comfortable. He rummaged in his bag for a bolt cutter. "Right, here we go."

He carefully placed the tool round the padlock holding the flap down and went to apply pressure when he suddenly jumped back.

"Bloody hell fire!"

Dawkins was horrified not only at the outburst but it appeared the man had been thrown back by an unseen force.

"Is this wired?" Thomas shouted.

"Well of course it isn't."

"Then why did I get a bloody shock?" He was rubbing his arm as if to get the life back into it.

"Impossible. You must have imagined it." Dawkins retorted. "Now try again."

"You must be jesting. I'm not going near that thing again. Not on your life."

Dawkins had to try another approach.

"May I remind you that you are employed here to carry out your orders which you have done diligently I might add for all the time you have been here. So why are you now being so belligerent?"

"Because there's something not right here Mr Dawkins. Can't you feel it?"

This caused a problem because obviously they could both sense something was wrong. It was almost as though something was trying to stop them opening the chest.

After a moment Thomas looked up and said "I'll give it one more try Mr Dawkins."

"Good man." The relief was obvious.

Again the bolt cutter was put in place but before he could squeeze the handles he jumped back again but this time for a totally different reason. He and Dawkins stared at the chest in disbelief. All three padlocks were hanging there unlocked.

"This is black magic. I don't touch this." Thomas was gathering up his bag and trying to get away.

"I'm sure it's nothing of the sort." Dawkins was trying to sound firm. "Now, if it bothers you, I will open the lid but you stay here as witness to anything I remove."

Thomas had tried a few tricks to keep the chest closed but now he thought that if the man was daft enough to pursue this then let him. He stood erect by the bed and watched as his superior took on this foolhardy action.

Unbeknown to Dawkins, Thomas was protecting himself with a force shield to keep him from the evil that would shortly erupt, because at this precise moment, he didn't know its purpose but he wasn't sure if it was anything he had encountered previously. There was always the chance it had a score to settle which made him extra cautious as he had crossed swords with many of his kind in the past. It didn't matter how long it took, they would always seek you out.

So this was the moment for which everyone had been waiting, although for different reasons.

Amy and Maud were annoyed at having been forced from the bedroom as they had assumed they would be in the front row when it came to anything interesting. They'd done the hard work of clearing out drawers, cupboards and wardrobes, and even found a few unsavoury books under the bed. But everyone was curious to know what had been hidden away all this time.

"Well, I'm not standing here like a lemon." Maud stated and made her way to the door.

"Just what I was thinking." Amy was glad the suggestion had been made because she was itching to go and listen.

Quietly they tiptoed along the passage until they were outside the door.

"If they come out," Amy whispered, "we'll say we thought they called us."

For once Maud had to appreciate the forethought and nodded. They both leaned with their ears to the panels but these doors were quite thick and it was difficult to pick out much. But when Thomas shouted they heard that and looked at each other wondering what was going on. Amy tried to look through the keyhole but to no avail.

Suddenly they both felt a force not pushing them but pulling them away, and much as they tried to fight it, the power increased and before long they were at the end of the corridor almost clinging to each other. Something was holding them with such a power it was frightening, but in fact it was keeping them out of the immediate onslaught of the evil release.

Cook stood at the kitchen table, her knife in her hand with a faraway look as though she was in a trance as she held the two ladies away from the room. It was quite an easy task to her but she knew every bit of concentration was needed as they were not up against any low form of spiritual power. It was also essential to release them as soon as she could or she could be recognised, not only by the escaping fiends but by Thomas.

Kam was flitting in and out of the area but not remaining still for a moment. His playthings seemed unimportant now and he was anxious to learn what had possibly been stalking him, and for how long. It was certain after his cursory look, that the spirits were simply using the chest as a waiting room and they could have come and gone at will had they so wished, which could mean only one thing. They were in control of the game and would move when they decided, so perhaps they wouldn't make a grand entrance now. They could be waiting for another time. This didn't make him feel much better because, as usual it was the uncertainty that always wore people down.

Dawkins bent over and tried to lift the lid.

"It's much heavier than I thought it would be."

He turned to Thomas who was staring straight ahead and not looking at it.

"It has to come up, there's nothing holding it." Again he struggled to raise it but it remained firm.

Thomas spoke now. "Probably a good spirit holding it down so the bad can't get out."

Dawkins looked at him again. "Now we don't want any of that mumbo jumbo here, let's just keep calm."

As he spoke Thomas's eyes widened in terror and he turned and ran to the door trying to pull it open.

"Let me get out. Let me out of here." He was yelling frantically but the door didn't budge.

What Dawkins had failed to notice while his attention was on the other man, was that the lid was now fully open and the immense feeling of evil was pouring out past him.

The women still held at a safe distance heard the banging on the door and could make out the cries but were helpless to do anything. It may have been doubtful if they would have had the nerve to move if they really had the chance.

Dawkins was held on the spot, and although he couldn't see anything, he had never felt such a horrible presence before. The whole room stank so badly of the putrid odour, he felt himself on the point of vomiting. Although he knew that this house had witnessed many strange events in the past, he felt sure this was the worst it could have known.

Kam emitted a spiritual sigh of relief.

"So. It wasn't me that they were waiting for after all. That's a relief."

This hard hearted person had no feeling for others and watched as the physical life was drained out of Thomas bit by bit.

"Who'd have thought there was a score to settle there? He must have been a bad lot." He mused, but it was of no importance. If the man was up to no good, then it had been dealt with and he was free to get on with his own ambitions. As soon as his belongings were accounted for he could be off and never have to frequent this dreadful place again.

"Wonder if the ones he had crossed will leave now." He thought as he circled above the house at a safe distance.

"The foolish creature." Abe was watching from way above.

"Makes you almost feel sorry for him, but he is so busy fobbing that attack off he hasn't seen what's staring him in the face, so to speak." Danny was also observing.

"Doesn't deserve pity. He should have his wits about him. Thinks he's clever but he misses the obvious."

Danny's thought pattern was in the chest which would appear to be empty spirit wise except for what was lurking in the thing that nobody had even noticed.

"Is Julius due to return?" Abe asked.

Danny was quick to reply. "He's already there."

"When?" Abe was wondering how he hadn't spotted him.

"Just arrived." Danny was happier with this than Julius but that wouldn't stop him carrying out his role to the bitter end.

When Cook knew the women were in no danger, she released them. While Amy was keen to see what had gone on in the room, Maud was a little more hesitant, for although she hadn't always experienced things first hand, she had heard of the past unrest from older servants long departed.

Tapping gently on the door, Amy called out softly.

"Are you alright in there Mr Dawkins?"

There was a pause and some shuffling then the door opened a tiny bit and Dawkins whispered "You mustn't come in here, either of you."

"We heard a yell. Who was it?" She wasn't leaving it there although she knew she was pushing it.

"Just a moment."

He closed the door for a moment and there were more sliding noises as if something was being dragged. When he opened it again he was flushed and not his normal composed self. Seeing the state of him Amy called to Maud.

"Come here quick, something's not right with Mr. Dawkins."

Maud was still hesitant but she needed to know what was going on, especially as her junior seemed one step ahead of her.

"What is it?" Maud arrived at her side then gasped. "What on earth happened to you?"

Dawkins almost slid out of the room so that he didn't have to open the door any wider than necessary. He leant against the wall of the corridor.

"I want you to do something without question please."

They both nodded, thinking they would learn the truth.

"Go and fetch Cook up here and you both wait in the servant's room."

"But," Maud was searching for a reason to stay, "why Cook?"

Amy jumped in "Wouldn't it be better if one of us stayed with you and the other went for Cook? You do look a bit seedy Mr Dawkins if you don't mind my saying so."

He took a deep breath. "As I said, I want you to send Cook, no, ask Cook to join me here and you please….both stay there until you get further orders. Make yourself a cup of tea or something."

The shrug that passed between them was obvious, but there was no other option, although as they hurried downstairs, they agreed that Cook wouldn't know what their instructions were, so one would appear to come back with her while the other stayed behind, and then follow at a safe distance. But they didn't know of Cook's alter ego and she had spiritually witnessed the whole episode

"You wanted me Mr Dawkins?"

The voice made them jump for she was standing behind them. Both wanted to ask how she could possibly know but she covered that quickly.

"You've all been up here a long time and your tea is getting cold and you did ask me to remind you of the time Mr Dawkins as you have an important telephone call to make."

He was about to question this but something told him to accept the remark while his brain did a quick retake of her transformation in the sitting room.

"I did indeed Cook. Thank you. Well ladies you can go and get your tea and we will be down in a moment."

He gave a little shoving movement with both hands as if he was ushering them to a given place so they had no option but to leave.

As soon as they were out of sight he beckoned to Cook and whispered "This isn't a pretty sight."

She dismissed the remark and indicated for him to lead the way into the room. Thomas lay slumped partly on the floor and the rest of him wedged against the wall, his eyes staring in terror. Cook held up her hand for Dawkins to remain silent and she stood motionless but was transmitting every detail of the body, and then the most important fact. The soul had been wrenched away and what was left was no more than an empty shell. Whatever had been waiting for the moment to pounce, had got what it came for. There was no answer as to why it had to be this moment, but maybe that was unimportant. Thomas had gone.

After the initial shock, Dawkins realised that this would be classed as a sudden death and the police would have to be informed. Although he was more than aware that there was more going on here than just the physical aspect, there would be no need to mention it. He was the only witness to the fact that the man had just cried out then dropped down dead. Cook, with her insight calmed him slightly by explaining that any examination would simply prove he had died from a heart attack.

It was late afternoon and Janet was getting ready for Amy's return. She knew it wouldn't be long for she could sense it, she thought. Of course she wouldn't mention her fee until the woman was well and truly hooked, then it would be too late. She didn't imagine she would have much in the way of savings but it was better than nothing. Then of course there was the brother. Maybe she could talk her into bringing him along sometime and see if he too had the power. It can run in families especially if it suited her purpose to convince her. That would mean double the income and if the man was anything like his sister, they would be a pushover. This new client awakened the greed by which she had practiced before and she wasn't about to let it slip away.

The spirits surrounding her abode mocked her. They had helped lead Amy to her as they had all the others. None of it had been coincidence, but all carefully set up. Unfortunately this area had been drained but they were about to revive the fashion, starting with this maid who didn't seem to have much about her. But they hadn't studied Amy and thought she would be putty in their hands so things could get interesting.

"What the hell is that?"

Amy went outside to empty some rubbish and came face to face with a pair of eyes staring at her and the most enormous set of horns which looked very ominous. Maud came hurrying out then laughed.

"It's a goat."

"But where did it come from?"

They both looked as the creature helped itself to some foliage and stood chewing happily.

"I don't know." Amy was very wary, she'd been frightened by one as a child and never trusted them.

"They're alright when you get familiar with them. I used to milk some that belonged to a neighbour."

"Well I wouldn't try milking that, it's got a dick." Amy let her trained image slip a little.

Julius was not amused by this latest image, and he didn't like having his private parts referred to in such a common way. But there was a job to be done.

"What are we going to do with it?" Amy was standing stock still in case it charged.

"We aren't going to do anything." Maud was quick to answer. "It must belong to someone from around here and it's just wandered in. Was probably tethered somewhere to graze and….." she stopped.

"What is it?" Amy still hadn't moved.

"They always have a collar, but this one hasn't got one. Well there's still an answer to that."

"Can't wait." Amy wasn't happy.

Maud ignored it and continued.

"Sometimes the owner would ask me to go and fetch one in from grazing. Now, he used to put the tethering chain through the collar and to get it off I had to undo the collar to get it out then do the collar back up then walk the beast back to its little stable."

Amy would normally have yawned by now but she daren't move as the thing held her in its gaze continuing its slow chewing.

"Anyway," Maud carried on regardless "the damn thing waited for me to undo the collar and as soon as the chain was off, the goat took off with me running at the side trying to do the collar up again. I'd got the ends, one in each hand but could I do it? It ran me all the way like that, it knew where it lived you see. I did feel a fool. Bet the owner was amused to see me flying along at that speed. I never did it again."

Amy sighed now. "And the point of the story is?"

"Don't you see? If someone undid his collar and he ran off, the collar is still lying on the ground somewhere."

"On purpose you mean?" Amy was still staring the goat in the eye.

"Well, could be but not necessarily. But it would explain why it doesn't have one."

"Wouldn't there be a mark on its neck, if it normally wore one I mean?"

Maud looked a bit closer. "No sign of one." She took a couple of steps nearer. "Now then Billy."

"How do you know it's called Billy?"

"They're all called that, if they're male of course."

"I don't care what it's bloody… I mean blooming well called. Get it to stop looking at me." Amy still daren't move.

At that moment Cook appeared at the doorway, took in the scene and hastily returned indoors.

"Well that was a great help." Amy sneered.

"Perhaps she's gone to get it some greens to draw it away. You know she doesn't overdo the words but she thinks pretty straight." Maud seemed happy with that.

The minutes rolled on and Amy was sure the thing was getting nearer although it hadn't moved. Just when she was about to risk it and run Cook came back with Dawkins in tow.

"There. What did I tell you?"

"You could be right." He looked a bit doubtful but added "Heaven sent."

Although Julius would have considered it a menial task, the fact he was able to keep the two ladies away from the room had worked long enough to fulfil the purpose, and now he prayed that he could be given an image befitting his talents. But who could ever know what his superiors had lined up?

Kam had been flitting back and forth because he just had to know what these two would do with this situation. Not that it bothered him but it was good entertainment and he was relieved the evil force hadn't been after him. And he could always use his bit of spare when the opportunity arose. Good way of celebrating he thought. But he still hadn't realised what still lurked in the chest, and if he had, he would not have been so complacent.

Maud had tried to coax the goat away from the house but it stood firm, so she persuaded Amy, with a bit of help from Dawkins to return to the servant's room.

Dawkins told them to be seated while he had a word with them.

"I'm afraid I have some very sad news for you. It seems Thomas was taken ill upstairs and," he looked at Cook, "he has died."

Maud seemed very shocked but Amy asked "Was it him who yelled?"

"It was. He must have had a sharp pain or something, and it was very quick."

There was silence for a moment while it sank in then Cook stood up.

"It must have been an awful shock for Mr Dawkins and he has asked me to continue." She looked from one to the other. "Of course the police will have to be called and a doctor to confirm, well you know. And then he will have to be taken away."

Dawkins took over. "Thank you Cook. I'm afraid it means you will all have to stay here in case there are any questions but you can only say what you know. After such time, you can go home for today."

He coughed before continuing "We will carry on in the morning as usual but I'm afraid we still have to clear out the chest, so if it won't be too unpleasant ladies, you may both be present when I empty the contents."

He knew full well they wanted to poke their noses in, but in truth he didn't fancy being alone in the room after what had happened.

Before leaving the room Cook asked that they stood and offered a prayer for Thomas and that his soul may rest peacefully.

"Wherever you are." She added to herself.

Chapter 8

After the police were satisfied with the facts, Maud and Amy were allowed to go home but it was pointed out that they should speak to no one about the unfortunate incident for the moment, and they may have to answer further questions the following day.

"Could you check that goat isn't anywhere about before I get my bike?" Amy had visions of being chased full pelt down the drive.

"If it makes you happy." Maud went to the door but muttered loud enough to be heard "A 'please' wouldn't go amiss."

She looked all around then returned saying "Can't see it anywhere. Must have wandered off."

"Thanks anyway." Amy thought she had better show some manners.

Dawkins was still upstairs and so Cook reminded them "Make sure you're on time tomorrow ladies, going to be busy."

"I always am." Was Maud's aside with a meaningful glance.

As she cycled quickly down to the road, just in case the animal was lurking anywhere, Amy mocked the last remark.

"I always am. Cocky cow."

Bryn had just got home and was having his wash. As he heard her come in, he called down.

"Won't be long."

"That's Ok," she called back "got lots to tell you."

He knew he couldn't spend too long in the bathroom now and was a little disappointed that he hadn't felt any of the caresses he enjoyed so much but he would have to be patient and wait for the right moment.

As Amy peeled the potatoes to make some chips, her mind kept going back to the house. She still felt uneasy about the way she and Maud had been almost invisibly held away from the room. Of all people she should be the one allowed in there at any time, after all, wasn't she Kameron's beloved? Well fate had worked in her favour and she would be witness to what was in the chest.

"Why all the secrecy anyway?" She thought. "You'd think the crown jewels were in there. Bet it's only a pile of old clothes anyway. Ah probably some fancy dress costumes."

"Want anything doing?" Bryn's voice made her jump.

"Oh, No thanks. I thought we'd just have egg and chips tonight."

"Lovely. Those that Mrs 'chicken lady' gave us?"

"They're the ones. Anyway, never mind about that. You wait till I tell you what's happened, only you're not to say anything because I'm not allowed to speak about it."

"Should you be telling me then?" He sat on the stool.

"Well, you won't let me down now, will you?"

"Course I won't."

As she started cutting the chips she lowered her voice automatically.

"You know Thomas, that old black chap that does our odd jobs? He's dead."

"What?" His mouth hung open.

"There, what do you think of that then?"

"Well, when did it happen?"

"Today of course, we were asked to leave the bedroom that was Kamer…..the young master's while they opened a chest and the next thing was we were told he was dead."

"But what happened?"

"Well the police came and a doctor and we think he had a stroke or heart attack or something, anyway Mr Dawkins was there and he says he just went down, but I heard him cry out."

"Oh dear. Poor man. Never saw him much. Kept himself to himself but never hurt anyone."

They were quiet for a minute then Bryn asked "But why can't you speak about it? Everyone's going to know some time. Can't keep that sort of thing quiet."

"Don't know, we were just told that's all. But I had to tell you."

As she was frying the chips she said casually "You don't mind if I go over to Eastcott tonight do you?"

"What? Where you went last time when you didn't come home?" He felt uneasy. There was a bad feeling about this although couldn't place it.

"Oh don't worry, I'll be back. Been warned not to be late in tomorrow, you know with all that went on today. And the master will be back in the evening."

"Well you be careful." He warned her, but at the same time was rather excited about being on his own for a while. He needed another session as soon as possible for his danglers were gagging for it.

Abe and Danny had decided to monitor Kam and Amy separately, but if the two were brought together with the help of Janet's spirits, only one of them would remain in situ while the other kept a close watch on the house. In the meantime they would be making fleeting checks on the chest to make sure the evil attached to the item hadn't moved.

It seemed that the evil entities that had targeted Thomas had left the area. This was unsettling because they had to be a high enough power to cloak themselves from Kam which meant they were capable of wiping their trail as they went.

"You know what this means?" Abe wasn't falling for the trap.

"Yes. They want us to follow. They know that because they have taken control of Thomas's soul and we will want to retrieve it." Danny had experienced this many times.

"Very carefully planned. This was no chance soul snatch. He's been targeted for a reason."

Danny mused. "But from which of his lives?"

Abe knew his next comment would cause even more concern.

"Do you know? I think his last one,."

"What makes you say that?"

"Think about it." Abe had to be very basic now. "He was from the Haiti part of the Caribbean, the home of voodoo and the like. Now we know that the way those spirits operate is different from the way we do."

Danny was recalling what they had learned about him.

"And he was instrumental in rescuing innocent victims from the clutches of the various sects before they could torture them, and we thought he was a good spirit."

Abe agreed "Until it seemed he may be only taking them for his own purpose, which was much more sadistic, but we won't go into that now."

"But wait," Danny was turning it all over "in that case wouldn't it make more sense for the good ones to want justice because it was their kin that he was accused of putting through the most heinous practices for his own gratification."

"I see your point, but it was never proved and the original captors were robbed of the spoils, so they wouldn't let that go, however long it took. But the outcome is that one of the groups has got his soul and our angels are on the track."

Danny was looking at it from an earthly sense now.

"You know what is so sad about all this?"

Abe knew where this was going so answered immediately.

"The fact that Capt Shaw's father took pity on the young man and brought him here for a better life, where he has hidden up until now. But has he? It's more likely he was tailed all along and his predators have known exactly his position, then struck when they were ready."

"But why now?"

Abe answered with another question. "Why don't you ask them?"

Danny didn't see any humour in the retort but knew that Abe was pointing out that for now, only they knew.

Dawkins and Cook were trying to have a moments' relaxation in their sitting room.

"Well, that's a fine thing to have to spring on them isn't it?" Dawkins was fussing with his jacket pocket.

"Can only tell them the truth, but I don't think it will have much effect if you ask me." Cook was mending a tear in her apron.

"Oh I think the master will be devastated, especially after…..well you know."

"That's exactly why I think it will pass over their heads." Cook didn't look up. They got enough to think about. Of course it does mean another funeral, so don't be surprised if you're expected to organise that."

He jumped. "I hadn't got round to thinking about that."

"Well, I'd give it a bit of thought if I were you."

Dawkins looked worried. "Of course I shall have to wait for them to ask me."

They sat in silence for a moment then he said very quietly "I am very grateful for your support today Cook."

"We do what we have to do." Was the simple reply.

He would like to have queried the 'we' but thought better of it so just said "I think we must try and get as much rest as possible tonight. We could be very busy this time tomorrow."

She nodded in agreement and went off to her own room.

Dawkins was still pondering the events of the day until his brain seemed in a whirl. His constant guardian calmed his mind and relaxed him into a state ready for sleep.

The first thing Cook did on entering her bedroom was to go to the window which looked out over the rear of the house. In direct line of her vision, the goat was standing looking up at her. Her acknowledgement of thanks wafted over him, and with the slightest inclination of his head he turned and disappeared into the bushes.

"Thank you." Was the unseen message she directed to Abe.

Julius was relieved to have been released from this present façade and almost dreaded what Danny had in mind for him next, for he knew he was still needed here for now. Before he could wonder he felt the communication which surprised him.

"We need you back in the house. Do you have a preference?"

He was staggered. "They are actually letting me chose my image!"

"I would suggest either something small which could be overlooked, or I could merge with Kam's belongings and flit from one item to the other."

There was a pause and he wondered if he had put his proverbial finger on an important fact.

"Stay put for the moment." Was the rather sharp reaction.

This made Julius extra curious. Why didn't they want him hidden in an inanimate item? It was his forte and had proved very successful on numerous occasions.

Danny and Abe, on examining the chest earlier had found a long piece of lilac silk which at a glance simply appeared to be a lining at the bottom of the chest, or something long discarded. But they had picked up a strong evil presence within its fibres, and not wanting to alert it had kept the knowledge out of their current thought patterns. But now at a safe distance they discussed the possibility that Julius could easily get drawn into its clutches if he started flitting from one item to another. Also it appeared to be very powerful and even he might not be able to cope if it realised he was snooping. At the present time, they were not sure what it was doing there, or what anything hiding in it might be waiting for.

"It looks like one of Kam's scarves he used to use to strangle his victims in his past lives." Danny thought.

"Perhaps it's not in the past tense."

Abe was always waiting for the old habits to rear their ugly heads. The attempts through the years to cleanse Kam's soul had been futile, almost as though a more powerful force waited for them to get him back on track, then immediately veered him off again.

"But he hasn't taken that route yet. You think he has someone lined up?" Danny was turning it over.

"Maybe, but I don't think he is probably paying it too much attention. He's been concentrating on the sexual thrills. It's when he gets bored with that and he wants to spice things up a bit he resorts to murder, and he won't have changed."

Danny added "And he's still a fairly young man or feels he is if he's staying grounded to this life span."

"Getting back to our prodigy." Abe knew they had to make a decision now. "As we can't be sure that even Kam is aware of the presence in the silk, we must protect Julius at all costs. Take up his suggestion for a small image."

Together they scanned the bedroom from afar and came up with a possible answer. If he was stationery he could be detected but also movement could attract so they would try something not often used.

"You want me to be what?" Julius thought he was misunderstanding his orders.

"We have to warn you that there is a presence in the room, so cloak your thoughts constantly and if it gets to dangerous we will pull you out." Abe was firm.

"If Danny had told me I'd have thought he was joking, but you aren't are you?"

The silence gave him his answer so Julius discarded the goat image and re-entered the house as dust settling on any surface high enough to be out of reach for normal cleaning. So now he was in position with a grandstand view while the wait began.

Bryn had said "TaTa" to his sister and welcomed the time on his own in the hopes he may be well and truly satisfied by someone nice. Little guessing her brother was discovering the delights he had been deprived of for so long, Amy left with her thoughts on her own objective. It never crossed her mind that the woman may not welcome her back, for something was pulling her to the bungalow with the sole purpose of communicating with Kameron.

As she navigated the small roads she tried to recall details of her last visit but it all seemed a bit hazy, but that didn't deter her. This was what she had been waiting for and now she would enjoy it. Sadly she still believed that he was hers for the taking and her mind was becoming so sick, that if she had been told that she could be with him for eternity when she died, she would have gladly taken her life.

So intent was she on her goal, she hardly noticed anything in the village until she arrived at the gate in the wall. This time, she didn't even have to try and open it for as she approached it swung back to allow her access, then slammed shut when she was safely inside. Slowly she pushed her bike up to the side wall and left it much in the same position as previously, then walked to the front door.

"I was expecting you, come in."

The door was already open and Janet stood there beaming. She looked very different to what Amy had remembered but guessed she was now in her 'medium' attire ready for business.

"Oh, I didn't say I was coming."

Amy was eying her up and down, taking in the details of her dress which seemed to be of a very floating material, various chains and necklaces around her neck, large rings and some sort of braid around her head.

"Bit over the top." She thought but smiled and muttered something to the effect that she had been looking forward to it.

The door shut behind her as though she was trapped but her mind was still on meeting her beloved and she hardly noticed.

"Please follow me." Janet had turned and was leading the way to the small room used for sittings.

"I've been looking forward to this." Amy's comment was ignored.

The woman stopped abruptly at a small table placed just outside the door.

"You have brought payment." It wasn't a question.

"Oh. I didn't realise, I mean I didn't know……um how much is it?"

"Depends how far you want to go."

"Far?"

"The basic contribution is £20, and after that, well who can say?"

Amy was rather taken aback. The idea of paying had never entered her head. So obsessed was she with meeting with Kameron in spirit, she never dreamt she would have to part with money.

"Does that mean I may not meet the person I am intended to make contact with?"

She wanted to know before she went any further. This woman could take her money and basically do nothing for it, but tempt her to come back in order to achieve her dream, and expect another £20 and possibly more.

"My dear child, you don't think I am simply here for pleasure do you? I have to scrape an existence out of my talents. Now with your gift, I could ask why come to me? You must feel that you are capable of making contact yourself."

Amy opened her mouth to answer but Janet carried on.

"I'll tell you. You can't do it. You haven't the experience and it's not all good over there, on the other side. There are bad things lurking waiting to trap innocent young women like you, that's why you need us to protect you from harm."

"Just what do I get for £20, if I have it on me that is?" Amy was feeling defensive now but knew she couldn't give up.

"Oh you get a full sitting and we see what happens. If you make a connection with someone you want to interact with on a more permanent basis, obviously that would entail a further amount."

"I notice you don't say fee, or charge, but that's what it is." Amy kept these thoughts to herself as she didn't want to antagonise her, but the air held a definite hostile feel.

"I'll just check." She fumbled in her bag and produced a £10 note, six pound coins, and counted out the rest in change, hurriedly retrieving a 20p coupon and shoving it back in her purse.

"Lovely." Janet seemed relieved as she scooped up the loot and deposited it in a small draw in the table. "Now we can proceed. Follow me please."

The spirits controlling the so called medium were getting impatient. They were always in a hurry to get on with things and this candidate looked promising. Far from being idle they had already done their homework and followed Amy noting the connection with Kam. Bryn had also caught the eye of one of the group who was now on his way to pay him a visit for his own enjoyment, although he could take on the appearance of the most desirable female imaginable.

There were about six evil visitors in presence as Amy followed Janet into the room and was beckoned to sit in a certain chair at the table. The little lights were giving a pleasant relaxing atmosphere to the place and Amy started to feel a bit more at ease. She put her bag on he floor then rested her hands on her lap. Janet slowly sat facing her, eyes fixed in a hypnotic stare.

The spirits were always amused at this for it had no effect on any mortal being and was purely for effect, but this silly woman really believed she was now getting her newcomer under her power.

"Let's stir it up a bit." One of them urged.

"My turn." A young female spirit pushed forward but was pulled back with some force by one of the elders.

"You will watch and learn or you will ruin it."

Feeling told off, the young one retreated and had no option but to obey. She wasn't one to stay in the shadows and was determined to do her 'thing' as she called it whenever the opportunity arose. She was always an embarrassment to most of the group but she had an attachment with the leader and so all the others had to go along with it.

Janet went through some preliminaries that she assumed were expected of her and had stood her in good stead in the past so was using them on Amy now. She told her to put her hands on the table palms upward and relax her mind. After a moment she began to hum softly gently swaying to and fro. Suddenly she stopped.

"There is a strong presence. Someone is here with you."

One of the evil ones moved forward and gently placed the feeling of hands on Amy's shoulders which made her jump and she involuntary felt the rush of wind as a silent fart escaped.

The spirits were highly amused knowing they could have fun with this victim whether it be here or elsewhere.

"Who are you?" Janet was chanting in a very low tone now.

Another evil moved up and started stroking Amy's breasts while another was fiddling around in her lady garden. She was wriggling in her chair and her body was reacting vigorously which didn't go unnoticed by Janet who felt she was really on form with this one.

"Do you have a name?"

The spirits gave it a moment then transmitted the word which Janet repeated.

"Kameron. I have come for you Amy. I want you by my side. I am lost without you."

The hilarity as the evil watched the manipulating of the silly recipient could have been entertaining except for one thing. They were not there for her good or to bring her closer to Kam. She was now their puppet and would dance to their tune, believing she was calling the shots.

"Got a right pair here." They all gloated. "Neither have got a scrap of talent in them, just receivers for what anything anyone wants to feed them."

"Move it on." The leader ordered.

Amy watched in awe as the image of Kam appeared hovering above the table. He floated down to the side of her, took her hand and led her to the small space at the side of her chair. Now he was facing her looking lovingly into her eyes and she was too far gone to realise that he had never looked at her that way when he was alive.

"I want you to be my spirit bride." He sank to one knee, looked up at her with his hands together and whispered "Please say 'Yes'."

The group were ecstatic. She was putty. They could get her to do anything.

"Of course Yes." she was beaming. "I've always been yours Kameron, you know that."

Janet was observing all this although trying to appear in a trance. She could only see Amy but knew something must be going on and was annoyed she couldn't be part of it. She didn't understand why. She'd seen things before but only because the spirits allowed her to. But what was happening now?

"Will you prove it too me?" The spirit emulating Kam was on top form and wasn't going to let any opportunity pass.

"Of course." Amy would have done anything.

He gently made her lie on the floor and remove her clothes, then he really went to work, but the others were not there as bystanders and soon were all joining in, except the young female.

"What about me?" She complained.

One of the evil looked at her then at Janet.

"You can have her."

"I don't want that!" she screamed but was soon quietened so as not to spoil the vibes in the air.

With the promise that she could be first with the next one they had lined up, she calmed down but then asked "Why can't I have her brother as well?"

"Because 'Lady' as they called the one who had left, "is servicing him, but you can pick up the scraps when he's finished."

"I'll see."

This session was going on longer than expected and Janet was getting a bit fed up. The evil was sending her images totally different to what was now going on down on the floor. Her mind turned to money. By rights she should be charging this woman overtime, but she obviously hadn't got enough money to pay now so she would be in her debt.

Amy came back to reality with her hands back on the table but confident in the fact she had met her Kameron and would be his forever. The evil had enjoyed the exchange and now had her in their power where she would prove to be a very useful tool. Janet would make sure she booked another session before she left with the understanding she paid the balance for tonight which had amounted to £30.

Although everyone is believed to have one or several guardian angels to protect them, the individual still has the power to follow their own wishes. Many times the person has such a strong will or desire for something that, however much their guardian may try and veer them away from it, they will either ignore the warning, or may be so intent on their objective, they become oblivious to any help being offered.

Such was the case with Bryn. For the first time in this earth life, he was being awakened to the joys of the flesh, albeit his own, and there was no way anything was going to stand in his way. As often happens with sexual appetite, it becomes a drug, and the more the addict has, the more they crave. His mind was transported to such a euphoric place that he actually believed he was having physical sex while he was actually jollying himself.

The session with 'Lady' had been a real eye opener. He'd discovered parts of the female anatomy he didn't even know existed. Of course he'd seen pictures of naked women but that was nothing to actually fiddling around with the ins and outs as he called it. For the first time in his life he had been introduced to the G spot, and that did it, he was hooked. Whoever this visitor was, could come again, anytime, all the time.

'Lady' was about to depart when the young female spirit joined him.

"Got bored with what was going on so I've come for a look." She announced.

"Well, if you can find any pickings from that dear, you're welcome." Then with a sneer "When I do a job, I do it. But I guess you're content with the leftovers."

The young one wasn't going to be treated like dirt from this old slag so she cast a glance at Bryn and retorted "No thanks, I prefer a bit more class, but I suppose he's more your sort, if you're that desperate."

Bryn was unaware of this battle going on over his head and as they left, still throwing insults at each other, he was left in the care of his angel who was sad to see this happening to such a nice man. Although every attempt had been made to ward off the visitors, Bryn's hunger had taken over and his resilience to the protection was building. The angel would have to seek back up next time an onslaught was imminent.

He lay back on his bed clutching his ding dong as if someone would steal it.

"Oh God. Oh my word. Oh Yes."

He was trying to relive every moment in his mind which was the best thing as his tanks were well and truly drained and he couldn't have raised a gallop for anyone. He reached for a handkerchief and wrapped his soft marshmallow in it before he went to the bathroom. As he washed away the evidence, he began to worry about being able to be alone enough for this to become a regular enjoyment. He daren't attempt anything because his sister was only in the next room and he was sure he was shouting at one point.

"Oh! What if she comes when Amy is here and I can't stop it." It began to be a major problem for he knew he wouldn't have the willpower to refuse whatever was being offered.

He finished in the bathroom and went downstairs. He had no idea of time so looked at his watch as he put the kettle on. It was almost half past eight and was dark now. Before he could wonder if Amy was going to stay out again, he heard her coming in the front door.

"I was just thinking about you." He said with relief.

"Yes, it's getting very dark on that road now but as soon as the lights of Eastcott are gone I see ours and I've got a good light on the bike."

"Well better be careful anyway."

It was almost as though they were both making polite conversation so as not to divulge what they had both been up to. Bryn wanted to ask if she had been to see the woman again but didn't know quite how to broach the subject, He still didn't understand what had happened before, apart from the fact she must have been a bit tipsy, but she seemed alright now. Most people would have wanted to know more. Where she had been and why, and more importantly why return to see someone who had obviously given her too much to drink? A husband would have wanted names and details and probably would have forbidden her to go again, especially as sunset was getting earlier all the time. Those country roads were no place for a woman on her own to be cycling. But Bryn didn't pry, much to her relief for she knew he wouldn't have agreed with what she was doing, especially trying to contact Kameron of all people.

If Janet felt her session had been successful, it was nothing to the elation shared by the visiting spirit group for it certainly was a section of the Dark Demons that had been 'playing' with Kam and now let him think he may be off the hook. They were not always active in the same place, especial with such menial characters as this woman, but used any venue to gather their harvest. The likes of Janet were custom made for they knew she would have no idea that they were even there, let alone what they were doing. All she would see was a silly client rolling around on the floor and the only thing she was really keen on was how much cash she could scrape out of anyone.

More experienced mediums would home in on them immediately and order them to leave the area.

Knowing of Kam's association with Amy she, along with many others he had pleasured, were being rounded up, not for their specific use, but as a powerful tool when they were ready to strike.

The constant fight between good and evil is an ongoing business, but many people fail to realise that the war between bad entities is much more vicious. Each tries to outdo the other and in the majority of cases, there is an old score to settle.

Now, the Dark Demons were playing Kam as if he were a fish with tasty morsels of bait being lined up. Then, when he had taken the last titbit, they would play him on the end of the line until they were ready to land him. Then he would learn his fate which would be worse than anything anyone could possibly imagine.

The spies had been out and Abe had been kept up to date with various movements. Danny had wanted sentinels on hand when Amy went on her trip to Janet, but it was decided they had to hold back until they could see the whole picture. Now they knew and it would be their job to not only keep Amy protected without them being discovered, but they also had to try and retrieve Kam now or his soul would never know peace.

Chapter 9

"Let her have a go at me now."

Amy was just in the mood for one of Maud's snide remarks. She had made a special effort to get to work early today as everyone would be a bit on edge with Capt and Mrs Shaw due to return home that evening.

Thinking that she had been visited by Kam's spirit, it gave her a feeling of power over the other members of staff and wouldn't they be surprised if they only knew?

Dawkins retained his outer calm but inside he was churning. It would be his job to break the news to his boss about Thomas's unfortunate demise and he had no idea what reaction it would bring. Also he quite expected an announcement about their future time at the place which must be reducing quickly.

"Good morning Mr Dawkins," Maud bustled in and without stopping made her way to the servant's room, glancing round to make sure she was there before her junior and a self-satisfied look was on her face as she entered.

"Good morning Maud."

Amy stood fully dressed ready for work smiling at her.

"Oh, Oh .. you're here then. Very good."

Amy was in a mischievous mood and looked around, then back down at herself and said "Yes, I do believe you are correct on that point."

As Maud opened her mouth to deliver some cutting reply, Cook appeared from the kitchen as Dawkins came in from the other door.

"Ah good," he started "we have a very busy day ahead of us…." and went on to give his normal summing up of the situation which they all knew off by heart but tried to look as if they were paying attention. Eventually he got to the bit they had all been waiting for.

"Right, Well you Maud and you Amy will accompany me to the late young master's room and finish the job we started."

"We all go through Kameron's stuff." Amy silently did a quick précis of his drawn out order.

"And Cook," Dawkins paused almost at a loss for words "will do whatever Cook normally does."

It was with very apprehensive feelings the trio made their way up the stairs to the dreaded room. Cook watched them go then went into the kitchen and stood with her arms leaning on the table, her eyes closed but she was ahead of them on the landing. When she was certain it was safe for them to enter she returned in thought to the kitchen, opened her eyes and took out a large dish ready for making her pie.

Danny was watching from afar but Julius now had a grandstand view, and in his dust form could move around a little just floating in the air unnoticed. His protection was at maximum for it was obvious that whatever was embedded in the silk was no amateur.

The trio entered the room and Dawkins had to steel himself from looking at the spot where Thomas had fallen.

"Right, let's get this over with." He muttered almost to himself.

Maud was a little hesitant and held back but Amy didn't need a second telling and was there at the side of the chest in a flash.

"It's unlocked!" She was shocked. "I didn't know you had done that."

Dawkins had to think fast.

"Well as you know, in the absence of a key, Thomas was going to force the padlocks but......um but the strange thing was, they weren't actually locked."

"What are you saying?" Maud had come closer and was peering at them.

Dawkins coughed. He hated lying but this was merely bending the truth.

"We all assumed, without examining them closely, that they would be locked whereas now we find they weren't."

Both women looked straight at him and Amy was having none of it. If they had been unlocked, she would have had a rummage around long before now.

"Oh Mr Dawkins. Now you know and I know that isn't quite right." Her smile was very smug.

"Don't be rude." Maud cut in then added "There is no excuse for not respecting your superiors, even in this situation."

"Ladies please. Whatever misunderstanding there was, let us get on with this without further delay." Dawkins was getting very nervous.

"I'll do it." Amy leant to open the first lock.

"You'll do no such thing, getting a bit above your station aren't you?" Maud wished they could leave the wretched thing as it was and just ship it out untouched.

Dawkins held up his hand. "Stand back please."

Before anyone else could move he had taken the locks off and the lid was open.

There was silence for a moment and while the trio waited for the first item to be removed, Julius was looking deeper.

"It's still there. Can't make out anything definite but you can feel it." he reported.

Danny didn't respond in thought but immediately strengthened the cloaking shield around him. As Abe joined him they decided to still keep at a distance as they didn't want it to sense their presence, and also they were concerned for the safety of the ones in body as well as Julius.

Dawkins reached into the chest and stopped.

"What is it?" Maud hardly dare ask but would have to face it sooner or later.

"Um, I'm not sure but maybe something we shouldn't all be examining."

Dawkins stood with his back to the chest but Amy was quick and had gone to the side her hands already on one leather item. She pulled it out and held it on high trying to put it in a position in which it would be worn but that wasn't easy.

"Where would this bit go? Stone me, it's all straps."

Maud's face was a picture. Her mouth hung open in horror and she looked rooted to the spot.

Dawkins gave one of his embarrassing nervous coughs and tried to take it from her but Amy had turned and was now exposing the next item.

"Well we all know what this is don't we?" The whip was swinging from side to side as she just missed the other two with it.

"I think that's quite enough." Maud looked as though she was going to burst into tears. "We get the picture, at least, well, I'm not familiar with those things."

Amy now stood with items in each hands that it would have been anyone's guess as to their purpose. She was on a roll and pulled out more leather. Sniffing one part she pulled a face.

"Smells a bit fishy to me. Ha ha." Then turning to Maud whispered "She hadn't washed for a while I can tell you."

That did it. With a quick "Excuse me" Maud rushed from the room.

"What did I say?" Amy tried to look innocent and then again bent over the chest.

Dawkins was furious and scolded her for her obnoxious behaviour but then her mood changed.

"Oh, what have we here? Someone's left a memento. Now this I could use."

She turned back and draped the silk scarf round her neck.

"Put that back at once. It isn't yours and you are defiling the young master's memory." Dawkins was furious at her lack of respect.

But Amy had an ulterior motive and she wasn't about to part with it. She had to come up with something.

"And how do you know that Mr Dawkins? You see you are wrong. This just happens to be mine. He kept it after we….well you know."

"I..I…I don't believe you for one moment. You've never mentioned it before."

"Well, you wouldn't expect me to would you, think of the young master's memory." She mocked.

She sidled away almost doing an exotic dance but that way she could remove the leather pouch, used for covering Kameron's condiment set, which she had concealed in the scarf, and put it in her pocket.

Although this was an innocent enough move on its own, and the item had now served its purpose, the damage was done. The evil had been willingly removed and made contact with her bare skin around her neck and also her hands. It was out of the chest.

Dawkins main concern now was how he was going to dispose of the collection of sex toys. Some were very obvious as to their purpose, but most were something he'd rather not have explained to him. He decided to pack them into a black waste sack and put them out with the rubbish for collection, then they would be gone and that was an end to it.

"I will ask you once more for the scarf." Without turning he held out his hand towards Amy who surprisingly draped it over his arm.

"You know why they use silk for tying people up?" She purred.

"I've no idea thank you." He didn't want to get into any conversation about any of the unsavoury items,

"Well," she bent so she could whisper "I only know what I've been told, but it doesn't burn, you know when you slide it across anything, skin and the like."

That was it, he'd heard enough and dismissed her telling her to fetch some black sacks and then she and Maud could check everything was in place for the Captain and his wife's return. He knew it had all been done but he had to get rid of her somewhere.

As if on cue, Maud re-entered the room apologising for her hasty departure but said she hadn't felt too well. He told her it was quite understandable as it had been traumatic for all of them and repeated his request regarding what he wanted her and Amy to do.

"I'm sure everything is perfect as usual Maud, but I know you like to double check."

She didn't mind for she had been glad of his response without making a fuss and anywhere was better than here at the moment.

He could never have explained why, but as Dawkins stood alone in the room waiting for Amy to return, he felt as though a weight had been lifted. The air felt fresher, the pressure had eased and he felt a gentle breeze waft across his face is if the whole place was being cleansed.

Julius had been moved to hover about the house at a safe distance and split himself as much as he felt was necessary. It was possible that this evil which had transferred itself to Amy could be aware of any surveillance but would give no sign of it.

Abe and Danny were chastising themselves that they had let Amy get near enough to be the contact but Abe always came back to the probability that she was the target in the first place.

"But why didn't it just go and possess her, I'm sure it's powerful enough." Danny was recalling the vibes they had picked up.

"I guess it's one that has to make the connection through physical touch, so she had to pick up the scarf." Abe knew that it didn't mean the force was any less of a threat, because some of the higher powers would play deceiving games to let one think there was no danger, resulting in innocent souls walking straight into the trap. Then it was too late.

"Which is why they couldn't get into the chest when she wasn't around." Danny thought he had the answer but then remembered Thomas.

"Hang on. The handyman was trying not to open it, but he wouldn't have been protecting Amy, because he sensed something in there which did get him in the end."

"And," Abe said "he may not have been aware of the other one in the scarf."

"Two separate stake outs but not connected?"

"Nothing new."

Both of them were only too well aware that they now had a much harder task. Amy had an attachment as they called it, and it would be apparent to any power of a certain standard.

"I've got a feeling that this is connected to the dark demons who still have Kam in their sights." Danny was musing.

Abe agreed. "From what I've been observing, very much so. But I don't know the exact reason except she could be used as bait."

"Thought he might have gone off her."

"Depends if that's all that's available at the time."

Danny remonstrated "But come on, she was only one of his bits of spare and he was bored with her. She wasn't one of his playthings. Can't imagine him using his leathers on her."

"I've a feeling she isn't the innocent young lady she may appear. Did you notice her reaction to the straps etc. I think she was regretting that she hadn't been part of it. It's one thing to have been broken in and poked now and again, but I think her appetite has been whetted."

"This could get interesting," Danny thought, "but we're dealing with pretty high evil here so it won't be nice."

They were interrupted by the arrival of Kam as he floated around the open chest. He was almost relieved to notice there seemed to be no presence there, either in or out of it, so that was an end to it. He'd missed the display of his goods due to an unexpected moment but even the fact of shocking the staff had lost its appeal.

Having made many previous visits to the house, Kam had been closely monitored by the Dark Demons and every so often they would lead him to a desirable female to enjoy his talents. He hadn't realised he wasn't using his free will but was just a pawn in the game. He had been thus employed resulting in his missing of the grand opening. Now it all seemed a bit tame and he wondered why he had been so bothered about it.

Things that seem highly important in this earth life, often have little meaning when one is totally in spirit. Often the physical doesn't matter as it is all capable of being destroyed, whereas in the other world everything is eternal.

Not so long ago he would have sought out Amy for a quick 'how's your father' in some corner, but with his recent climaxes still fresh in his thoughts, he couldn't be bothered. What he didn't know was that Amy believed they had made intimate contact at Janet's and now she had a very different outlook on their relationship. He had chosen her to be his spirit bride and although she didn't know what to expect next, this was enough for her to put everything into achieving her dream. But the demons had made sure he was elsewhere while she was under their power.

Maud had fussed around until there was nothing more to fuss over. Amy was feeling quite special now and her self-assurance was increasing by the minute and as Dawkins joined them and requested they meet in the servant's room she didn't even acknowledge his remark which didn't go unnoticed.

Cook was well aware of what had taken Amy over and made sure her protection was on full strength. It was almost dinner time and Dawkins was feeling the pressure of the recent events, but was also particular that everything would be perfect for the family's return.

"I know this has been a very difficult time for us all, in so many ways," he began "and I want you to be assured that you have all coped with it extremely well."

Maud and Cook gave a small whisper of an acknowledgement while Amy stood looking from one to another.

"I think we should all have a little time to settle ourselves and I won't be asking anything of you until after lunch." He looked at Cook. "Would you like Amy to give you a hand?"

"I've always managed, I'll manage now. Don't like folks under my feet but I appreciate your offer Mr Dawkins."

Cook was portraying the image everyone expected. While it would have been a good chance to keep an eye on the young woman, she daren't appear too eager and so had to keep up the façade.

Kam had floated down to the room and watched them almost with contempt, but then he noticed Amy in a new light. There was something about her that he hadn't been aware of before. She was coming over as very desirable indeed and then he noticed what she had slipped into her pocket. It was his favourite pouch which was made of such soft leather it gave him the urge just by putting it on and there was only just enough room for him to stand up in. Now this was more like it. He could use a bit of this right now.

As she stood there, Amy felt the sudden urge that made her squeeze her thighs together and thought she would burst if she didn't get out of here now. Thankfully Dawkins had dismissed them to relax until lunch and she was almost cross legged as she made her way to the toilet. For Kam was massaging parts he had never bothered with before and she was almost delirious. So as not to be disturbed she hurried to the outside privy where she could enjoy this moment to the full but so far gone was she, that as soon as she had shut the door behind her she reached the most fulfilment she had ever known.

Kam was actually enjoying this and the Demons knew he would be back for more which was just what they had planned. Amy could only think of the meeting at Janet's and knew that this was because of Kam's proposal. But if this was the way of things, she wouldn't need the medium any more because she was having it all anyway. Janet had done her job, thank you very much, but she wouldn't be required again.

Amy had to learn that she was not in control of her own thoughts or movements, and as far as Janet believed, she certainly would be going back for reasons yet to be revealed.

Julius had been recalled temporarily, partly for debriefing and also to give him a short break. When a spirit takes on an unusual form, the concentration in the field is enormous for they have to be on constant alert and yet cloak every emotion or reaction.

He had gleaned that the evil which had used the scarf as a physical base was a scout they had come across before. They didn't think it had been taken over by the Dark Demons then but it certainly had to be in their pay now. It wasn't one to be dismissed lightly, as it was a clever operator and one day may become one of the most feared evil entity in its own right. It wouldn't be part of a group, it would rule the group. It would be god.

"If it could be destroyed at this stage, think what could be prevented in later centuries and zones." Julius was always hopeful but the others had to be practical.

"We wish." Abe agreed but was forced to add "You can't just destroy them. It doesn't work that way. There will always be a fragment or something that has hooked onto another host where it can wait for ever if needs be."

Danny said "Or flit from one base to another for eternity if it wants."

"And that's what makes them hard to track down sometimes." Julius knew what they were saying. "Wishful thinking."

Abe was wondering when the last time was that they came across this scout.

"Don't think it was recent, but I'll work on it." Danny was curious too.

"Will it make a difference?" Julius wondered.

Danny answered that. "You never know. We've had things turn up, quite innocently but then found it was an old adversary that wasn't there just for the pleasure of it."

"Think this one is up to something of its own then?" Julius wanted to get to the bottom of this one.

Abe broke into their discussion. "What I wonder is, why did two share the same refuge, and why did they emerge so close to each other. And don't say because the lid was opened, that had nothing to do with it. They could have got out at any time."

The air went still as they all pondered that one.

They decided to keep Julius in his present image for now but were ready to change him at any moment. Danny was returning to his human form for a while but decided to take advantage of any source of likely information and would do some digging around on the internet. Abe was free, and of such a high level he could search any place on the earth without being traced and although he didn't feel his colleague could turn up anything new, he respected his decisions.

Although they may not have appeared to have taken too much interest in Thomas's sudden death, Abe had been in constant touch with Cook ever since the moment it happened. Even Danny hadn't realised, for the communication was above even his level but this was essential due to the strange circumstances.

She could be apparently intent on her daily duties, not having much conversation with anyone, but simultaneously be in deep conference with other realms.

There were many anomalies concerning the current event of which she and Abe were both aware. Firstly, the man's soul appeared to have been stripped from his mortal remains in a second and although this wasn't always unusual, it did raise a big question. Captain Shaw's father had presumably brought Thomas in, and therefore it shouldn't be easy for any other entity to get him out unless……..this led several ways.

1. The Captain's father had removed him.
2. Thomas was powerful enough to flee when the evil attacked.
3. The evil was so strong it overtook the basic rules.

They needed the answers to all three possibilities before they could get a clear picture. But then Cook came up with her own thought.

"He hasn't left the place at all."

Abe asked her to explain but could see the way this was going.

"Oh he's left his body alright, but I feel he gave the visitors the slip regarding his soul. He might even have pre-empted it."

"Knew they were there and gunning for him. Just had to be ready, lie low and wait." Abe could accept this but it presented another question. "And where do you think he is now?"

"I've a good idea, but cannot let my thoughts go that way."

"Still around though."

The silence gave him his answer and he pushed it no further.

As they closed the connection, he felt there was a lot that had either been taken for granted or believed because it had been handed down, but nobody had ever thought to check it out.

"I have to admit," he mused "maybe Cook could have just hit on something."

But the questions remained. Who is, or was Thomas? Where is he now?

It was late afternoon and the weather had turned nasty with a chilly wind and the rain bucketing down. Bryn had just about finished his work for the day and would be glad to get home and have a bath. He was just on his way to let the farmer know he was going off when one of the pigs got loose and grabbing a wooden paddle he ended up chasing it back to its sty. He cursed the delay for he wanted to get home and he knew Amy could be late, with the family returning to the big house any time. He needed his moments alone more than ever now.

Eventually he cycled home. It was one of the most uncomfortable rides he had known, the wet clothes rubbing against his skin and a totem pole that seemed to be growing with every turn of the peddle. Quickly leaning his bike he hurried to the front door and took off his outer clothes and boots in the porch. As soon as he got in he scooped them up and got them into the kitchen as they were dripping everywhere.

They had a little covered area outside the back door where Amy would hang washing if the weather looked unsettled and she daren't risk leaving it out all day. This was ideal and Bryn soon transferred the wet things onto the line and left his boots outside. He grabbed a mop which was always out there and quickly ran it over the floor.

Now he could get on with the matter in hand. There was a warm feeling across his back as though something or someone was soothing his skin. He couldn't get to the bathroom quick enough and peeled away the rest of his clothing. There was no doubt what was happening and he realised who it was as the familiar massaging of his special places was having a very intense effect.

Where his mind went next was anyone's guess. He was in absolute heaven and he wished it would never end. She was so in control of every inch of him and although he thought he couldn't wait any longer, she seemed to have the knack of just holding him on the edge. When he did finally explode, his yell of relief was indescribable. His breath was coming in short bursts and he could feel a tight band closing round his head. He sat on the toilet to regain his senses as he felt he would fall over if he remained standing. Then, as nature took over he realised how much he needed a pee but nothing would trickle yet. Now he was desperate for another reason. When he finally managed to go he thought he would never stop and sat there gasping as he tried to work out just what was going on and fearing it was his imagination. But it couldn't be. Someone had been there with him, he'd felt her but why him and why now?

He sat and mulled it over for a moment then decided that it was so good, it didn't matter who or why. He was wanted, and he had never known such a thrill or a feeling of wellbeing in all his born days, so he told himself not to question it, but enjoy it because he couldn't be sure how long it would last. The thing he could be sure of was that he couldn't wait until the next time, but not just yet, he'd got to refill his dangle bags first.

"So, you've got him in the bag?"

The Dark Demons knew would have no problem keeping Bryn's attention while they followed their plans concerning Amy and Kam so it had worked to their advantage when 'she' (as he now preferred to be called) got him in her sights.

"He won't even realise when his sibling isn't there. When I am in charge, they are tunnel visioned." she informed them but then added "As long as I am left alone to work it."

She was assured she would have no interference from any source provided she saw the job through to the end, then she would not be required anymore and could leave what was left of the man to his own devices.

The interaction between 'Lady' and Bryn was being monitored from a distance by Abe but there was one operative that would not be allowed anywhere near the couple at the moment, however it may prove a very interesting encounter if the good powers decided to stir things up a bit. That would be a drama not to be missed, the meeting of 'Lady' and Powl. Both travelling on the same bus, but on the other one so to speak.

Chapter 10

It was early evening when the master and his lady arrived at the house and nobody was allowed off duty until they were told. Cook had the food prepared, Dawkins was almost running after himself with anxiety while Maud seemed to be rather quiet.

"You Ok Maud?" Amy asked as they stood by waiting to be called.

"Of course." Was all the reply she got but couldn't help noticing that this woman was on edge about something.

"Getting to all of us."

"What is? "Maud turned on her.

"Well you know. Thomas, the goat, the master coming back, with his wife." She added the last bit to make it effective.

"What are you saying?" Maud was red faced now.

Amy looked at her, smiled and said "Never mind."

Dawkins appeared at that moment and sent Maud up to prepare for the food arriving which he would do as usual.

"You can help me carry it and then take away the dirty plates once that course has finished." He said to Amy. "And then keep out of the way. They don't want everyone staring at them."

Maud had gone up to the dining room and positioned herself ready. Soon Dawkins arrived and put the salvers on the sideboard then hurried Amy off to wait in the corridor. When the couple entered the room from their sitting room, Maud kept her eyes lowered and waited for Dawkins to pour the wine before placing the starters ready for him to serve.

The meal continued in a very quiet manner with the couple hardly speaking and certainly not looking at each other. The atmosphere was exceptionally tense and it was obvious it wasn't just because of Kameron's death, although it played a major part in their relationship.

It was therefore quite a relief when it was over and they got up separately and returned to their drawing room.

The Captain beckoned Dawkins and said very quietly "You can dismiss the other two now. I will call you if we need anything else."

Amy was clearing the table in the room and Dawkins saw Maud in the corridor. Out of earshot he whispered "You did very well, it won't be long now."

Without speaking she gave a little nod and he noticed she was very tight lipped but it wasn't over yet. There was still a lot to be done.

"You go now, we can finish up here," he said kindly.

"It's alright. I don't want snide remarks from her." She cast a look toward the door.

"I will handle that. See you tomorrow."

Reluctantly she agreed but was still glad to be out of the place. It was having an effect on her nerves and she didn't know how much longer she could stand it.

Cook was preparing a light supper in case it was required and was just covering it up when Amy breezed in.

"How do you like that? She's gone. Left me to do all the work."

"By her, I take it you mean Maud?"

"Well of course. Who else?"

It was becoming increasingly apparent that this young woman was getting a bit cocky and rather above herself and this didn't go down well.

"Then I expect there is a very good reason for it." She retorted

"But why should I have to do it?"

"Young lady, when you get to Maud's age, things change."

"Well I know that. Oh she's on the turn is she? So what?"

"You'll know when the time comes and it's worse for some than others. So don't mock what you don't understand." Cook was having none of it.

"She does go a bit red now you mention it."

"I didn't."

"No but……."

The tone was sharp "And that's an end of it and you won't refer to it tomorrow. Do you understand?"

Even Amy had the sense to know when she was up against a brick wall so she finished her chores and left.

When Dawkins came down, Cook asked if Maud was alright and they both exchanged knowing looks.

"I gave the idea it could be the change."

"Good. That should cover it. Thank you." Dawkins looked relieved and hoped it would keep Amy from asking too many questions. But knowing what she was like, you never could tell.

Amy got home later than usual and, although she felt a strange urge visit Janet, common sense told her that not only would it be foolish to go when it was already dark meaning both journeys would hold risk, but Bryn might question her returning so soon.

"I put your dinner on a plate on top of the saucepan, shouldn't take long to heat through." He thought she looked tired after her long day so asked "Shall I switch it on?"

"No I'll do it. Thanks."

She was grateful for his thoughtfulness as usual and had always appreciated he was a good man that would have made some homely girl a good husband.

As she left the room she noticed his cheeks had an extra flush to them. Having always worked outside, his body had become quite weathered and brown but there was definitely a glow about him. At one time she would have pursued the matter with a "Tell me more" third degree session, but now her mind was set on her own goals.

She returned to the living room to wait for her dinner to heat and said "Nothing on the telly then?"

"Nah. All repeats. I was just enjoying doing nothing." Then to change the subject "How did it go then?"

"What? Oh, them two returning." Maud would have pulled her up on her grammar but now in her own home she occasionally relaxed the strict rules that had been drummed into her.

"How were they?" He always had a caring side.

"Well it was tense I can tell you. Hardly spoke to each other I understand and then Maud went funny."

"How?"

"Well she was on edge all the time and got sent off before me, and Cook says she's on the change."

"Oh, I see," he coughed feeling a bit uncomfortable as he didn't like to discuss women's things, as he called them.

Amy was feeling smug.

"Well, we'll just see who might be late tomorrow then won't we?" and went to get her dinner.

Bryn was desperate to be alone soon. This ache in his groin was getting worse and he knew there was only one answer. If help didn't come quickly he would have to take himself in hand. As soon as he could he said he thought he might have an early night. Amy didn't question it assuming he'd had a tiring day too and that would give her the chance to try something that had been niggling at her.

She waited for him to be upstairs long enough to be settled in bed then sat in the armchair and closed her eyes. If she had the gift, now was the time to test it and if it worked without help, she wouldn't be needing the Janet woman and that would save a lot of money. After all, why should she pay for what she could do herself, possibly in time but you had to start somewhere?

The Dark Demons were watching with some degree of amusement, but were still aware of their sinister purpose. What they had in store for her and Kam would drop them both to the depths of utter depravity and they would never be able to face anything decent again, for the shame would rule them forever. They were not the only targets, demon cells were operating all over the place and by the time the victims were honed to perfection, there would be no way they could ever return to any existence as they had known it.

She had turned the lights off so that the room was in complete darkness. Her mind was floating and she was aware of a presence behind her, its hands slowly massaging her neck and calming her from head to toe. Her guardians were surrounding her with a protective force aware of the evil presence and had called in extra power to protect her. But the demons could overcome anything they had set up and the group infiltrated within moments. 'Lady' without any delay went upstairs to give Bryn the benefit of her experience with instructions the young one stayed where she was.

The image of Kam was being wafted in front of Amy until she was reaching out to him thinking she had brought him here. When she started begging him to stop playing and get on with it, he was immediately placed on top of her in the chair, his naked pole inches away from her face. She was so amazed that her special power had worked so quickly she didn't notice what else was going on as she enjoyed the lollypop. The other members of the group were having their own bit of enjoyment but one was always on watch, a bit like a lookout meercat sitting on top of the highest piece of vegetation to give the alert of approaching danger.

How long the session went on she had no idea, all she knew was that she didn't want it to stop, even when she was exhausted. 'Lady' picked up the vibration that it was time to leave but Bryn had been more than well serviced so her pleasure job was done.

What people fail to realise when they are on a high, is that this kind of interaction not only drains their body but their spirit. It bears a vague resemblance to the myth of vampires sucking the life blood from their prey, but is invisible to the human eye. The evil destroys the soul which is considered to be a conquest. Although the human may revel in the euphoria for a while, the person only realises too late that there is no way back. They are trapped in eternal hell. Hence the work of the good powers is not so much trying to retrieve them, but prevent it from happening from the onset. Although both sides are powerful beyond our understanding, there is an everlasting battle with one appearing to outwit the other, but it is a seesaw situation with no eventual result.

It had been a mentally tiring day and Dawkins knew that, although the master and his wife had retired, he could be called upon should anything unexpected be required. He hadn't undressed but lay on his bed reflecting the past years.

This house, 'The Lonely Elms' to give it its proper address, but known locally as 'The Elms' was fairly large and in its early days had been used to capacity with a full quota of servants employed to provide the needs of the family and the many friends who came to visit. Being well tucked away from the village road, virtually anything could be going on without the slightest suspicion of the locals. The small hamlet was originally built by the owner to house the non resident staff but as the numbers had dwindled, the houses had been sold, either to business people wanting a retreat at weekends from their hectic schedules, or the odd one or two by property developers who bought the place to rip it to bits inside and modernise it purely with the purpose of selling it again.

Now Thomas's cottage was empty and it would have to be cleared before anyone could buy it, but the sale would bring in a welcome amount for the Captain and his wife. When the main house was sold of course it meant that Dawkins and Cook would have to find alternative accommodation, while Maud and Amy would have to leave their homes.

It was common knowledge that the house had been home to many strange happenings over the years but nobody was allowed to discuss it. Naturally there was gossip below stairs but not when the butler was about. There had been strange apparitions which had been passed off as the person having been at the cooking sherry, things moved which it was deemed were done for a joke to initiate any newcomers, but the most disturbing was that young maids had been touched up. As it always happened when they were alone, they were accused of romancing and wishful thinking and to not suggest such a rude thing.

But something had happened that had shaken everyone from the top right down to the scullery maid. Dawkins was just a young servant starting at the very bottom so he was not privy to a lot of gossip but he kept his ears open and acted as though he hadn't heard much. Most tales became Chinese whispers and in no time the story going round would bear little resemblance to the truth.

There had been occasions when the Captains late father would return from a trip abroad with some trophy in tow, namely an attractive maiden. Although his wife tried to cope with his antics, the embarrassment of it eventually became too much for her and she took her own life. The master had put on a good show of grief, but nobody was taken in by it and never forgave him. They all had great respect for their mistress and were disgusted with his behaviour but they needed their jobs so had to hide their emotions and get on with the everyday requirements.

At the time of this tragedy, the 'import' was viewed with great suspicion. She would sit in her room chanting and had a strange collection of weird objects which were hurriedly removed from sight if she thought anyone was near. But servants have a way of noticing things and it soon became apparent that she had brought more to this house than her body.

"She's a witch and no mistake."

"I don't feel safe with her here."

"Why did he have to bring her in the first place?"

"I think she's casting spells and if she doesn't like you, you've had it."

The comments were flying around but there was more to it than conjecture. The whole atmosphere was changing and everyone could feel it. Cook was a kitchen maid at the time but was relaying all she could back to base without anyone's knowledge until one day the 'visitor' was walking through the herb garden as Cook was picking thyme and she noticed the woman had stopped in front of her. She knew she was being scanned so kept her human image as strong as she could before looking up.

"Can I help you?" she sniffed the thyme as she stood with a slight smile on her face.

There was no reply but the stare was so intense that Cook knew the intruder would sense the barrier she had raised. This called for more protection. Suddenly a blackbird flew between them breaking the connection, thanks to help from afar.

"Oh silly bird. Always doing that." Cook laughed and shook her fist in the air.

The other woman turned and walked into the house. It had been a close call but Cook wiped it from her thoughts and concentrated on picking parsley to go in the stuffing but she would have to be on her guard.

Abe had monitored the 'visitor' and realised that although fairly competent in her own field of devil worship, she was no match for Cook and the evil powers above her would remove her as soon as possible and replace her with someone much more efficient, then the fight would be on.

About this time there had been many sightings of what the staff believed to be their beloved late mistress who sadly was not at peace. In time they got used to it and would speak to her if she passed them in the corridor. There was never a bad feeling and nobody was frightened but they all wished she could rest. It was assumed that she wanted something sorted out before she could move on, and if they could have done it, they would.

Cook daren't make contact as she was only there to observe and report at this stage but her thought patterns were being relayed to Abe for reference. It would be more important than ever soon, for the master would be returning with the one who had been selected as the replacement. He would be accompanied by Thomas.

The visitor had been sent back to her own country and as Thomas seemed to have settled in quickly, went about his own business and did his jobs, things settled down a bit and even the mistress appeared to have found rest.

But then matters took a more physical turn. Dawkins had tried to put much of it out of his mind but there were everyday reminders which would never let him.

As a young man he had taken a fancy to Muriel, a young parlour maid just a few years older than her sister Maud who had only been there about a year. Both liked him but his preference was always for the older one. As things progressed, they started to express their love in a physical way, that is they had sex whenever possible. He was so smitten with her he didn't really notice how much of an effect it was having on Maud who was eating her heart out over him, hoping that he would go off her sister and notice her.

How much further it would have gone, he would never know. They had been out for a walk and he was going to open the subject of marriage when they could afford it. He was hoping she still loved him as they hadn't done anything for some time and he had noticed a slight distance in her manner.

They had stopped at a gate leading onto a field and she stood looking into the distance. He slipped his arm round her waist but she didn't respond.

"I've got something to tell you." She began.

There was something in her tone that made the warning bells go off.

"She's going to say she doesn't want me anymore." He thought.

"I um, I think, well I know, I'm expecting."

The word pregnant didn't crop up in conversation back then.

He felt a sense of relief. So that's what she had been worrying about.

"Well we'll get married straight away so it will be alright. When are you having it?"

"In six months."

He was doing some quick sums in his head trying to think when it could have happened, and he'd been so careful, but he would stand by her, and he wanted to marry her anyway so she couldn't refuse now. Suddenly the thought hit him. He would be a father. They would have to find somewhere to live. Everything was racing through his mind when she turned to him and said something that poured cold water over all his elation.

"You don't have to. You see I don't think it's yours."

The silence was only broken by the wind and the occasional bird.

After a while he whispered "So there was someone else."

She wanted to say "Obviously" but that seemed harsh so she took a breath and said "Look, I think a lot of you but we're not exactly made for each other. Now Maud adores you. Why don't you court her?"

He was stunned, not only at the truth but the callous way she would happily fob him off with someone else, and her sister no less. Didn't she have any respect for her either. His hurt turned to anger.

"Any more?"

"What do you mean? Any more? You calling me a loose woman now?"

"Well, I'm beginning to wonder. How could you?"

After a few moments he moved a few steps away and said "I feel like walking away and never seeing you again, but I will do the gentlemanly thing and take you back."

"Don't bother. I can look after myself."

"So it would appear." He still stood his ground.

She turned in a huff. "Oh go on then but no questions."

If he thought that was bad enough, it was nothing to what he learned about a month later. Although the father had kept it under wraps, it emerged that it was the young Captain himself just recently married. Suspicions were aroused when he and his new wife decided to go to their Corfu home for a while and take Muriel as a personal maid. The excuse was that the mistress hadn't been too well of late and needed taking care of.

The situation had just about torn the marriage apart there and then and they had long discussions about the next move. The Captain's father had not been travelling quite so much and agreed to be around to run the place' while they all went and sorted the mess out', as he put it. Muriel would normally have lost her job immediately had it been anyone else, but in the circumstances the man was just as responsible so he had to do what he could and still try and keep the actual facts quiet.

Adoption was suggested but the fact remained that this was still a descendant and it didn't seem right for the child to end up just anywhere. But then another fact emerged. The Captain's wife was also pregnant, so there would be two heirs.

They were still deciding what to do with Muriel's child when events took a strange turn. The wife had a miscarriage and was told that she may not be able to bear any more children. She was devastated and didn't want Muriel anywhere near her so the two lived in separate parts of the villa.

Then came the time for the delivery and Muriel gave birth to a lovely baby boy, but sadly she died a few days later.

This caused a proper dilemma but the Captain, after taking orders from his father told his wife what would happen, basically whether she liked it or not. Muriel would be taken back to England where she would be given a proper funeral. The Captain and his wife would return with their new baby boy. At first she was hysterical and refused point blank saying she could never bond with the child and could never treat him as her own, because of course he wasn't, plus she was still grieving for her own, which had been a girl.

After much persuasion he talked her round but she made it quite clear that as far as she was concerned their personal life was over, it would all be for show, but only because the child was his and he had a responsibility. It didn't suit her to have to find somewhere else to live when she had everything here so she would cope, as long as, and this was a big proviso, he hired a nanny. And so baby Kameron entered the family.

Maud had been devastated at being informed that her sister and the baby had both died but as the months passed she noticed a likeness in Kameron and after many probing questions learned the truth on the understanding she never told anyone. In a very low moment, she confided in Dawkins who had suspected for some time. It was possible the rest of the staff had noticed but nothing had been said. As the two sisters weren't alike, the similarity had not been noticed over the years as new servants came and went and it became something of the past.

When Amy had questioned Maud about her outburst in Kameron's bedroom, in a fit of temper she had referred to Muriel having sex with her master.

"That's how you were conceived in the first place," was directed at Kameron even though he was totally in spirit.

Obviously Kameron's death had shaken the household but Dawkins now lay there wondering how much of the Captain's marriage was retrievable. For his poor wife, everything about it was terribly sad and she must wonder if she could spend much more of her life being reminded of it.

As expected, the Captain wanted Thomas's funeral to be arranged by the staff, and although he would foot the bill, he wanted as little as possible to do with it. Coming so soon after the death of his son was bad enough but he had other issues with this.

Although it had not been obvious to most, Captain Shaw had never felt at ease with the man ever since he arrived. His late father's antics were an embarrassment, and he was glad when the latest female had been sent packing and hoped the home would return to some degree of normality. There was no fault with Thomas that he could identify. The man did as he was ordered without question, was courteous and knew his place, but there was something that never felt right.

There had been times when he seemed to look into your soul, and one got the impression he knew everything without being told. The Captain was unaware of Cook's apprehension and it may have made him feel better if he had known. But after his parents died everything seemed to settle into place and as he was away quite a lot in the army, it drifted to the back of his mind.

The strange thing was, that when Dawkins broke the news, he wasn't altogether surprised, which was strange in itself. You'd think the sudden death of a long and trusted servant would be upsetting, but somehow it wasn't. He put it down to the fact he was still grieving for Kameron and nothing else could hurt him now. His wife seemed more upset and that annoyed him.

An onlooker could very well have thought that the lady should have had a medal for the way she had tried to bring up the child, although she was always going to fight a loosing battle which became obvious as he grew into manhood. Now it was as though the weight had been lifted and she was no longer responsible for him. So her heart went out to one whom she believed deserved her sympathy.

The funeral would be arranged as soon as possible and held at the tiny church which was on the edge of the estate. There would be no gathering afterwards much to Cook's surprise as she was already planning what to serve. Respects would be paid and thanks given for Thomas's life and that would be it. But they had forgotten one important fact. When he left his physical roots behind, Thomas didn't leave his religion, and his familiar rituals would not be practiced, therefore according to his birth family, his soul would not be properly prepared for the journey.

Although our ultimate existence is in spirit, many hang on to their earthly upbringings and beliefs, hence the variety of ways of saying farewell to the body and wishing a safe passage of the spirit to the next life. But it isn't the next life. It is one continual one whether using a body for a short while to gain experience and tackle the tests we are set, or to be existing in spirit on a permanent basis.

At the moment, as it was unclear as to Thomas's spiritual whereabouts Abe called for extra sentinels to be in place for the service as he expected some sort of presence and anything could happen.

Chapter 11

Janet was getting angry. The woman hadn't been back yet and she owed her £30 which was the figure she invented off the top of her head.

"Why should I use my talents and not get paid for them?" she thought.

The trouble with having to practice almost under cover was that you couldn't go round asking if someone had been seen or where they lived. There hadn't been many clients of late and money was getting short so she tried to hang on to anybody who ventured there.

It had started off alright on the first strange encounter with Amy although Janet hadn't been too sure just what happened that night as there seemed to be something going on but she couldn't identify it but put it down to her powers not focusing properly.

"Well she came back, and look what happened. It would be a strange person who didn't want to have more." She thought as she dusted round the small room. "Perhaps she's had to work, it's only been a couple of days."

She carried on cleaning but her mind was working on how she could find this source of income. Of course! The woman had said she lived in Narrow Brook with her brother so that shouldn't be too difficult to trace.

What she didn't realise was that the demons didn't need her. Amy had been fooled into believing she had been visited by Kameron, during the session and at her home, but the demons had impregnated her entire being with something that he couldn't resist.

He had already had a sniff of it when he saw her in the kitchen with his pouch in her pocket and had acted upon a sudden powerful impulse which was not what the senior demons had planned, so heads had rolled and those who had been left in charge of him had been severely reprimanded.

He was the kind of person that would take what he wanted but if it was put in his lap he would soon get tired of it. But keep him dangling for a while, tempting him a bit at a time, he would go for the kill and then they had their working couple ready for action. He would keep feeling a pull to the area where she was, get a scent of the aphrodisiac, then be like a dog chasing a bitch on heat.

The staff had been summoned to the dining room.

"Oh what now?" Amy muttered expecting another long drawn out lecture which could be squashed into thirty seconds.

"Show some respect." Maud frowned.

Before Amy had time to come up with some retort Dawkins called them to order with one of his 'ahem' coughs.

Although it was a difficult subject, for once he seemed to want to get it over and done with as quickly as possible.

"Firstly, the subject of the late Thomas's funeral. On the master's instruction I am making all the necessary arrangements as you know. We will all be required to attend the short service at the church, he will then be taken to be cremated and his ashes scattered in the grounds of the estate. We expect there may be a few villagers there as well, at the service of course, not the cremation, being as they are the remaining few elderly employees who are still occupying the cottages owned by the family."

Amy asked what the others were wondering although there was a slight gasp from Maud.

"Are the master and mistress going?"

"Um, at the moment no specific plans have been made but certainly one of them will."

"Only I was thinking that if we are all at the church, who's going to be here?"

Maud cut in "I'm sure Mr Dawkins has taken the necessary steps for security."

Cook was observing all this in silence but was also aware of a presence floating near Amy. The demons were dangling the carrot again and had manoeuvred Kam into the area and he had picked up the scent. Amy was virtually glowing with femininity and he wanted it. The whole of his senses were on high alert and he had got to take her. But he was being stage managed and was not in control as much as he believed.

Without warning he felt himself sucked away from the scene at such a force, it took him a moment to realise he wasn't even in the earth's atmosphere.

Whilst Cook was regaining her earthly composure, the whole event was now being discussed by Abe and Danny who had been recalled from one of his earth body visits.

"I am concerned." Abe opened the communication. "The likes of the Dark Demons don't play, they control and they possess. We've known for centuries they have him in their sights and have used him for their sadistic plans, so this is no gentle encounter. Something big is on the cards."

"Well, I've been digging around on the internet and I feel certain people have more to do with this that we imagined." Danny was musing.

Abe was never convinced that his obsession with using physical means could turn up anything that they hadn't learned from spirit.

"Now what have you been wasting your time on?"

"As I've often said, some things are not always obvious. There are times when we are not the 'all seeing, all knowing' force we like to think we are."

Abe now hoped he would get to the point.

"Go on."

"The evil can be just as devious as we are and things that seem too clear can be hiding important factors."

"Could you elaborate," Abe almost sighed "like now?"

Danny knew that when he first laid out the information it would probably be disregarded, but he knew that Abe had more sense than to ignore it completely and would chew it over himself then probably come up with the answer as though it was his deduction. But that didn't matter.

"Can I start with Captain Shaw's father? Now he seemed to have many ranks in the army but there is no trace of him on record. He was known as 'Major' quite often and wore some sort of tropical uniform abroad, even sported some medal ribbons, but he was never awarded anything."

"Brought disrespect to his family." Abe acknowledged. "So he was never in the army as everyone, even the Captain himself believed?"

Danny added "The army, navy, air force, marines, you name it he was never in any of it. How he got away with it I can't understand."

"So why was he always travelling the world? How could he afford it?" Abe was getting the gist of it.

"Exactly what I thought. " Danny knew he had his attention now. "So I began digging in a different area. Why would he be always hanging around certain areas of the world but never visiting others? There had to be a connection."

"And did you find one?"

"Opium for a start, then other such narcotics. Remember what his son found in his belongs. That little pipe in a long wooden tube with the round lidded pot attached to it with string, and because it was unused he assumed his father had brought it back as a souvenir."

"So basically he was a full time dealer." Abe wished he had come to the point earlier but that was Danny.

"Had to be and that's where his money came from. He would go over there, collect the stuff, then travel somewhere else and sell it."

Abe had been considering a lot in this short time. Firstly he needed to trace the spiritual guides that had monitored the man during his activities. And secondly, did the Captain know? But there was another important factor they couldn't overlook.

"And where do you think Thomas fits into all this?" He had a feeling Danny already had the answer.

"Well, there has to be a connection and I feel it must be when they were together on Haiti, but I'm sure it goes back before that."

"What makes you say that?" Abe always liked a reason.

"That's what I'm working on now and I shall browse again as soon as I go back down."

They parted, both with their thoughts on the conversation but their paths may take different routes trying to get to the bottom of it.

Maud and Amy had gone through most of the clothes in the bedrooms and had been told to now pack any ornaments etc as best as they could but to leave large items where they were.

"I wonder how much longer we've got." Amy said as they used old linen to protect the more delicate items.

"For what?"

"To work here of course."

Not long ago she was horrified at the thought of having to leave the house where she felt close to Kameron and his physical belongings, especially his underwear. But now she thought she had the gift to contact him, it didn't seem so important.

"I suppose you've considered that we will have nowhere to live. They will sell all the remaining houses you know." Maud was abrupt.

"Hadn't really thought of that." Amy seemed absent minded.

"Well you had better start making plans like the rest of us."

As they worked, Amy knew that if she could bring Kameron close to her at home, she could do it no matter where she was because he was a spirit and all she had to do was call him. Janet flashed into her mind and the fact that her parting shot had been that she owed her some money.

"Oh sod her. She can run for it. I don't need her."

Maud on the other hand was thinking on more practical terms. Many years ago she would have set her cap at Dawkins, but with the history, although she still liked him, there would be no way she could ever have any sort of relationship with him. He had shown his kind side to her recently but it was all too late. So, although she had to take her own advice, she had no idea what she would do or where she could go.

Cook gave an outward show of expecting to end up in a home somewhere but didn't elaborate, whereas Dawkins was obviously worried as to his future home.

People were noticing how Bryn seemed to have changed recently. He had spruced himself up and had a very happy demeanour. The lads at the farm were commenting in his hearing.

"He's got a lass on."

"Looks as though he hasn't had much sleep lately."

"Or he's seen too much of his bed. Eh? Eh?"

It was always accompanied by rather course laughter but Bryn just turned and patted the side of his nose and gave them a knowing wink.

"Who'd have thought it.?" One lad would say.

"Not seen him with anyone."

"Have to keep an eye on him, see if there's any more going."

Being a good generation below him it was unlikely they would be moving in the same circles so he didn't worry about the banter, in fact he got quite a buzz from it and started winding them up when he could.

"What's her name Bryn?" One called form the pigsty.

"Which one?" Was the retort which started another round of whoops and comments.

The one thing he did worry about was that he couldn't be sure that his spirit partners would return or be faithful to him. After they had finished the job they left with no promises of future commitment and he would have liked a permanent partner of whom he could be sure. Of course he enjoyed every sex laden moment but he needed to know there was feeling for him. If he only knew that if there was, it wasn't what he'd expect. Lady or Powl could vouch for that.

As little was required from the staff over the week end, the two ladies were told to report back on Monday. Dawkins as usual would be on hand for taking care of any business and serving meals, while Cook would simply prepare them.

The house seemed exceptionally quiet now and Dawkins felt he had to tip toe everywhere so as not to disturb the peace and quiet but was grateful in some ways after recent events. But sometimes it felt too silent and he was getting the feeling of not being alone. The only sound from the master and mistress came when they seemed to be arguing, but they had little to say to each other in his presence and you could cut the air with a knife. He thought maybe their attitude was causing an uncomfortable feeling but as the hours went by he knew something was wrong. Wherever he went there was something shadowing him until it seemed to be touching him.

In need of company he went down to Cook to try and shake this thing off. As he entered the servant's room he saw her watching him from the kitchen.

"Come in and sit down. We need some tea." She was giving a command and he willingly obeyed.

It was almost as though she had been waiting for him and knew exactly when he would arrive because the cups were on the table and the tea had brewed. He felt as though he didn't have to explain because she already knew and as he sipped his tea the presence seemed to be leaving him.

"The emptiness must be getting to me." He attempted a false laugh.

"It's not surprising, lot going on." Was all she would say, but she was reinforcing the shield around them and alerting Abe that they had company.

Julius had been hovering around since his last instruction and found that the dirt image was quite useful because he could spread into the tiniest bits then reform at will. He was now instructed to waft into the main entrance hall and keep a close watch on the door leading down to the kitchen and servant's area. He had only just positioned himself on the hat stand when he saw a movement which even to him was indistinct but it seemed very familiar and not evil so he ventured nearer.

"What are you doing here?" He almost yelled at Vard who was hovering in front of him.

"Been sent on a training course."

"Where?" Julius was wondering why the visit.

"Here, with you, but strict instructions to watch and observe, no moving without orders."

"In which case you had better do something about your image."

Vard laughed "I see they gave you a good one." But before he had time to wait for a reply, he too was transformed into similar particles. "Oh God."

"He won't help you." Julius was amused at Danny's tactics. "Hang in here, you'll get quite used to it. Now, we have to be on high alert."

For a few moments they conferred as to what had gone on in the place and Vard had been given very strict instructions to follow Julius's lead and not try anything clever. It wasn't that kind of an operation, this was the big stuff and if he didn't feel up to it to leave now, but there was no way that was going to happen.

Cook drank her tea with mixed feelings. Nice to have another one in situ but this pup could just be too eager and put them all at risk. She would have to monitor them closely.

It was like the lull before the storm. Everyone was trying to carry on as usual but everyone connected with the house, whether bodily or spiritually could sense it, and they were all sure in their own way that the calm wouldn't be lasting much longer.

The legal requirements regarding Thomas's sudden death had been dealt with and his funeral was to take place the following Friday. Even the simplest plans seemed to stir up their share of hiccups, but as the week progressed and everything was in place, most were secretly looking forward to it being over.

Abe had back up on standby at a safe distance so as not to arouse suspicion but the air was so active with bad vibes, he knew something was brewing and it had to be during the service or just after when Thomas was taken away. Cook had been kept up to date and although she would be going to the church in person, she would keep half of her soul at the house to warn of any unusual activity. It was suggested that any evil force could use the empty house to plant new seeds while their defences were down.

Danny had pointed out that they could do it anyway if they were that strong, but Abe in his wisdom reminded him that they would always use any weak moment, especially when inhabitants were absent. Although it didn't totally convince his friend, he was drawing on experience and had learned never to underestimate anything, however insignificant it may appear at that moment.

It came as a shock when the staff learned that the Captain would not be attending the service but his good lady would be. There were mumblings of surprise but that was the decision and they had to accept it.

The morning of the funeral arrived and there was quite a nip in the air. The hearse was at the front door along with one mourner's car. Although the church was on the estate, it was too far to walk. The Captain's wife, accompanied by Dawkins, surprised the female staff by how well she appeared. She greeted them with a quiet 'Good morning ladies' and got into the car followed by the others.

The local vicar stood waiting at the porch door along with Bryn and a handful of villagers. As Thomas was carried in, everyone felt a strange wave of power which seemed to be coming directly from the coffin. The Captain's wife and Dawkins being directly behind felt as though it was pushing them away and he had to steady her to stop her from falling. They managed to take their places and when the undertakers had placed Thomas on a small stand, they felt they couldn't get to the back of the place quick enough exchanging meaningful glances. This was something they had never experienced in all their years in the business.

The vicar started the service but something seemed to be gagging him and his words were i. distinct at first but then something happened that shook the whole congregation. His voice changed until he was chanting in a foreign tongue and music was filling the air, not from the small organ but more like steel drums. The rhythm was getting more powerful by the second and for no reason everyone was standing.

A colourful mist was floating round until it was hard to make out what was going on. Dawkins strained his eyes and could only just see the vicar who was motionless and the sound now wasn't coming from him but from every direction. It was too much for some of the older people and they tried to get out of the door but couldn't reach it but it would have been no use for it was firmly closed.

The sound was increasing to such a point it was hurting everyone's ears and apart from the thickening mist, there was a horrible smell of rotting flesh. Everyone was feeling faint and thought they must be dreaming but suddenly they were brought back to reality. Although nobody could see, they heard the most horrendous scream and a strange sliding sound followed by a crash.

From above now, the voice was low and menacing.

"You are not fit to be in this place. Did you think you had beaten me?

Go now. Go to hell where you belong."

If that wasn't enough to scare them it was followed by a voice that was recognised by everyone.

"You can destroy my body, but you haven't got my soul yet." It was as if Thomas was standing in front of them.

All of a sudden, the place was still. As everyone came back to their senses, they looked around, at each other, at the vicar then to the coffin which was on the floor, its lid slightly to one side. Immediately the undertakers rushed forward and asked everyone to go to the back of the church. After they had checked that all was alright they replaced the lid and put it back on the stand then indicated to the vicar that he could continue.

To say that the short service was hurried through as quickly as possible would be an understatement, but everyone just wanted to get it over and get out of the place. The vicar spoke to everyone outside and they had left before the undertakers dare remove the box, just in case it wasn't properly secure. There would be an enquiry into why the fasteners hadn't been properly tightened.

The mistress and household were driven back to the house in silence and as they entered the hall she turned and shook hands with them one by one and thanked them for their loyalty and discretion. Then she asked Maud to accompany to her room but added "I think we all need a cup of tea."

This was more than many staff had ever heard her speak especially to them. But she was a new lady, and they liked her.

Cook had put all the tea things ready along with a small tray of snacks and as soon as the kettle had boiled she asked Dawkins who would be taking it up.

"I'll do it," he said quickly as he didn't want Amy nosing about which she would if she thought there might be a titbit of gossip going.

He was soon carrying the tray upstairs which left Cook alone with Amy.

"Well I must start lunch." She said without looking at her,

"That was scary. What do you think it was?" Amy was following her about.

"Now you know I don't like folks under my feet." Cook almost pushed her out of the way. "Sit down and drink your tea."

But Amy wasn't letting go that easily.

"Why does everything wash over you?" She was almost rude.

Cook stopped at a cupboard in the kitchen then turned and came back to face her.

"There are a lot of things that it's best not to question young lady. Also it's very rude to be inquisitive." The look she gave her was something Amy hadn't seen before and it unnerved her a bit.

"Alright. Alright I only asked." She huffed and took a sip of her tea.

Cook didn't reply and went back to the kitchen. As soon as this youngster had gone she would need to communicate but must be alone.

Mrs Shaw had been a little bit crafty by asking Maud to go with her and also to have tea brought up to her sitting room. She guessed her husband would be in a foul mood and she had had enough of it. If there were other people there, he wouldn't dare sound off in front of them so it would give her some breathing space. The events at the church had shaken all of them and she didn't need him yelling.

They got to the door of the room and Maud went to open it but she stopped her.

"Just a moment."

They both stood and listened then Mrs Shaw indicated for her to carry on and open it. The room was empty much to her relief and as they entered she asked Maud to help her off with her coat. She kept her there until Dawkins arrived then dismissed her. As he poured the tea she made light conversation about the diminishing staff and asked if everything was in hand, but kept off the subject of the funeral. Only then, when he had left the room was she ready for the onslaught.

"What has got into you woman?"

The outburst shook the ornaments as he came storming into the room.

"You will be inviting them for dinner next."

Knowing she had him just where she wanted him she retorted "Oh what a marvellous idea. How did you manage to think of it?"

"What….?"

"Let's get one thing straight. Everything is going to change from now on. I've lived your nasty little lie for all these years. Well no more. I am not the Captain's wife any more. I am me. So you had better get used to it." Her strength grew with every word and the look on his face gave her all the satisfaction she needed. It was time to start living.

One would have thought that getting this sad event out of the way, would have eased the atmosphere in the house but it seemed to have the opposite effect. Cook had used her skills to monitor every change in the place while she was away and had been relaying it to Abe. Julius and Vard had found the need to move their positions several times as they felt they were being observed.

Being left on her own in the kitchen Cook went into conference with Abe who confirmed there certainly was something very evil hovering around and it had manifested itself during the service, left for a moment then returned but much stronger.

"What's its target?" she asked.

"That's the strange thing. It seemed to be after Thomas, but we wonder if it is still trying to trace his spirit. He's doing a good job of concealment."

"Must have some big score to settle, its not letting go." She didn't feel at ease with this.

"Feel it goes back to the time before he came here, or even further. But Danny's digging into that."

He warned her to stay alert as this was something at present unknown but they had to expose it by some means before it caused permanent damage.

Dawkins was fending off any questions about what might have happened at the funeral saying that none of them knew, and it was best forgotten and everyone should get on with what they had to do. But underneath he was becoming rather paranoid. Every shadow, every slight noise was beginning to work its way into his mind and he was even becoming scared to climb the stairs to his room. Cook had picked up on this and made the excuse she needed someone with her in case she slipped, thus ensuring he always had company, especially in the dark.

"It's so cold everywhere." Amy was talking to Maud as they continued with the sorting and packing.

"What do you expect? It's autumn."

"I don't mean that." Amy shivered. "It's sort of creepy. I don't like it."

Although Maud was feeling the same, she wasn't going to admit it.

"All these old houses are the same, but its only people's imagination. It's only a building, just remember that."

No sooner had she uttered the words, when the room went icy.

"Th..that's not normal." Amy shuddered. "I'm getting out of here."

Before Maud could speak a tremendous force lifted her and threw her across the room. Amy screamed and tried to get to the door but it held her where she was. Everything had gone dark and both women felt they were being crushed until they couldn't breathe.

"Maud, Amy, which room are you in?

As quickly as it came, the presence left and the room was light again. The door opened and Dawkins stood there.

"It's best to leave the doors open so that you can hear me. What has been going on?" He couldn't help but notice the state of the two.

"There was something in here Mr Dawkins, wasn't there Maud?" Amy was crying now.

"Well Maud, what happened?" he spun round to her.

"I'm not sure, Mr Dawkins, it…it….." and with that she fainted in front of him.

Amy was almost hysterical. "I've had enough, something's not right, it's bad, I want to leave and never come back."

Maud was starting to come round but was as white as a sheet.

"It was him." She breathed.

"What was?" He hardly dare ask.

"It…." her voice trailed off and the tears ran down her face.

As if on cue Cook appeared at the door.

"Now what's going on?" she asked with quite a matter of fact tone. "Oh dear, passed out. Well you two go and leave her to me, she'll be alright in a minute."

With a little brush of her hand she waved Dawkins and Amy out of the room, pulled up a stool and sat by Maud.

"Now you take your time." It was more of an order.

"I'm not ill."

"Of course you're not. Just a bit overcome."

Cook wasn't putting an arm round her to comfort her physically but she was trying to look into her brain patterns. She soon had her answer and although appeared to be looking into space passed the information to Abe.

"So it is him. What is he doing here?" Was the reply.

"Come for some sort of justice I would imagine. Don't know what yet." She knew this was going to be a battle and she was only too well aware that she had to strengthen her shield even more against this level of evil.

Bryn had been visited by several willing parties and was quite enjoying himself despite still seeking the ultimate partner, but he might as well enjoy the sexual ride while he had it. He didn't realise that it could peter out, but the more he was available, the longer it would be active. He could live the rest of his earth life in such ecstasy if he wanted.

He was sitting at home with Amy and discussing the funeral.

"They are trying to pretend it never happened." She said.

"Well, something did. Not nice. Wouldn't want to go through that again."

He tried to say the right things but was wondering if it was some sort of personal punishment. He was in the house of God, and he would know that he had been sinning by having sex with things not of this earth. So it was probably aimed at him. Amy didn't feel that way at all, in fact it never crossed her mind that she would be admonished for her antics with Kameron.

As they sat there, both felt the familiar sexual presence but how could they react with their sibling only a few feet away. The demons had put 'Lady' on Bryn's lap while the image of Kam was rubbing himself round Amy's face.

"I need the toilet," Amy cried as she rushed from the room brushing her face to get the presence away for a moment but as she did so, the demons replaced it with Kam himself and by the time she had got to the bathroom, he had her juices well and truly flowing. She was not in control and somehow this was different, it was more intense and it reminded her so much of their sex when he was alive, but it was much more passionate.

Downstairs Bryn's equipment was fully exposed and was being worked to fulfilment. It wasn't a long drawn out business, in fact it was over quicker than usual but he just couldn't hang on to it this time. In a panic he rushed to the kitchen and grabbed some kitchen paper to wipe away the evidence. It was a bit harsh but would have to do, then he noticed something. His dick was bigger. It must be his imagination because just using it a lot couldn't do that, or could it? The old problem, you couldn't just go and ask anyone, and certainly not the lads at work.

He made it back to the room before Amy returned, and pretended to be looking through the tv guide. She seemed very quiet but for some reason he didn't ask if she was alright.

The Dark Demons were more than satisfied with the upstairs performance and could now put the next step of the plan into action.

Chapter 12

Amy and Maud had the week-end off, just leaving Cook and Dawkins in the house with Captain and Mrs Shaw. The place seemed too quiet and the general feeling was, that now the two women were out of the way things were about to happen. The ones upstairs were about to have one almighty bust up, while below stairs things were very different.

Cook was in almost constant touch with Abe, while Dawkins was churning inside so much, she sensed he was on the edge of a nervous breakdown, which would have been very sad as he had been the stalwart head of the staff for so long. But she would do all she could to prevent that from happening.

Her attention was also on the situation upstairs. She had felt the change in Mrs Shaw immediately Kam had died and knew this woman had found new strength from some source and things were going to be different from now on, for as long as they were there. After that, who could know?

Dawkins entering the kitchen brought her back to the physical.

"Well, that's a new one." He seemed surprised.

"Oh. What's that?"

"I've got the meal requirements for today." He waved a piece of paper towards her.

"Well, are you going to tell me, or do I have to guess?" She was purposely abrupt.

"They've ordered completely different things." He put the paper on the table in front of her.

"What's this? Steak medium rare, well that's for him but spaghetti?"

"Bolognese." He finished.

"Yes I know what it is. But she's never asked for that before."

"Have you got the ingredients?" He wondered.

"That's for me to sort." She said without smiling for there was more to this than a simple meal order.

He sensed the barrier she had put up and so asked quietly "What are we having?"

"Sausage and mash."

"Oh lovely." He smiled.

She knew it was one of his favourites and had already made up her mind to keep his spirits up in any small way possible.

Danny had been digging around on the internet again and was still convinced that the 'Major' had been a drug dealer and that Thomas was more than just a manservant, in fact he had tied him in with one of the local suppliers. But this still begged the question as to why he would be brought back to this house as an underling. One of them must have had a significant hold on the other. The 'Major' would be the obvious choice, but these evil entities were clever and could turn a situation upside down so as to throw any watcher off the scent. Thomas must have been pretty powerful for Cook not to be able to pin point just what he was.

But one fact was crystal clear. The 'Major' was back. It wasn't by chance that his presence coincided with Thomas's death and the question now was, did he instigate it, but hadn't succeeded in capturing his soul, for Thomas removed it at just the right moment. It did suggest that maybe one was good and the other evil, but which? Abe pointed out that it needn't be so, and they could just be fighting on the same side but against each other if there was a score to settle.

"Well, things have changed up there." Dawkins was eager to share his knowledge with Cook.

"Didn't they like the food?" She wasn't going to be drawn.

"No. Not that. But she's giving the orders, not him. Sat there like a naughty boy that had been told off."

"Oh well, we expected change."

Dawkins was getting frustrated at her bland replies.

"But something's going on. I'm telling you. Things are going to blow."

She looked at him closely.

"You said he was quiet. Doesn't sound like a blow up to me." And got on busying about the kitchen.

"You know what I mean. You can feel the tension, but she's all smiles. Like a different person, in fact she's quite attractive when you look at her."

Cook now gave him a hard look.

"Well, perhaps you shouldn't be looking at her."

"What are you saying?"

"Her husband 'looked' at Muriel if you remember."

Dawkins pulled himself up to his normal stature and retorted "I meant nothing of the sort, and you should know that."

The slightest suggestion of a smile proved she had knocked him out of his nervous state for now just by putting his back up. But she would continue to watch him closely.

The lady of the house had changed into something very casual, but was wearing makeup and making sure her hair was in place. The pair were both in their late 50's but now she looked a good deal younger with this attention to her appearance.

"Where are you going?" the Captain almost demanded to know as he entered the room.

"Nowhere. Why should I be going anywhere?" She turned away and looked out of the window.

"Then what are you all dolled up for?" He was getting angry.

"Am I? Well fancy you noticing." She turned now her eyes flashing. "It will be the first time."

"Me? Who's been the one that didn't want sex? Was cold as ice in bed and not the wife I expected when I married you."

She moved closer now her face set and even he took a step back.

"Oh yes, people thought I was the mouse, the one who didn't like mixing with people. Never liked going out. But if they only knew the truth."

She was on full power and he was going to get all the pent up emotions from more than thirty years.

"I was brought up to put a face on things to the outside world, it wasn't the done thing to air your dirty filthy washing in public, but you really put that to the test didn't you when you got caught out. Oh dear, how careless of you."

"Look Hilary, I thought we had sorted that." He used her name for the first time in months.

"No, you sorted it, I had to go along with it. But let us not stop there."

"Look dear , there's really no need….."

"I haven't finished, in fact I haven't even started, and do not under any circumstances call me 'dear'. I am not your dear, darling or any tag you have used on your playthings."

"Why now?" He still didn't see where she was going with this.

She walked round in a circle making him feel so uneasy he sat down on the nearest chair, so now she was standing towering over him.

"All these years, I've had to watch your despicable son" then she repeated with force "your son, grow into the most useless yard of pump water I've ever seen and I was glad to say he didn't have one drop of my blood in him." She paused to take breath then added, "While mine was buried abroad. And still is. My own child."

"Well, I..I..." He was at a loss for words and this new person frightened him, whereas he had always had the upper hand.

"And let us not forget the finishing touches."

Although she was wearing an attractive blouse, she had a scarf round her neck which she slowly untied and pulled it away until the bare flesh was revealed. Then she slowly undid the buttons and opened the front to expose her chest. He turned away and pushed his fist into his mouth.

"I've had to live with this," she spat, "having to always wear a high neck so that your cruelty wasn't on show. Oh, how convenient for you that I was brought up not to put my dirty washing on view."

The words now took on a totally different meaning, which was just what she intended but she didn't stop there.

"If people only knew why your dear little wife was always hidden away, even from the servants at times." She paused. "And let's not forget that I could never have anything done about it because it would all have come out and been terrible for your reputation, and I use the word very loosely."

Cook was in tune with this rant and thought "About time lady. You go girl." She had always known what had been going on, but it was always the drink to blame. When he was sober, you couldn't have met a nicer kinder man, but put a glass to his lips and he turned into a beast. This made her take stock now. It had started after his father, the fake major had come back from one of his trips. That's when he got vicious with her.

Abe had picked up on this thought and immediately contacted Danny. Things were beginning to fall into place slightly.

"The 'Major' was slipping drugs into him, without his knowledge." Abe was sure now.

"His own son?" Danny was hoping it wasn't the case but he knew Abe was rarely wrong.

"And I wouldn't be surprised if it didn't follow on with Kam."

Danny thought then said "Hang on a minute."

"I'm ahead of you." Abe wanted to put everything in order. "Now we know that Kam has an evil past, so when he was born to Muriel and the Captain, he was a prime target."

"Now wait a minute though," Danny was also looking at every angle "that would mean that every force, good or bad knew about it."

"Could almost have engineered it."

"That's going a bit far." Danny wanted to know why.

"Go back, someone would know." Abe wanted him to work it out as well. There was only a second's pause before the truth hit.

"Oh heavens! One of them was a very high up evil, even another branch of the Dark Demons."

"Got it now?" Abe was sure they were on the right track.

"Because although this goes back years, it makes no difference in spirit, they plan for centuries sometimes."

"But now the question. Who?"

"Don't you mean which?" Danny was only looking at two possibilities.

Abe was taking a wider view but agreed that the most likely had to be the 'Major' or Thomas. And if so, one of them at least was indeed high level evil, or they could both be.

"That would explain why Thomas is around still, although we haven't located him yet, and the 'Major' has come back, or has been in hiding and has now come into the game."

They were both now deep in thought, churning all the possible answers over and over.

"We've got to be one step ahead of them." Abe stated emphatically.

"Agree, but I'll be happier when we know exactly who and how powerful."

"Always start at the top and come down," Abe reminded him "then we are at least prepared for the worst."

Danny asked "Should we get Julius and Vard to snoop?"

"Bit risky. If it's as high as we think they would be no match and could be overcome in an instant, but they are good detectives so they can stay put for now, but be ready to get them out immediately."

"Surprised they haven't been sussed." Danny was still thinking but didn't expect Abe's reply.

"Almost sure they have."

"What? Oh no. You're letting Julius do his thing. Master of decoy, and he's training Vard. You do fly close to the wind."

"We've all had to learn the hard way, that's why some don't make it." Abe was very blunt at times and appeared to have no feeling but that's why he was of the level he was.

The argument had been over for some time when Dawkins was summoned to Mrs Shaw's sitting room.

"Do come in Dawkins. Please sit down."

"Excuse me ma'am?" It wasn't his place to sit unless something important was coming.

She pointed to an easy chair opposite to the one she was occupying.

"Sit, please."

"Very well ma'am."

He was most uncomfortable. Servants never sat and on the odd occasion when instructed, they were expected to take a dining chair and sit upright, never in an easy chair. It was unheard of and old habits died hard with him.

"You've been with the family for many years now Dawkins and seen a lot of changes."

"Indeed I have ma'am."

He guessed the time had come for him to be given his notice but was surprised that it wasn't the master telling him. She stood up and moved to the back of his chair and leaned over him.

"You have proved yourself to be invaluable Dawkins."

He tried to turn to answer to her face but she seemed to be moving from one side to the other and his words were lost.

"In fact," she was talking in very dulcet tones now "I really don't think I could manage without you."

"Oh." He was relieved but that soon changed when he realised she was speaking in the first person and would have expected 'we'.

Her hand was now on his shoulder and he jumped.

"Don't be nervous." she was breathing down his neck and he was at a loss to know what to do without causing offence, for his instinct was to get up and dash from the room.

It was a relief when she moved her hand but then she sat on a pouffe just in front of him so he had no option but to look at her.

"You wouldn't want to work for anyone else would you. I mean where would you go when this mausoleum is sold?"

"Oh, oh I thought you were dismissing me ma'am." He almost laughed but wasn't sure what was coming next.

"On the contrary." She was smiling at him. "I'm sure you would like to stay in my employment, indefinitely."

Now the bells were ringing.

"Your employment, don't you mean you and your husband ma'am?"

"I most certainly do not. I mean you will work for me, as my manservant."

"But, I thought you were both going to your villa……..."

She cut him short. "We are but we will have our own space. It's big you see and we can easily live under the same roof, but apart."

"I'm sorry, I thought you shared, um well everything." He didn't quite know how to put it.

"Not for a long time, and certainly not now. Things have changed Dawkins and I will have my own staff, namely you."

She stood up and went to the drinks cabinet.

"You will have a drink with me to celebrate." It wasn't a question.

"Oh no thank you, I'm still on duty and …. um, it isn't considered fitting to ….well…"

"Oh things are changing, you can forget all those silly old rules, except for when you take up residence in your new post, then of course you will do anything I ask." She turned to look at him. "Won't you?"

Although he had felt most uncomfortable up to now, the last innuendo settled it for him.

"I'm sorry," he stood up "I would have to think it over carefully." he was edging his way to the door but she was there before him.

"There is nothing to think about. It is settled, you will have a job, I will have my companion. There is nothing more to be said."

"But I haven't agreed." He found the courage from somewhere and his reply came out quite forcibly.

"Oh, we are seeing different side to you aren't we? My word, I think this will be a very interesting, shall we say, arrangement?" Her eyes were sparkling as though she liked a bit of resistance.

"If you will excuse me ma'am I have a lot of work to do."

Before she could argue he had left the room and was hurrying down the stairs.

"Got time for a coffee?" Cook was ready for him and indicated to the cups on the table.

"Do you know, I think that would hit the spot. Thank you."

She poured out the drink and pushed his towards him.

"Giving you a hard time?" She looked very knowingly at him as she sat down.

As she couldn't possibly have known the exchange that had taken place upstairs he took it as a passing pleasantry.

"Well, you know how it is. I think the whole selling up and moving business is getting to everyone. It's the uncertainty for us isn't it?"

His mind was still full of the conversation that had just taken place but kept everything as simple as he could.

"What will you do?" she asked

That made him jump. "Do?"

"Well haven't you got any family or anything?"

"Oh I see. No not really, well not anyone I could go and live with."

His mind suddenly realised the choice that lay before him. He could take up the mistress's offer and have a job and a roof over his head, or start again having to find somewhere to rent on his own. Both prospects seemed a bit daunting but somehow the latter was preferable. If he did choose the job, he could always be terminated when he was too old to want to look for somewhere else, whereas now he still had a bit of energy and all his faculties.

"I might go into one of those flats on the edge of town." Cook broke into his thoughts. "Too old to work anymore. This has been my life and although I'll miss it in some ways, I'm ready to put my feet up. Should have done before really."

Although it seemed like a casual conversation, she didn't want to put any pressure on him, but she knew only too well what was going through his mind.

"You know something." Danny was studying Abe's vibrations.

"Maybe. Just watching for now."

There was no point in trying to prise anything out of him for when Abe went into one of these modes, he was weighing up everything from all angles and he usually was spot on, but wouldn't voice his thoughts until absolutely sure. Also it didn't attract the attention from high level powers as to his deductions. Although Danny was having a few suspicions of his own he knew better than to push it just now and also keep his own ideas cloaked.

Throughout the weekend, both Bryn and Amy were having enough spiritual intercourse to last a lifetime, but the more they had the more they craved. The real Kam was now servicing Amy while Bryn seemed to be enjoying a few newcomers. The brother and sister both had their own excuses for wanting to be alone but as their pressing needs were uppermost in their minds, neither queried the other and were grateful for the chance to indulge.

Bryn had been pretty naïve up to now, but by this time there wasn't much he didn't know and when two spirits appeared to be fighting over him he invited both to join him, which led to even greater numbers until suddenly something brought that to an abrupt end.

'Lady' had been letting him learn a few tricks from these one night stands, or day as the case may be, but it was time to sweep them all out and move in on a permanent basis. This wasn't just for pleasure now, she had a very important job to do and nobody was going to mess it up. Little did Bryn realise that she was taking up twenty four hour residence and there was nothing he could do about it, even if he wanted to.

Amy had found her ultimate dream. Kameron, as she still called him, wanted her for who she was, not just as a prodding tool. If only she had known how she appeared to the onlookers, still the cheap bit of spare she had always been but he had been impregnated with the image that she was hot stuff and couldn't get enough of her. She was doing all the weird and wonderful things he had enjoyed through the years, and here it was in one package.

The distant memory of having been brought over to cleanse his soul had been long forgotten, but while he chose not to remember, it was playing a big part in the overall picture.

Danny was still waiting for Abe to enlighten him but all he got was

"Yes, it is going to plan." Or "It's all falling into place. All parts of the picture are coming together and it's gathering momentum."

But Danny was watching and comparing notes and he too realised a pattern was forming, but he wouldn't voice it until Abe was ready to discuss it.

It will come as no surprise that all the players were being carefully stage managed by the Dark Demons, or another such power group, for nothing could be taken for granted. Just because this sect had acted in such a way before didn't mean they were necessarily running this operation. It could be a copy cat cell. And that meant there could be more, not just at this location but worldwide, which was always a possibility.

In a bold moment Danny did ask if Abe had traced the guardians on Haiti and environs, when 'Major' and Thomas were living there.

"I have." Was all he got in return.

He refrained from thinking "Sorry I asked."

"I'm thinking of pulling Julius and Vard out."

This sudden decision came as a shock.

"Why? They are well cloaked." Danny couldn't see the sense.

"It needs to be as empty as possible. They've done good surveillance but they can be used elsewhere and it will give a clearer picture."

"Where will they go?"

Abe was silent for a moment then said "Everywhere, but not together."

"Well, I'm at a loss." Danny was trying to puzzle it out then realised he was being tested. "Wait a minute."

"Yes?"

"I think you are going to be moving them from one person to another, buzzing about, nobody knowing where they will turn up next and more or less in full view."

"Keep going. The reason is……"

"Got it. Decoys. You want them to be noticed, cause a bit of confusion. But is that necessary?"

"Absolutely."

Danny had his doubts. "Julius will have no problem, but that Vard, I can see him taking risks. Could jeopardise the whole thing."

"Then he will have to learn the hard way."

"What?" That's a bit callous." Danny didn't like throwing spirits into the arena.

"Good distraction. But don't fret, help will be at hand."

"You've got it all worked out haven't you?" Danny would love to have probed but knew it was of no use.

So now it was time for them to wait for the next performer to step forward and place their piece into the jigsaw.

No sooner had Julius and Vard been removed and cast off their dust images, when the next act started. The weekend may have been energetic for Amy but Maud had spent quite a miserable couple of days on her own. Nothing had gone right from the start. A bag of sugar had fallen to the floor and just when she had cleaned that up, the kitchen tap started dripping which didn't seem too bad at first but after a while it began to get on her nerves and she put a cloth in the sink to soften the plop..plop..plop. She would have to ask Dawkins to send someone to get it fixed, then realised there wasn't anyone. As the events took their toll she sat in her armchair, buried her head in her hands and sobbed.

As she arrived for work on Monday she felt drained and although it was the end of an era, she was beginning to look forward to leaving the place. It wasn't the same any more, even the house seemed different and you could feel as though you were completely alone, but it was watching your every move. She jumped at the slightest sound and was noticeably on edge.

"I'm sick of packing. Covering things up. Cleaning up the dirt it all leaves." She was sounding off to Cook as she took off her coat.

"All in the same boat." Was the short reply.

"I don't know how you can say that. You haven't had to break your back bending over, having to sort what is kept and what isn't."

Cook stopped what she was doing.

"I've spent most of my life here, bending over, the table, the stove, you name it. And before that I was bent over scrubbing, then cleaning until I was put in the kitchen. So there's not much you can tell be about 'bending over' lady."

Maud was in such a state she daren't answer for fear of losing her cool and certainly didn't want to let herself down in from of this woman.

"Oh good." Dawkins' voice cut into her thoughts. "Master has asked you to go up to his study, pronto."

"Pardon? The Master?"

"That's what I said. Now don't keep him waiting."

Maud was tempted to say "No Mr Dawkins, Yes Mr Dawkins, three bags full Mr Dawkins." But instead straightened her apron, patted her hair and left with a definite sniff.

Dawkins eyed Cook half expecting her to say something but wasn't surprised when all he got was a 'Hmm'.

"Um, just so you know," he said, "the house is on the market but there won't be a sale sign up. Looks a bit common you see."

"So how will folks know?" she tried to sound a bit thick.

"Oh it's with the estate agent so it will be in their showrooms and in the very best magazines."

"Funny way of going on." She grunted and got on with the breakfast trays. "They're eating in their own rooms now."

"Um, yes I am aware thank you." Dawkins didn't want to be reminded of the situation after his last private encounter then added "I'll get Maud to take the mistress's when she comes back and I'll take the master's.

Cook gave him a look but her spirit was observing elsewhere for she knew very well what was coming next.

The Captain was sitting at his writing desk and swivelled his chair round as he called "Come In" for Maud to enter the room.

"You wanted me Captain."

She stood just inside the room and he beckoned her over and pointed to a chair at the side of the desk.

"Sit down."

"I don't sit." She was already feeling uncomfortable.

"Well I don't want to strain my neck looking up at you, and I also don't wish to stand at the moment as my back is playing up, so please humour me and sit on that chair." The last part was almost given like an order on the barrack square.

"Very well."

Cook was observing thinking the Captain and his wife were both playing the same scene which in itself smacked of manipulation.

"Now Maud, you are very well aware of what is going on here at the moment and you must have wondered about your future."

"Well, it would be unusual if I didn't." She was stern faced and wondered what was coming next.

"Of course." He smiled but it wasn't returned. He wheeled his chair a little nearer to her. "Well I want you to listen very carefully to what I have to say."

If Dawkins had divulged his conversation with Hilary, Maud would have already been on her feet now and out of the door.

"As you know, my wife and I are going to permanently live in our villa in Corfu, which means that when this estate, along with all the cottages in the village which we still own are sold, you will have nowhere to live."

He looked at her closely to see if she had already made arrangements but she stared back in silence.

"Right, well I may have the answer. You see I will need a personal assistant whom I can trust and I think you would be the obvious choice. You have a long track record and I don't want strangers knowing my business. You would have your own quarters and a small salary and live in the sun." Then added quickly "For the rest of your days."

He studied her closely trying to read her expression but she wasn't giving anything away. He moved closer and before she could resist he laid his hand upon hers. She pulled it from under his grasp where it fell and touched her leg, but he had made contact and that was all that was needed.

At first, disgust filled her mind. He had got her only sister pregnant and then Muriel had died giving birth to his child, which meant living a lie watching her nephew turn into the most objectionable man. And now he too was dead. This man had ruined her life and she had only stayed in his employment to be near her own flesh and blood, and the security of a job and a home.

But the turmoil in her mind showed her another aspect. Yes, she would have a job and a home, if he could be trusted to keep his word, which was very probable as it would ensure her mouth stayed permanently shut. Plus the fact she would be under his roof, and one day justice could be done, especially if she gave it a little nudge.

"That is a very generous offer, may I think it over please?"

"Very wise, that's what I like, you don't jump in without weighing up all the facts. Take as long as you like then we will discuss money and your exact duties."

He pulled his chair back and waved her off.

"Let me know as soon as you have decided."

She left the room without further comment but her mind was churning as she went back downstairs.

Cook and Dawkins were in the servant's room and looked round as she entered.

"Ah Maud, I've sent Amy to tidy up outside, it was getting a bit sad looking with Thomas not being here, and I wondered if you could dust round the remaining servant's rooms on the top floor. You can leave ours, and the sitting room, just the others please."

"Of course Mr Dawkins."

As she turned to leave, Cook said very quietly "Why don't you two have a drink first, maybe you have something in common you'd like to talk about." Then giving Dawkins a knowing look, she turned and went into the kitchen and shut the door.

"What was that all about?" Maud had stopped with her hand on the door.

Dawkins mind had been prodded to remember that Cook had a few hidden talents and he said "Not sure but the drink is a good idea. Sit down Maud."

"Hm. Second time I've been told that this morning." As soon as the words left her mouth she regretted it. "Oh ignore me. I don't know why I said that."

Dawkins wasn't stupid and soon put two and two together.

"I think you do, and if it makes you feel any better may I say that I may be in the same position."

"I don't understand Mr Dawkins."

"Today you were called to the master's room, and I think he offered you a job,"

"How in creation do you know, I mean, what makes you think that?"

He smiled. "I thought so."

"So you were listening." She looked very annoyed.

"Nothing of the sort. I don't do that Maud."

"I'm sorry, I shouldn't have said that. But I don't understand."

He looked straight at her before delivering the blow.

"Because it happened to me at the weekend."

"Oh that's alright then. He wants both of us."

"Not him. Her."

It took a moment then she sat open mouthed for a minute.

"What?"

"Exactly. Now do you see?"

She thought before answering.

"They both want us to work for them at the villa and we will have our own rooms and be paid. Right?"

"Wrong, well right in one way."

"Now you're going to have to spell it out. I'm lost."

He took a breath. "He has one part and she has another part, and they live separately, so we would not be working for both, you would be with him, and she wants me with her."

"Oh, hold on a minute. They've got this the wrong way round. Surely I should be her maid and you would be his butler."

When he didn't reply she added "Wouldn't we?"

He just shook his head. "I'm pretty sure I know what he would want off you, because I am in no doubt as to what my services will be."

You could have heard a pin drop.

They both sat looking at each other for some time then she said "Would you mind if I asked what you are going to do? Not that it's any of my business really."

"Well, there is the good side, jobs, a place to live, I certainly haven't got anyone here and the weather is a lot to be desired. But, at what price?"

"It doesn't sit right in my brain." She looked into space. "He touched me you know, first time ever and I haven't any personal respect for him, in fact I still despise the man."

"Touched you? You mean....."

"Oh nothing like that, not personal."

"Only, she touched me, like you say not in a private way, but I had the feeling that it could lead that way once we were in the villa."

"Oh, yes I think you have something there."

Again they mused, churning the pros and cons over.

"Could be burning our boats." He almost whispered. "Go over there and if it doesn't work out, what have we got to come back to?"

She nodded.

"I'm going to have to think this through. Can't give a snap decision."

He agreed. "I wouldn't mind if they had asked us both, as servants to cover the whole place, not spilt."

"I know." She was quiet for a moment then ventured "Could I ask a favour please Mr Dawkins?"

"What's that?"

"You know when you've made up your mind, would you mind telling me?"

"I think I would be glad to, and you will do the same?"

"Yes, I'd like that. Thank you."

They agreed to keep it to themselves because it was really nothing to do with anyone else. At that point Amy breezed in from outside, took off her overall and said "It getting nippy, I'm chilled, any tea going?"

While Cook smiled and thought "A gathering of forces won't go amiss."

Chapter 13

"It's only the beginning isn't it? They are activating all the pieces then putting them on hold until they bring them all together for the final onslaught." Danny was beginning to get the picture.

"That's right, this in itself doesn't seem too significant," Abe agreed, "but we know where it ends to some extent, or at least where it has before."

"And now we have to stop it getting to that stage." Danny agreed.

Abe was still worried. "Correct, but don't forget that these attacks can start in a similar fashion, but the end can be totally different from any other."

"And that's the bit you are not sure of?"

"Not at this present time. Can you do a bit more digging regarding the 'Major' and Thomas? Something came up from one of the guardians that I think could give us a bit more insight into their goal."

"Of course. And you think those two are leading this?" Danny didn't see any other possibility.

"Let's keep our options open for now. If they are, then they have to be either working alone in which case it isn't as big as we thought, or," he paused "they are part of the Dark Demon clique, or a similar one as we have already guessed."

"I'll go back down and have a dig around." Danny was about to leave.

"Have a look into any so called religious clans, or families with several women, you know, where one man seems to be playing God."

"Got it." And he was gone.

Abe knew that having drawn the easy couples together, the next move would not be so simple. He formed a list in his mind.

1. Hilary, the Captain's wife had made a play for Dawkins and had secured a contact with him.

2. 'Lady' had now taken full control of Bryn with his approval.

3. Kam and Amy were well and truly a spiritual item.

4. The Captain had made Maud an offer which she was considering, and had also made physical contact.

5. This was the one that worried him. It was the unknown factor but it had to involve the 'Major' or Thomas somewhere.

Many of the main characters thought they were following their own desires, little aware that all their strings were being pulled from a high source that was not only powerful enough to take full control, but was evil of the highest order.

Julius and Vard were now repositioned as immature little spirits that wandered about, being nosey but not interfering with anything. There were always many of these novices wherever you went and nobody took much notice of them. If they got in the way, they were brushed aside. Many could be mischievous but these two had been warned not to draw too much attention to themselves unless instructed. As they passed each other they didn't communicate but their observations were closely monitored.

"Where's the other one?" Danny asked, meaning Powl.

"On loan."

"Good. Wouldn't want him mucking it up now. The further away the better."

"He will be out of the zone for a while."

"What's he posing as this time?"

"The usual I expect."

The area had been carefully sifted to leave the essential workers but there was more than enough experienced back up when required.

"So are you going to divulge any more?" Danny was keen to know where all this was going.

Abe wasn't one to share until the moment was right so he passed the question right back.

"You seemed to be doing a good job of working it out. So how far are you along now?"

Danny seemed disappointed. "I am sure of what is going on but not why? That is, I haven't got the objective yet, and it has to be something big and threatening."

"Bigger than you have estimated. Remember when we worked on that commune business, the big one in the States?"

"How could I forget? Hang on, this doesn't fit with that."

"Doesn't have to. But it's got a similarity.

Danny knew that Abe was way ahead of him but wouldn't part with any more knowledge until there was proof.

It was getting near to lunchtime in the house, when suddenly the pair got an emergency call through one of their secret routes. Cook was being attacked not physically but through a high powered spirit. She cloaked her true self while pushing her physical image to the fore but this thing was penetrating even her strong shield. She could fool many high levels, so if this was getting through, it meant it was of an extremely sophisticated source.

Abe did an instantaneous scan of the area and was horrified when he saw that the entity had completely enveloped her and seemed to be crushing her soul. Immediately he called in his back up but as they attacked from all angles to trap it, the evil simply evaporated leaving nothing, not even a trail.

The guardians left except one who checked that Cook was alright and when satisfied vacated the area as quickly as possible.

"That was a test run wasn't it?" Danny soon recognised the tactic.

"Checking how powerful she is, plus how quickly we could arrive." Abe was a little annoyed at falling into the trap, but they couldn't leave her to cope alone. Then added "It will be back."

"It knows what it's up against having done a reconnoitre." Danny was well aware of what had just happened.

They were both silent as the same question hung over them. Who?

It was late afternoon and everything about the house was very still. Dawkins made sure Amy was well occupied and indicated for Maud to follow him to one of the empty rooms well away from anyone else.

"Have you made up your mind Maud? I most certainly have."

"I know what I feel is right Mr Dawkins but I should be very pleased to hear your decision."

"Very well. I will refuse the offer. There is nothing about it that feels very wholesome, but please, don't let my thoughts influence you."

"Oh." She breathed a sigh of relief. "That's exactly my sentiments. What a relief. Oh dear me." She seemed as though she didn't know how to express herself but after a moment she added "I don't mind a bit refusing now, seeing as how you are. I was a bit worried in case he told me to leave straight away."

Dawkins smiled. "That thought had crossed my mind, but can I say that it made me feel very cheap. A feeling I have never experienced in this house since I became butler."

"Yes, I think that is it. There was a lecherous feel to it, well at least that's what I felt."

"Are you happy telling him on your own, because I would be pleased to be in attendance if it would give you reassurance. After all, what can they do to us now?"

She looked away deep in thought then turned suddenly and said "That's very kind, but no, I will stand up to him. I've got nothing to be ashamed of."

"Good for you." He touched her lightly on the shoulder. "And I will be very polite but take great pleasure in refusing my post, whatever it was going to be."

She smiled now, relief flooding her face.

"Should we do it at the same time?"

He smirked. "Why not? Should be all over within about two minutes flat. Then we can meet and compare notes."

She was about to leave when a thought struck her.

"I don't suppose we could have Amy out of the way first could we?"

"I will arrange that." He looked at his watch. "Only half an hour to go. I'll dismiss her now. Wait here." And he left the room quicker than she had seen him move for many years.

In no time he was back and moved to the window where he could confirm that Amy had left the premises then beckoned to Maud who followed him to the house phone. First he rang Hilary and asked that he see her which was agreed immediately, then he rang the Captain and said that Maud had requested a word with him and that too was accepted.

They checked their appearance as usual and made their way up the stairs until they were outside the Captain's study. Tapping on the door, Dawkins waiting for permission to enter, went in and announced "Maud to see you Captain." The master nodded and indicated for her to come in and once deposited, Dawkins closed the door and made his way to the mistress's sitting room. Again a gentle tap was followed by a request to enter. Both were on a mission but guessed it would not be accepted graciously.

Danny was watching closely to see the reactions from each room but knew that whatever decision had been made it would have little bearing on the whole plan of things. The connection had been made and the pairing done and there was no way back. It didn't matter where their bodies were placed, their souls had been caught and now they would be under the instruction of whoever was running the operation.

Dawkins was first back in the room but Maud joined him only minutes later.

"Well?" he enquired.

"Not what I expected." She seemed quite pleased and relieved. "He just said it was my choice and he accepted it. Oh and that he would be sorry when I wasn't working for them any more as I had been a loyal servant. And that was about it really." She gave a little shrug then asked "How about you?"

For a moment he was a little taken aback. "Well, that is a surprise. You see they could have been reading a script. She said exactly the same to me."

"That is strange." She looked a bit bemused but then rubbed her hands together and said "But at least it's all alright. Do you think I over reacted?"

"Well, if you did, so did I. That's what I don't understand."

"What?"

"Why didn't they get together, have us both in and ask us jointly? You could say that wouldn't have been etiquette as I am of a higher position, so they could have asked us separately but making it clear that we would both be servants in their villa."

"As I said, it seemed cock eyed to me. I was the obvious choice for her, and you for him."

They paused for a moment thinking over what had gone on then Dawkins looked at his watch and said "Time you were off Maud. I wouldn't think too deeply about it. See you in the morning."

But as he made his way up to his room later, it was very much on his mind. Something had changed but he couldn't work out what. He felt different and Muriel came into his mind. That was it. He felt as though he had a connection with a female or was in a relationship but that was ludicrous and he tried to sweep it from his thoughts, but it was festering inside him and wasn't going to leave.

Cook went straight to her own room instead of going to the sitting room and took off all her working clothes. Now wearing a very plain full length nightdress she lay on her back on the bed and to any observer was fast asleep. Even her spirit seemed to be hovering just above her with her guardians at her head and feet. But she had detached the part which was only visible to extreme levels and was in conference.

"I know who it was, or rather who they were."

Abe was very attentive and indicated for her to divulge all she had learned in the brief mode, which meant she just imparted the smallest amount of information but enough for him to piece together. This was used in cases where they had to keep the meeting even shorter than the instantaneous version.

"Sudden. Surprise. Overwhelmed. Controlling. Tried to plant soul cell. First 'Major' then Thomas. Fighting for possession."

With that she was gone. Even the blink of an eye would have been at least ten times longer than this exchange.

Abe had got the loose end he'd been waiting for. Now the picture was clear and although it was horrendous to even contemplate, he knew he had a fight on his hands and he had to work quickly.

Danny had come across some old news reports which at first seemed to have no bearing on the case but then the similarities had to be more than just coincidence. Through the years there had been stories about two people, sometimes husband and wife, two men, or two women who had been on the 'wanted' list but never traced. They had gone by many names but the underlying factors were identical. Not only were they sought by earthly means but also spiritual and they seemed to have the skill of completely going to ground. The police reports marked them as 'cold case, file closed'. In spirit they were considered to be 'pending until reappearing'.

With this information Abe was able to trace the guardians that had been assigned to each earth life and sure enough in every case, the evil had overcome them. This meant that if 'Major' and Thomas were now active they could destroy not only the bodily forms but the hope of spiritual peace.

The fact that they had both attempted to place a control cell in Cook showed that they may be working together and if the first didn't succeed, the second one came in to finish the job. But it appeared that neither had been successful. Then he considered Cook's final statement. "Fighting for possession." Could it be they were actually fighting each other? Now that threw a different light on it.

Amy had got home a bit earlier, having been dismissed by Dawkins, and hoped for a quick session with Kameron before Bryn showed up but her lover was already with her as she entered the house and steered her upstairs to her room, dragged her to the window where he started massaging her before her clothes were even off. Then she felt every item been torn from her until she was absolutely naked. As her room was at the front, she could see directly onto the road and as there were no net curtains, any passer by would have had a full view of her and assumed she was alone, or accompanied by a very short man, or even one on his knees out of sight.

At first this embarrassed her in case she was seen but after a while the sheer thrill and enjoyment took over and she didn't even care, in fact she would have enjoyed watching their faces. When he gave her a moment before starting again, her dignity had evaporated for he had succeeded very quickly in stripping it from her, using her desire to have him for herself. But Kam still thought he was in control and not being governed by the dark forces.

For the time being this pair was completely tuned into the part they had to play along with all the others in their situation across the globe. And each couple merely started off by one of them wanting the other for their use only. Sexual possession. They ignored the warning 'careful what you wish for' which had been relayed to them many times by their guardians but sexual craving is one of the strongest desires and people will not listen, even to their own instincts. Now it was too late.

The Captain was now suggesting to his wife that, when the estate was sold, he paid her a substantial amount and she found a place of her own, in fact he would help her. If he expected her to fall in with his wishes he should have known better so for the time being had to settle for her living in the villa, but in her own part.

They had both half expected the servants to decline their offers of work, but it didn't matter for the seeds had been planted and for the time being they had their subjects under their roof and that would be enough. They were still ignorant of the fact that they had been impregnated with the evil seed long ago and now it had been activated, so they had no will of their own and would merely be following orders subconsciously.

Day had crept into night and Dawkins was ready to try and relax and forget a lot of what had been going on. He just wanted to drift off into a peaceful world with no worries. He was in that beautiful half way stage when he felt someone within his room and reached for the bedside light. A hand came down on top of his and started to move up his arm. Frantically he fought back as he thought it must be an intruder, but if it was it was female and very desirable for he could now smell her perfume and feel her soft touch exploring places under the sheet.

Now she was breathing in his ear and he wasn't fighting any more. It crossed his mind that it couldn't be Cook unless she was using her alto image, so it must be Hilary.

That was enough. The message went straight back to the demons that Cook was of a high level, and Dawkins' momentary thought had divulged it although of course he was completely unaware of it, as was Hilary. While she had been given the urge to seduce him, the main objective was to open his mind and it had been so easy, so while she carried on enjoying the delights on offer, her part for now was done.

Whether or not he would regret it in the morning never entered his head. Having been a fairly sexually active young man, he had been celibate for the last few years due to lack of suitable partners so all the pent up desires came out in a rush and she wasn't complaining either.

It was only when she had left and he lay back contemplating the unexpected visit, he realised the purpose of her previous offer and he now knew exactly what his job description would have been. Then it occurred to him that Maud would have been asked for the same reason. So he would be bonking his mistress in one part of the villa while the Captain was knocking Maud senseless in the other. Sounded a bit basic when you put it like that.

If he had enjoyed the episode he wasn't alone. Maud went to bed also wanting to clear her head, but as she tossed and turned unable to sleep, she felt a presence in her room and it was very near to her. She lay perfectly still for a moment hoping it would go away but there was a warm feeling on her neck and it was creeping down to her chest. Then a heavy weight seemed to be holding her to the bed and she distinctly felt something pushing where it shouldn't have been. As she tried to cry out, hot lips covered her mouth and she felt the movement of going up and down in the bed. Something was happening inside her that had to be satisfied but at the same time she was terrified. It was soon over and the presence had gone leaving her thinking she must have had a naughty dream but when she felt down to her thighs she knew it was a bit more than that.

The Captain in his own bed had just 'arrived' as he called it politely and was holding onto his prodder with satisfaction. This was good. He now had honed his skills so that he didn't even have to move his body to enjoy the delights of whoever he wished. It had taken a bit of practice but this proved he had made the grade. For some reason he had been drawn to Maud and she was now his. But none of this had been by chance. His father had seen to that.

Abe was in a tight spot. Whether to pull Cook out now, not only for her own spiritual safety, but for fear the demons could trace her source which was secretly guarded. She had been invaluable in that position but things were coming to a head and she was in the firing line. He would have to make a decision soon.

Danny was also attempting to sort out something which hadn't quite made sense. When he tried to compare the earth lives of the 'Major' and Thomas to see how far they went back together, there seemed to be a gap. He listed everything he had in chronological order and although the 'Major could be traced continuously, Thomas seemed to disappear at least twice with no trace of physical or spiritual activity. Even when a soul passes over, they are accounted for, but he completely vanished leaving no trail whatever. This could only mean he had to be of an extremely high level.

Danny ran his findings by Abe.

"If he's that high, why is he bothering with what seems a trivial matter in a small village this time?"

Abe was quick with his reply.

"Because it is exactly that. Something small which he hopes nobody will take too seriously. But as we have already gathered, it is only part of a much larger picture. All these little cells will be activated and then the evil will take over, or hope to."

"So what do we do? Scan the whole world?"

"My friend, your diligence has come up with some valuable information, but while you were occupied, we have done just that. And you won't be surprised to learn that the earth is riddled with the same tiny little cells."

Danny had a thought. "But you're not suggesting that one almighty evil power is in complete control of all these little units."

Abe answered that with one word. "Pyramid."

"Ah. The one at the top passes to the next level then the next etc. Is this one at the very bottom then?"

"Could well be." Abe concluded

They were quiet for a moment then Danny brought up the question of the commune that Abe had mentioned on a previous meeting.

"They all died. By agreement."

"Correct." Abe was waiting for his friend to move onto the next step.

"But, that can't be. He's not going to get everyone to kill their allotted partner then destroy themselves. They wouldn't do it."

"It's been done many times on a small scale."

Danny thought for a moment then said "But they were brainwashed through some fake religious sect, not because they were enjoying sex."

"Doesn't matter how it's done. Hypnotism, brain washing, terrorism, sexual control or fanatical possession."

"You mean he intends to wipe out all human life on earth?"

Abe only had to give a spiritual indication to confirm Danny's assumptions.

"But I don't see the point. If he wants control and power, there would be no one left to rule."

Abe paused to let his next remark sink in.

"It isn't as simple as that. His initial objective is to infiltrate solid relationships whether they be heterosexual, gay, bisexual, it doesn't matter but he goes for couples. Then he gradually destroys the love, trust and companionship and leaves the earth with hatred, jealousy and lust in its place. People then use each other with no thought for feelings, loyalty, heartbreak or respect. The single people are gradually drawn into this callous existence he has created until it destroys itself."

Danny had listened with horror. This was much worse than he had ever experienced on such a large scale.

"They kill each other." He said simply.

"Or themselves. Can't take it you see."

Danny went back to a previous question.

"But I say again, who will he have to rule? Everyone will all be gone. He will be king of nothing."

"He wants spiritual power, to control all the levels of existence. He will start at the bottom by destroying earth life, then move onto the lower levels and up as far as possible until he reigns supreme."

"But that still means he's wiping everyone out." Danny was insistent

"Oh he will be very selective. Just keep the ones he wants that he can manipulate." He paused again. "But there is still a chance that it could also destroy itself even at those levels."

After soaking up all this new conjecture it was obvious the good forces had quite a battle on their hands and they would be determined that this power of mass destruction would have to be taken out as soon as possible, but it would have to be very carefully planned.

Julius and Vard had been nosing around the area to pick up traces of anything unusual and had decided that Vard should keep a close watch on the area around the estate while Julius moved further afield but they would both be wary and keep their guards up.

The first place Vard wanted to check was the small church for he imagined a few spirits could be hanging around there and you never knew what they may have witnessed over the years. He floated round the inside looked at the memorial plaques on the walls and noticed the same surnames on several. So he went into the small graveyard to see if he could match up the plaques with the graves. As he drifted over the majority he noticed a corner where there were only two tombstones well away from the others. On close examination he found they only bore the letters RIP with no names or dates.

He knew he was being watched and called to the hovering spirits but they stayed way back near the church wall, so he moved over to them and asked about the two separate burial plots. None of them would give him an answer and they moved to a stone with a large cross on the top and merged with it. The message they were sending was "Leave alone."

Vard wasn't going to leave it there so moved back to the corner and turned to see what they would do. He was now directly over one plot and he could feel the vibration of the earth trembling beneath him. Suddenly he was being dragged down into the earth and was aware of two stone coffins with remains in each but the feeling creeping round him was of pure evil. He fought to see if there were any names on the lids but everything was getting blurred and just when his soul seemed to be trapped he felt a tremendous pull from above and he was being catapulted upwards.

"What do you think you were doing?" Julius had called for help to get this idiot out of danger. Cook seeing he was safe returned instantly to her physical body.

"I found something. I think the evil has a base there. Down in the earth."

Danny had called them away and was questioning Vard.

"Why didn't you ask? You would have been told that they date way back. They were family members who had brought the whole place into disrepute and had to be buried away from the church so they were put there."

"But stone coffins."

Danny knew he wouldn't rest without an explanation.

"They have been there for years, and well, the family unearthed them and reused them."

"They took them out and…….." Vard was still hooked on this.

"No." Danny continued, "They just dug down and lifted the lids and popped them in."

"But people would think that was unholy."

"They didn't know."

There was a pause and Julius who had been taking all this in asked "One wouldn't have been the 'Major' by any chance?"

Danny passed it off and said they had better get back but Vard must stay with Julius for now.

"I know when I'm being fobbed off. They know what's there and it's got something to do with this Kam business, I can feel it."

Julius was silent for a moment then said "Why don't we go and check out that medium that Amy went to?"

"Why not? Can't get into much trouble there." Vard thought it was a waste of time and had been suggested to get him out of the way but he made up his mind to go back whenever the opportunity arose.

Janet actually had a client when the two arrived and they couldn't help but notice that apart from her guardian, there were no more spirits near the place. They watched for a while and found it quite amusing the way she waffled on without a clue what she was talking about then suddenly the Dark Demons group arrived. Julius managed to pull Vard to a safe distance where they watched Janet being fed information. They pulled back even further when 'Lady' arrived but were interested in her part in these proceedings. They didn't have to wait long for she did her usual trick of leaving to visit Bryn.

Vard was about to follow but was held back.

"What do you think you're doing?" Julius wasn't letting go.

"Want to see where he goes. It's a bloke." Vard was still eager to be off.

Knowing their presence could be picked up Julius decided it would be easier to go along with it knowing full well where it would lead than to stay and argue.

In seconds 'Lady' was in Bryn's bed and Julius waited for the reaction.

"That's the one I was guarding after Powl messed up but look at him, he loves it." If Vard had possessed a mouth it would have been hanging open. "But I thought we were trying to stop that happening. What's going on?"

Julius took a moment to remind Vard about a person's will and how strong it could be. They moved a safe distance away and started to sum things up. Immediately a message was sent to Danny and Abe that they believed a small Dark Demons cell was using Janet's home as a base. It didn't take long to realise that it was on Amy's first visit that she had been impregnated and it begged the question as to just how innocent Janet was.

Dawkins was up early the next morning but knew that Cook would already be in the kitchen. She looked up as he entered the servant's room with the expression on her face that was asking for an explanation.

"How are you Mr Dawkins?"

"I am well thank you Cook." Then trying to veer her off asked "Did you have a good sleep?"

"I did thank you."

She said no more but he knew she was almost scanning him for information. He put on his jacket and checked his appearance in the mirror.

"I understand prospective buyers are due to arrive today so we have to keep well out of their way unless otherwise instructed. I will speak to Maud and Amy as soon as they arrive as the private rooms need a brush up."

"And just where will his lordship be while all this is going on?"

Dawkins was a little surprised at the bluntness of the question but calmly replied "The master and mistress will be going out for the day but will require dinner about 5pm."

She gave her usual little shrug which was her way of ending a conversation and went into the kitchen.

Maud arrived with rather a flush in her cheeks which surprised Dawkins.

"Ah Maud, at nine o'clock I want you to clean the mistress's room and Amy can do the same in the master's." He looked straight at her when he spoke and noticed her face drop. "Is that a problem?"

She would still have to do it but he wanted to know why she looked unwilling.

"Well, um Mr Dawkins, you see I've been thinking, and I wanted to have a word with the Captain first thing and it would be easier if I was to clean his room instead."

Thinking back to their previous conversation, something now alerted him that she may have changed her mind. He led her away from the servant's room as he knew Cook would be listening. When they were at a safe distance he turned her round to face him.

"What are you up to Maud? I thought it was settled?"

For a moment she looked like a naughty child that had been told off but then she took on a new personality.

She faced him, took a deep breath and said "Well I've been thinking. I have nothing, he took everything away. My sister, my nephew. So why shouldn't I reap the benefits of his lifestyle. I don't intend to be poor while he lives it up so I am going to accept his offer, whatever it may entail."

"Maud!" He was staggered. "You would share his bed, because that's what he wants you know, to get a roof over your head."

She gave a very cunning smile.

"Oh not a roof Mr Dawkins. My roof."

Dawkins looked her straight in the eye.

"I cannot believe what I am hearing. Never would I have thought you would stoop to such a level."

She smiled as she said very quietly "He took your girlfriend remember."

"Well…I .." He was lost for words as he knew she was right.

"Let me put it this way Mr Dawkins. For years, ever since we were first at work, we have been servants, doing the bidding of those with money. Well now it's time to have some of that, and if you have any sense you'll do the same if only to get your own back. What goes around comes around you know."

He was taken aback at her bluntness and with giving one of his usual little coughs said "I must remind you Maud that while you are still in this employment, I am your senior and I would ask that you respect that."

She didn't answer but gave him a very knowing look while a smirk crept over her face.

It was time for him to take charge of this situation so said very curtly "If you want to take that route, that is your business but for now you will follow orders. You will clean the mistress's room."

"Very well Mr Dawkins."

But jealousy and greed had been planted in her, and with the power behind her she would get exactly what she wanted, and the Captain would get what he deserved.

It had been a very uncomfortable exchange and Dawkins was feeling he was fighting double standards within himself. He almost envied Maud's attitude and wished he could have had the courage to say what he felt on many occasions, but he knew his place which is how he kept his job. When he was younger it was all that mattered without much thought for the future, but now it was staring him in the face. What future? The memory of last night kept flitting through his brain as if he was being reminded of it and mustn't ignore it. As soon as Amy arrived he despatched to her task then took a moment to weigh up his own situation.

He would have to leave this house, he would have no job with little prospects of finding another and no other skill for this was the only one he had ever known. It looked bleak indeed and Maud's suggestion wasn't sounding so bizarre now. But what should he do?

The rot was setting in, taking different forms but in each case was fuelled by deadly emotions and was spreading like a row of dominoes where all it needed was the first one to topple.

Amy was so engrossed in her relationship with Kam that she was oblivious to almost anything else, whether it was physical or spiritual. She went about her work with her mind in the clouds and when she was with her beloved she was part of him and that's how it would be forever. He had hinted that it would be more practical for her to join him on his side and although she was keen on the result, she was a bit apprehensive on how it would be achieved, but rather than loose him she would go along with it eventually.

As instructed by Dawkins she cleaned the Captain's room then made her way as if to go downstairs, but something made her do a detour to Kameron's old room. She was being drawn in and pulled to the bed which although stripped was still usable for their kind of antics.

"Oo, couldn't you wait?" she laughed to herself.

The next minute she was lying on her back with her clothes round her waist and the pair of them were enjoying the usual 'warm up' as she called it, which was a quickie before the long drawn out session. She was aware that this time it may be all they would get as she would be missed.

They had just finished when he roughly pulled away and she heard a sadistic laughter echoing round the room.

"Kameron, what's got into you?" she tried to whisper.

What came next shook her rigid.

"Kameron? I'm not Kameron. He's off with his latest bit. Mind you, he was right, you're not bad as a bit of spare." Again the eerie laughter floated around then faded into silence.

For several moments she didn't move. Then slowly she adjusted her clothes and sat trying to get her mind to think properly. After the anger and jealousy subsided a bit she tried to make excuses, then reasons why he would do this but then it hit her.

"Of course, it wasn't him. He would never do that now. Someone else was using me."

It didn't occur to her that she hadn't queried it until the end and had automatically accepted that it was Kameron. If she had, she may have wondered if he had been the one playing the game. But it was enough, the seed of doubt had been planted however much she tried to convince herself to the contrary. But she needed to meet him again soon for the two emotions were boiling to the surface, but which would be the stronger, jealousy or anger at being made to look silly, and not forgetting hatred and revenge that would be lurking in the wings waiting for their bite of the cake.

Cook had been observing all that was going on and was very aware of the change in personalities of the staff and was waiting to see how each one reacted to the current circumstances. Using her spiritual self she had covered most of the area surrounding the estate and was well aware of the demon cell in the next village but it didn't end there. It was now spreading like a river that had burst its banks but seemed to steer away from the major towns and cities. To her experienced senses she could even isolate the trigger points and was annoyed when Vard stumbled upon the one in the graveyard as she had hoped to keep a low profile on that so as not to alert them. Her only consolation was that they would see the young cub for what he was and may disregard him, but as many plans over the centuries had been scuppered by that minor oversight, they may just be keeping a watch on him which meant that Julius could also be tailed. She would politely suggest that the two be split again.

"I knew it," she thought as she returned to her physical image "they have to learn, but why does it always have to be on my patch?"

If Bryn seemed to have escaped being drawn into the deadly sin net up to now, that was about to change drastically. 'Lady' had taken great delight in tutoring this novice, but the gilt was wearing off and she was gasping to break in a few new ones. But that left him wide open to all passing entities to play their dirty little games.

He always hoped he would be home before Amy so that he could have a quickie before dinner, and it had become the habit to have another session before bedtime, and then the night was his to bonk his socks off. It was almost knocking off time and he had just moved some of the feed to the storeroom when he felt the familiar warmth smoothing its way round his groin area.

"Let me get home first." He breathed.

Before he had time to think he had been pushed to the ground, his pants were undone and his cucumber was looking to the roof.

"Hey, don't be so rough." He laughed but didn't want her to stop.

It then occurred to him that she wasn't alone, there were several of them and his entire body was getting the works. It was all too much and he erupted like a geyser, gasping and groaning at the top of his voice. It was only when he heard the giggles and opened his eyes he saw the other farmhands in a row nearly pissing themselves with laughter, but trying not to make too much noise in case the farmer heard.

Most of the comments were only for lads to enjoy but the embarrassment Bryn endured was something he'd never known before. Even all the jibes he used to suffer when he was young didn't come close to this.

"Shall I fetch you a cloth?" one of them asked before falling about clutching his sides.

"Wish I'd known, I'd have videoed it and put it on Intouch." which was the main social media site at the time.

"Not got a bad one has he? Could ride to York on that."

As one of them spotted the farmer coming out of a nearby barn they all made a hasty retreat but Bryn knew this was not the end of it by any means and he would now be the laughing stock of the whole village.

So apart from desperately needing continual sex, he had shame to contend with.

Dawkins made his way up to Hilary's room on the pretence of checking to see how Maud was doing. As he neared the door, she came out, cleaning materials in her arms.

"Oh, I've finished now Mr Dawkins." She said as she nearly bumped into him.

"Is the mistress there?" He asked as if checking every detail.

"She's in the bathroom and she sent you a message."

They both stood looking at each other for a moment then he tilted his head and said "And the message is?"

"Oh, just a minute." She put her equipment on the floor and pulled a note from her pocket. "She's sealed it." She said very meaningfully.

"So I see. Thank you Maud. You may go down for coffee now." He was almost abrupt and waited for her to disappear before opening the letter.

He stood with his mouth open as he read the words. It was from Hilary asking him to reconsider and agree to work for her at the villa but she would like him to keep it private for the moment.

As he slowly made his way down the stairs everything was going through his mind. Maud was now going for her own reasons so why shouldn't he look after his own future. If it had been Hilary in his bed, he had rather enjoyed it and if there was more where that came from, he would be silly to refuse. Most men wouldn't. Then he thought of her last request, to keep it private. His mind was made up, he would go and live the life he had only seen others enjoying, but he wouldn't tell even Maud.

Deceit had added its name to the list.

Chapter 14

The decision had been made. Cook must be removed. Her physical body could be found as though she had peacefully passed away in her sleep but her spirit must leave the area as she had now been targeted by the 'Major' and Thomas who would be back, either together or working separately.

"She's been a valuable source of information and protection." Danny seemed disappointed at having to move her.

"We knew it would come." Abe stated. "For all this time she's slid under the radar, but we don't know just what heights this pair have risen to, and what help they are calling on, so we can't leave her in there, its far too risky."

"When?" Danny wanted to know.

"Any time soon. We have back up who will replace her in spirit and that will confuse the opposition. We are up against the more powerful lot now."

"Yes, look how the emotions are building, and they aren't loving or benevolent, just the opposite."

Abe agreed "That's just what they planned. They do this. Use the strong energy that governs them, and when it is en masse it's quite a force to be fighting."

"From little acorns." Danny mused.

"Exactly."

Dawkins had been summoned by the Captain to gather the four remaining staff in the dining room as he wished to address them. It was very quiet as nobody seemed to want to offer any conjecture.

As the master entered the room they all went to stand but he beckoned them to remain seated.

"I've called you all here to thank you for the years of service you have given this family, and to keep you informed of what is going on at the present time."

Everyone looked straight at him without turning to see what anyone else's reaction would be.

"As I expect you are aware, my wife and I will be leaving for our villa in Corfu and we have decided not to wait until the house is sold, but to go very soon." He paused before the next bit. "This means the house will be left empty."

There was a hush as they waited for the obvious.

"Unfortunately it means that there will be no one residing or working here from that point. The property will be in the hands of the estate agent who will show prospective buyers around but there is no need for the house to be kept habitable. I would like to thank you for your hard work clearing and packing the various items and they will be removed next week."

Again silence fell over the room.

"I expect you are wondering how much longer you will be here and where you will live when the cottages have been sold. Basically you have one month to find alternative accommodation."

The gasp was expected and he quickly hurried with his next statement.

"You will all be paid until then as a token of your long service but you will not be working here after next week."

He looked round the group and to ease the tension Dawkins stood up and offered thanks on behalf of them all and said how sorry they would be that this era had come to an end, but privately knew he must answer Hilary's note as soon as he could, accepting her kind offer. Every man for himself now.

Cook was aware of the offers to him and Maud and their decisions and knew that Abe would possibly be recalling her as

Cook, but that left Amy. She would be the one who would have the biggest hurdle for her dreams of being lady of the manor had been dashed, and now she was nothing and had nothing. But she knew that underneath this woman wouldn't take anything lying down especially if she felt she had been thrown on the scrapheap, not only by the master but by Kam. Things could get interesting.

Dawkins waited for the master to leave the room and suggested the servants went about their business carrying on as normal for now. He made the excuse he had to see the master about the requirements for the following week but making sure there was no one about, quickly made his way to Hilary's room. He tapped gently on the door expecting to hear the familiar 'Come in' so was shocked when she opened the door herself and beckoned him inside.

"I knew you'd come. You've changed your mind haven't you?" She was beaming.

"Well," he began "if you will pardon me, you seem to have said it for me."

There was a friendly familiarity about the atmosphere and for a moment they were no longer employer and manservant.

"I am so pleased you saw sense. What have you got to stay here for?" she ushered him to a seat.

"Well, now you put it that way, nothing at all and this is the only job I know."

She smiled and he wondered what little gem was going to come now.

"Of course it will be too warm for you to wear that attire so you will have to get used to being in something a little more, shall we say comfortable."

"Oh, I see, I hadn't thought of that." He realised he hadn't given much thought to the details of the job.

"Don't you worry about a thing, it will all be taken care of."

"Oh well, thank you very much." He noticed she had smiled more in the last few moments than he had seen in a long time. But then her face grew serious.

"I suppose you know he's bringing along a companion." She followed this with a knowing look.

"You mean Maud. I had heard." He wasn't going to elaborate and preferred her to give any information.

"Well they won't bother us. Big place you know. You'll absolutely love it."

"May I ask a question?"

"Of course, you must have many."

He coughed uneasily. "What about cleaning, who would be expected to do that?"

She laughed now.

"Oh my dear man, certainly not you. No, we have a local woman comes in and cleans the place."

"And would I be over her?"

She looked him straight on.

"You really will have to forget the past. Things will be very different for you, it's a new beginning."

"Thank you, only you hadn't exactly laid out what my duties would be so I wondered…."

"You will be my attendant. That's all there is to it. He has his companion and I have mine."

It was a great temptation to say "Well make up your mind which am I?" but he wasn't going to spoil the possibility of a good thing and knew he would only know when he got there and he had settled into his new role.

After a few more pleasantries he left to go downstairs and Maud came into his mind. What a surprise it would be when she found out, but there was no need for her to know yet.

He went into the servant's room and noticed Cook watching him as if she had overheard the whole conversation. But he brushed the thought aside because it wouldn't matter soon.

Amy came dashing into the room.

"Mr Dawkins, there's a foul smell coming from the front sitting room downstairs. It's awful, it's like something's rotting. It's made me want to puke."

As she did look a bit of a funny colour he told her to sit down for a moment and grabbing a hand towel went up to the room. Her description was mild for what met him. The air was acrid and there seemed to be a haze floating everywhere. Although he had the towel to his nose and mouth, his eyes were stinging and he felt himself being overcome. Frantically he tried to find the door but there was nothing there and soon he lost all sense of direction and was stumbling about wildly. In his ears he could hear a chant he didn't recognise at first but then the melody became familiar. It was the one Thomas always hummed as he went about his work.

"Mr Dawkins. Mr Dawkins. Are you alright?" Cook was shaking him and slowly he could make out her face looking down on him. Then he could see Maud who was almost in tears.

"Get away. Get out of here." He tried to yell.

"It's alright. You are in the hallway." Cook tried to calm him. "We heard you and when we came we found you here."

"Did you hear anything else?" he whispered.

The two women looked at each other, then Maud said, "Nothing much."

He got up slowly and Cook decided he needed to go and sit in the servant's room and have a good strong cup of tea, with a spot of something in it.

They all sat trying to make sense of what had happened when Cook said "The sooner we are all out of this house the better if you ask me."

Amy was looking nervous. "There's been a lot of strange stuff going on recently hasn't there?"

Although she had enjoyed her moments of lust with Kameron, she hadn't been too happy with the other unexplained events and now she knew she didn't need the house to communicate with him, she wanted to get out as soon as possible. Also she needed to know what was going on in the spirit world. Things weren't as good as she thought now that she was unsure of Kameron's intentions, for it seemed he hadn't changed his ways now he was on the other side. Well, she would teach him a lesson, that is as soon as she knew that he was visiting and not some usurper.

"Where will you and your brother live?"

Maud's question brought her back to reality.

"Um, I don't know, we haven't got long to find somewhere. Can't stay in the village because we couldn't buy the house when they sell it. We will have to rent something. We'll have to start looking harder now."

Dawkins gave Maud a hard look which she returned little knowing they would be living under the same roof very soon.

The Captain had called Dawkins and it sounded rather urgent so instead of his usual butler speed, he hurried up to the study. The door was open and Captain was examining the lock.

"Ah Dawkins," he greeted him "something's gone wrong with this damn door. It won't lock and you know I must be able to secure all of my rooms."

It had always been a rule that the locks were constantly maintained which had fallen to Thomas as part of his regular routine.

"I'll have a look sir." Dawkins bent down and twisted the key in the lock which seemed to be perfectly alright. The bolt was coming in and out quite freely so he turned his attention to the housing in the doorframe.

Nothing was blocking the free running so he closed the door and turned the key.

"There we are." He announced.

The Captain gave him a strange look, waved him aside and opened the door.

"Well, that can't be. I've just locked it." Dawkins stood in amazement not believing his eyes.

"Exactly. It's happened each time, but why?"

"I'm at a complete loss. There is no reason why it shouldn't be working perfectly. When did you say it started being faulty?"

"Just now of course." The Captain was getting very frustrated and would take it out on whoever was near at the time. "You don't think I would have ignored it once it was faulty do you?"

Dawkins took a breath. "I had better arrange for a locksmith to come in at once."

"Well be careful who it is. Don't want just anyone snooping around here."

As Dawkins went to open the door he froze.

"Now what's the matter man?" The Captain was quite wound up and hadn't time for any dramatics.

"You just opened the door."

"Very good. Yes I just opened it. What about it?"

Dawkins stared at the door which was now closed.

"Well the wind must have blown it."

As the Captain uttered the words he knew how hollow they sounded for there was no wind in the room and while he was getting very fraught, Dawkins was becoming more uncomfortable by the minute especially following his recent experience.

His hand shaking he went to open the door but it was now firmly locked and no amount of twisting the key had any effect.

"You'll have to go out through the other room." The Captain ordered "and for Christ's sake get that door fixed."

He led Dawkins through his sitting room and out of the door leading to the hallway.

He was hurrying along the landing as he needed to get back to the kitchen area as soon as possible to try and gather his wits when he heard the sound of an argument ahead of him. The corridor led to Hilary's rooms and he recognised Amy's voice which was almost a shout.

"But I made it, as you asked and someone else must have stripped it."

He stopped outside the door and could hear Hilary screaming in reply.

"Who do you think you are you little slut? If you had made the bed it would still be made. What are you suggesting? That I have had a man in here?"

"I'm saying nothing of the sort and you know it."

This wasn't the kind of outburst that would have been heard in the house at one time, but what had Amy got to loose now?

"How dare you speak to me like that? Just because you thought master Kameron had eyes for you doesn't give you the right to get above yourself lady."

Dawkins felt he must intervene or the two would be tearing each others' hair out so he knocked quite loudly on the door.

"What?" Hilary screamed.

"Can I be of assistance madam?"

"Come in and sort this creature out."

He entered slowly for fear a missile might be aimed at him but they stood facing each other eyes blazing.

"Should I take Amy downstairs and speak to her?" He offered.

The reply came with vengeance.

"Put her where she belongs. In a brothel!"

That did it. Amy flew at her but she side stepped deftly and let her keep going at speed.

Dawkins held up his hand.

"Enough ladies. Amy come with me. Now!"

He pulled her by the arm but she wrenched it away and very slowly and deliberately walked through the doorway, but the look she gave Hilary could have turned her to stone.

Once outside the room he marched her quickly downstairs and stopped in the hallway.

"Right young lady, explain your behaviour."

"She accused me of not making her bed when I had done it. I reckon she stripped it off for spite so she could have a go at me."

"The mistress isn't given to falsehoods Amy, are you absolutely sure?"

He felt he was hearing the truth for Amy had no reason to have a pot at Hilary unless she had heard that Maud had been chosen to go to Corfu and not her.

"Yes I'm sure, and I don't lie either Mr Dawkins. I might not be what some people think of as perfect but I was brought up to tell the truth."

He had a strange feeling that something was unsettling the house and those that remained in it, but couldn't figure out what it could be.

Abe and Danny had watched the recent events and they were certain they knew the reason but were still undecided as to exactly who was causing the unrest. It was as if some force wanted everyone out of the house which presented another question.

"They will all be gone soon anyway," Danny was musing "so why the hurry?"

Abe had one theory. "Because whoever it is wants it cleared now."

"They need it for some specific purpose?" Danny couldn't think why the Dark Demons should have targeted the Lonely Elms unless there was unfinished business there.

"Could very well be. They don't want these people cluttering up the place, but as you say, why the urgency? This could be a vendetta that goes back years, so why the rush?"

They went over all the facts again but knew there was no action they could take at this precise moment.

"What about Cook?" Danny asked.

"Think we'll leave her but monitor constantly, then we can pull her in an instant if the situation demands."

They did a scan of the house and noticed distinct changes in the colour of the air. It started small then seemed to be spreading throughout the building, and everywhere it went it caused chaos, misunderstanding and distrust.

It was decided to keep Julius and Vard well away from the property now and they were told to flit about as though they had no specific purpose but keep a watch on Janet's house and also the home of Bryn and Amy in particular.

Maud was carrying some table linen to the storage chest in one of the downstairs rooms when suddenly she felt very heavy and the items weighed at least twice what they should. Her legs crumpled under her and she fell in a heap in the middle of the room. Everything was swimming in front of her and she felt very unwell. Suddenly she was aware of two strong arms lifting her and pulling her from the place and she came to her senses lying in the corridor. Her guardian had managed to ward off the evil presence and drag her to safety as it didn't seem to be able to leave the room.

She was surrounded by the linen and started to gather it together in a pile. But how was she going to re-enter the room to put it away. She considered asking Amy but that would have been unfair to her. Dawkins was walking along the corridor and ran to help.

"What happened Maud?"

"It sounds silly, but I don't know. One minute I was in there trying to put these in the chest and the next I was on the floor. But I seem to have been pulled out. It wasn't you then?"

"No I didn't. Let me help you up."

Maud looked embarrassed. "They'll blame the change again won't they?"

He looked straight at her. "Well I for one, don't."

"Oh?"

"There are too many strange things going on in this house and the sooner we have all left, the happier I will be."

"Oh don't say that, about the strange things I mean. I think we are all on edge."

"At least you can get out of here at night." He said without thinking.

"Why? What happens at night?" She looked really freaked out now.

"Oh, it's just, well I think with it being so empty, one can imagine all sorts of things." He tried to pass it off but he knew she didn't believe him for one second.

"I think you're right about getting out." She said quietly. "I'm sorry you aren't coming to Corfu."

He was quiet. Should he tell her or not? But this didn't seem quite the right moment and something seemed to be stopping him.

"Everything will work out, you'll see." He took her arm and walked her down to the servant's room where it was almost time for lunch.

Cook was well aware of what had happened in the house this morning and just looked knowingly at them both as they came in but didn't utter a word.

It was becoming obvious to all parties that certain rooms in the house were to be avoided. There had been so many unexplained unpleasant feelings that everyone confined their activities to the safe areas, but these were being reduced by the moment.

"It's as though the rooms have been let out to evil ghosts." Amy voiced as they gathered for lunch.

"That's enough of that kind of talk thank you very much." Maud tried to squash the subject but Amy was determined.

"Why aren't you all admitting it? Something's not right and I don't like it."

"Well go now. What's stopping you?" Maud was quick to say but given the chance she would have been first out of the door.

"All right ladies, we are all under a lot of pressure, so let's just finish these last few days in peace shall we?" Dawkins still felt he had to keep order although it didn't feel as though he had much control any more.

"Lunch." Cook brought the food to the table at the right moment to halt the antagonism.

As the Captain and his wife had planned to be out for a while, it gave the staff time to relax a bit. There wasn't much to do now and although they were grateful to be paid for another month, there seemed little point in them remaining. They kept the place clean and tidy and carried out any requests from upstairs, but it all seemed a bit futile and spirits were dropping.

Dawkins told Maud and Amy they wouldn't be required after tea time and that he and Cook could handle the evening meal when the couple returned. He felt that Amy could use the time looking for other employment and somewhere else to live. He knew what Maud would be doing considering her acceptance of the job.

Julius and Vard had been popping in and out of Janet's house and noticed that whereas the demons had also been making short visits when it suited, there was now quite a hive of activity around the place. The pair had been changing their images so as not to draw attention to themselves but Julius was getting the feeling that they were being monitored and suggested they kept away for a while. Danny agreed and said that he would do spot checks which would be instantaneous so they could concentrate on Bryn's place for now.

Again the same problem arose. There was quite a concentration of spiritual presence around his house and it wasn't just the visiting of willing females for Bryn and Kam having his bit of spare with Amy. There was a very strong evil there which was spreading over the whole village including Maud's house. But Julius noticed it seemed to emanate from the little churchyard and the stone coffins in particular which caused another problem. Vard was not supposed to be in that area.

Abe made a spot decision, Vard must be removed and leave Julius to his own skills of deception for as long as possible. Danny would also keep him under observation and it was agreed that at the first sign of serious threat, he must pull him out.

Much against his will Vard had been repositioned elsewhere and Julius felt free to work his own way. He had always been aware that, although his charge had to be trained to as high a level as possible, the spirit was always a liability and so Julius's attention wasn't wholly on the matter in hand, but now he was free to roam, change and observe unhindered.

It was evening and the sun had already set and darkness was creeping quickly over the landscape. To the untrained eye it was a beautiful sight but to those with insight into other existences, the evil was building making it an ugly place.

He stayed a short distance from Bryn's house and watched with some amusement as the female, or would be female entities lined up ready for their turn. A quick scan showed him that Amy was already fully occupied with Kam, at least she hoped it was Kam in her bedroom and the interchange was quite amusing but he hadn't time for sightseeing. She appeared to be in no immediate danger so he turned his attention to the next room.

Bryn was really getting the treatment and at first Julius had a job to see just how many clients he was servicing. Then he noticed something different and sent a thought image to Danny. These weren't single spirits, but one dark evil being that had split itself into many forms to give the impression of being a group. Bryn was in great danger. This was not providing sex for his fulfilment, this was taking over his very soul which would soon be used for their purposes and by the time the poor fool realised, it would be too late.

Abe wanted to know if the entity was known to them but although there was a familiarity about it, neither he nor Danny could identify it. The call went out to their equals in all over the globe and one reply made them stop in their tracks. They had come across this being not so long ago and now he was operating on full power. Whatever he had been waiting for, he had come to take but he seemed to be using an indirect route to his goal. Bryn was now under the control of Thomas.

A hefty discussion followed. Thomas would have nothing against Bryn but he was such an easy target. His connection with

Amy would give him free access back into the house by devious means. If he had gone straight in his presence would have been picked up immediately so he would enter via the 'wooden horse'.

The next question was why would he want to? He had nothing against anyone there so had he come back for something, or someone? Extra guards were called in to be at the ready should they be needed instantly. All they could do for the moment was wait until the next move.

Cook was asked to do a virtual scan of the whole house to see if she could pick up anything that seemed even slightly out of order or different. She had remarked that the moods were changing and soon they would have the seven deadly sins all under one roof. The staff were almost like strangers. She also felt as though something was closing in on them and the sooner the mortal ones had all left the place the better. She knew she would be going by other means which was all part of her work.

She then told them something via the secret route. The 'Major' was around, not all the time, but certainly popping in and out as if he was waiting for them to go, or maybe for another reason.

Abe decided to inform her of Thomas's close proximity so that she was ready in case he suddenly appeared.

"That's it?" She was certain of her assumptions now. "They are both meeting here but I don't know why or when."

Abe knew it had to be imminent, almost like the gathering of the clan and again warned her that she may be pulled out quickly for they may both realise she wasn't what her image portrayed.

"Does he hover round any particular room?" Danny had been taking all this in and was trying to work out the reason for the presence.

"Not particularly and not for long. Just short bursts then gone."

"He's weighing something up." Abe said.

"And choosing the right time." Danny added. "He's waiting for them to go, that's got to be it. He wants the place to himself where they can fight out, whatever it is they have a feud about."

Abe put a different light on it. "Or they're working together."

"No." Danny couldn't accept that but had no defence to back up his objection.

It was like playing a waiting game and when Friday came everyone knew they would be counting down the last week. It wasn't announced as to which day the Captain and his wife would be leaving but it was estimated to be very soon after the servants had been dismissed for good. Maud had kept very quiet about her new position and trusted Dawkins not to divulge her business. He still hadn't admitted to her that he would be accompanying them to Corfu and made up his mind to say that he thought it would be a nice surprise for her. Cook let it be known that she may have a little holiday by the sea before moving into any new accommodation.

"Be a bit chilly," Amy had pointed out "you'll need your thermals on."

Cook waved a spoon at her in play but said "You two found anything yet?"

"No. Bryn can still work at the farm but we will have to find a place where he can bike to it. I'm looking around for another job but there's not much about."

"Not round here." Cook said "But you've got the weekend to try and find something. Best get on your bike and ride round a bit, see what comes up."

It seemed a funny thing to say and Amy little realised that Cook was trying to get her as far away as possible at every opportunity.

Chapter 15

It was late afternoon and everyone was trying to find something to do to keep themselves occupied. The skies were thickening and storm clouds were building over the estate and the house became so dark that lights had to be put on.

"I hope it isn't pouring when we have to go home." Amy was looking out of the window.

Maud joined her. "Come away, if there's lightning it can blind you."

"I like watching it, I just don't like being out in it." Amy didn't move,

"I hate thunder, always have."

"What's he doing here?" Amy had spotted Bryn cycling up the drive to the house. "I'll go and see what's up."

Not wanting to be left out of anything interesting, Maud followed although she had a job to keep up with the younger woman.

"What's burning?" Cook asked as Amy dashed to the back door.

"Bryn's here." She opened the door as he burst in. "What's up?"

She noticed how different he looked. His eyes were ablaze and he was on a mission for he pushed her aside and strode upstairs to the main hallway.

"Where are you?" He boomed as his voice shook the place.

"Waiting for you." The voice seemed to come from the ceiling yet it was all around.

All the servants had appeared and stood together trembling, even Dawkins and they were soon joined by the Captain followed by his wife who was demanding to know who was making all the noise.

"What in hell's name do you think you are doing man?" Captain addressed Bryn then suddenly realised there was something very wrong about him. As he and Hilary reached the last few steps of the stairs, a terrific rush of air came from behind and blew them the rest of the way until they were huddled against the servants.

Bryn was now in the centre of the hall looking up the stairs where someone seemed to be standing. It was hazy at first but when it became clear Captain gasped "It's Father!"

The image floated slowly until it was half way down the stairs then stopped.

"What do you want?" It demanded.

"You know very well what I want. What I've been waiting for all these years." The voice now wasn't that of Bryn but Thomas's distinctive tones.

"Don't be foolish, what can you do?"

Bryn turned slowly and faced the assembled mortals.

"You will witness what happens when someone takes everything you hold dear, defiles it then lets you live with the memory. Well I have followed you across time for all the atrocities you have perpetrated and got away with, even let me take the blame."

The 'Major' seemed amused at this little drama but waited for the rant to finish.

Thomas, using Bryn pointed his finger up at him. "In your last earth life, you took everything I loved, you ruined it, you infected my female relatives with your sexual diseases, but that wasn't enough. You weren't content with the adults, you even had to take the girls. I watched them all die."

The whole place was hushed and the Captain looked horrified for this was his father that was being accused.

There was silence for a moment before Thomas continued.

"So you brought me here, to give me a job and a life and thought that would pay for my sorrow. I had no choice, but it meant I was living off your drug dealing which I despised you for. But I knew my time would come and I would bring you to justice. You took all I had and now it is my turn."

The laughter echoed eerily. "You always lived in a dream and nothing has changed. What can you take from me now?"

"Everything."

The reply was met with silence for a moment then the 'Major' mocked, "Oh I look forward to hearing this."

Bryn took a step forward and looked at each of the people, then turned his attention to his enemy.

"You used to laugh at my people's beliefs, our chants our rituals, well you should have taken more interest instead of turning your back. Many years ago you were given a special mark and it has identified you for the evil person you really are."

"Mark, what mark?"

"Oh you won't see it but those with the power recognise it straight away."

"You're making all this up. Just trying to frighten everyone. Well go and play your silly little games somewhere else and leave this place alone."

Thomas's voice boomed up the stairs.

"You are about to lose those you love and all the physical assets that came from your wicked life."

"Oh my wicked life eh? And you are so pure that evil forces killed you off if you remember." He was gloating now.

"No."

"They witnessed it." He indicated to the servants who were nodding,

"No." Thomas repeated. "Just one of my many skills. Yes I let my body go, to free myself but I was in control of it, every miniscule moment of it."

Now it was the mortal's turn to be shocked for this was something they hadn't reckoned on. The few seconds that followed seemed to last an eternity and even the 'Major' seemed uneasy wondering what the next move would be.

Abe and Danny were closely monitoring every word, each movement and had the guards as close as possible. Julius had been recalled for safety as they weren't too sure what the next move would be but it was obvious things were coming to a head.

"I am sure the assembled company would like to know my full reasons." Thomas was quieter now but more menacing.

Amy started to tremble. This was her beloved brother with whom she had been so close and was there for her after their parent's death. How could this be him speaking? Dawkins tried to catch her as she fell to the floor sobbing.

"So it begins," Thomas continued "quite a little patchwork of lies you have built here."

Captain moved forward. "I've had enough of this. I will call the vicar and have you exorcised."

"Stay where you are, I will come to you in a good time." The voice boomed.

Silence fell again.

"Let us start with you fake 'Major'. From your many partners you had a son that you admitted to along with many that you didn't but of course you just paid the mothers off and wanted nothing further to do with your offspring. But you decided to do the right thing and marry this one."

"But you also had a daughter. She worked here as a maid along with her husband who was a footman. I don't think you ever realised Freda Hall was your own flesh and blood, and nobody ever told her."

Amy gasped aloud "Mother, no it can't have been."

"Sorry my dear, yes that makes you the Captain's niece. I will leave you to work the rest out for yourselves."

There was a bit of muttering among the group then Amy yelled "So Kameron was my……"

"Cousin, that's right. Gets messy doesn't it?"

The Captain tried to move forward again as he begged "But this can't affect all of us, not what he has done surely?"

Thomas faced them as he said slowly "It touches each and every one of you. Why do you think you were the only ones remaining?"

He appeared to be rising from the floor as he pointed to each in turn.

"Captain, spawn of this devil. Your wife who lived with you off the profits of your father's drug dealing. Amy, your father's granddaughter who couldn't stop meddling in what she didn't understand, just like you. Maud the aunt of your grandson. Dawkins through his physical association with Muriel, Kameron's mother."

"Haven't you missed someone?" Captain cut in.

"If you are referring to your cook, I think you will find she has gone."

They all looked round but she certainly had left the room and her remains would be found later slumped over the kitchen table for she had relinquished her body when Abe recalled her spirit before they had time to capture it.

"But what are you thinking of doing?" The Captain was now demanding what was going to happen then turning said "This is ludicrous. What is stopping us moving? Nothing." But as he turned to face Thomas he was rooted to the ground.

The air was changing, it was getting stagnant and everyone was starting to heave. The women were crying and even the men felt ill.

The 'Major' was floating the rest of the way down the stairs.

"Alright, you've played your little games. Made your point, now clear off and let these good people be at peace. If you've got an issue with me then we will sort it like men even in spirit, not all these dramatics."

Thomas rose in the air and faced him.

"You want the finale. Then you shall have it. You took everything from me that I held dear. Now I will return the favour."

"I don't understand."

"You will. You have a grandstand seat. Enjoy the show."

As he vacated the body he had used, Bryn slumped to the floor. Amy rushed to him sobbing but he seemed unconscious. The 'Major' had also disappeared but the air was still heavy with their presences.

Now the two spirits were invisible but audible.

"You can't do this." 'Major' cried.

"Hurts does it?" Was the taunting reply.

"Are you going to follow them when they leave here and keep them in torment the rest of their lives?" 'Major' was begging.

"The rest of their lives? They have been brought here for a reason. They will never leave."

It wasn't only the 'Major' that gasped at the last statement.

"What does he mean, we won't leave?" Hilary was getting hysterical.

"Don't listen, he's trying to fool us. Of course we are leaving and as soon as possible." The Captain was trying to contain his anger.

The storm was above them and the thunder was shaking the windows. The rain was deafening and the lightning so bright that Maud reminded them not to look at it.

"What was that?" Dawkins shouted to be heard.

"Not sure." Captain yelled. "Sounds as though it was upstairs."

"Is that a crackling sound?" Maud was listening intently.

The house had been hit and fires were already getting out of control, some not obvious yet but still burning, in the attic, within the walls and following anything to give it a route such as the water pipes, telephone wires and electric cables. The people would not get out for the doors and windows would not open and even the glass refused to break. They were all trapped which was what Thomas had carefully planned and his words echoed round the condemned property.

"They will never leave."

Sadly this would always be one battle that Abe and Danny, plus their supporters would have to concede as a loss. They had failed in their combined efforts at intervention during the whole episode and it had proved again that evil forces could, on occasion outwit them. The invisible shield that Thomas had so successfully mastered with the help of his ancestors, was impenetrable.

....

And so the curtains slowly close on this insight into another dimension but it is not another world, it is all around us, controlling and affecting our lives.

So are we really in charge of our own fate?

About the Author

Tabbie Browne grew up in the Cotswolds in central England which is where she gets the inspiration for her novels. Her father had very strong spiritual beliefs and she feels he guides her but always with a warning to stay in control of your own mind.

Her earliest recollection of writing was at primary school and it has seemed to play a part at significant times during her life. She thinks it is only when we are forced to take step back and unclutter our minds for a while we realise our potential. This point was proved when she slipped a disc, and being very immobile had to write in pencil as the ink would not flow upwards! At this time she wrote many comical poems which, when able again, performed to many audiences. Comedy is very difficult but you know if you are a success with a live audience.

In 1991 as a collector of novelty salt and pepper shakers, she realised there was no book in the UK devoted entirely to the subject. So she wrote one. Which meant she achieved the fact that it was the first of its kind in the country and it sold well to like collectors not only in the UK but in the USA.

Another large upheaval came when she was diagnosed with breast cancer, and due to the extreme energy draining, found it difficult to work for an employer. So she took a freelance journalist course and was pleased to have articles accepted, her main joy being the piece about her father and his life in the village. Again the inspiration area.

But the novels were eating away inside and drawing on her experience at stamp and coin fairs she wrote *'A Fair Collection'* which she serialised in the magazine 'Squirrels' for people who hoard things.

When she wrote *'White Noise Is Heavenly Blue'* and its sequel *'The Spiral'* she sat at the keyboard and the titles just came to her, as did the content of the books. There is no way she could write the plot first as she never knew what was coming next, almost as if somebody was dictating, and for that reason she could never change anything.

Loves:
Animals,
Also performing in live theatre and working as a tv supporting artiste.

Hates:
Bad manners,
Insincere people.